Praise for the Remy Chandler Novels

Dancing on the Head of a Pin

"A powerful urban fantasy."   —Genre Go Round Reviews

A Kiss Before the Apocalypse

"The most inventive novel you'll buy this year . . . a hard-boiled noir fantasy by turns funny, unsettling, and heartbreaking. This is the story Sniegoski was born to write, and a character I can't wait to see again."
    —Christopher Golden, bestselling author of *The Lost Ones*

"Tightly focused and deftly handled, [*A Kiss Before the Apocalypse*] covers familiar ground in entertaining new ways. . . . Fans of urban fantasy and classic detective stories will enjoy this smart and playful story."
    —*Publishers Weekly*

"This reviewer prays there will be more novels starring Remy. . . . The audience will believe he is on Earth for a reason as he does great things for humanity. This heart-wrenching, beautiful urban fantasy will grip readers with its potent emotional fervor."   —*Midwest Book Review*

"It's kind of refreshing to see the holy side represented. . . . Fans of urban fantasy with a new twist are likely to enjoy Sniegoski's latest venture into that realm between humanity and angels."   —SFRevu

continued . . .

WHERE ANGELS FEAR TO TREAD

A REMY CHANDLER NOVEL

THOMAS E. SNIEGOSKI

A ROC BOOK

ROC
Published by New American Library, a division of
Penguin Group (USA) Inc., 375 Hudson Street,
New York, New York 10014, USA
Penguin Group (Canada), 90 Eglinton Avenue East, Suite 700, Toronto,
Ontario M4P 2Y3, Canada (a division of Pearson Penguin Canada Inc.)
Penguin Books Ltd., 80 Strand, London WC2R 0RL, England
Penguin Ireland, 25 St. Stephen's Green, Dublin 2,
Ireland (a division of Penguin Books Ltd.)
Penguin Group (Australia), 250 Camberwell Road, Camberwell, Victoria 3124,
Australia (a division of Pearson Australia Group Pty. Ltd.)
Penguin Books India Pvt. Ltd., 11 Community Centre, Panchsheel Park,
New Delhi - 110 017, India
Penguin Group (NZ), 67 Apollo Drive, Rosedale, North Shore 0632,
New Zealand (a division of Pearson New Zealand Ltd.)
Penguin Books (South Africa) (Pty.) Ltd., 24 Sturdee Avenue,
Rosebank, Johannesburg 2196, South Africa

Penguin Books Ltd., Registered Offices:
80 Strand, London WC2R 0RL, England

First published by Roc, an imprint of New American Library,
a division of Penguin Group (USA) Inc.

First Printing, March 2010
10 9 8 7 6 5 4 3 2 1

ROC REGISTERED TRADEMARK—MARCA REGISTRADA

LIBRARY OF CONGRESS CATALOGING-IN-PUBLICATION DATA:

Sniegoski, Tom.
  Where angels fear to tread : a Remy Chandler novel / by Thomas E. Sniegoski.
    p. cm.
  ISBN 978-0-451-46314-2
  1. Private investigators—Fiction. 2. Angels—Fiction. 3. Boston (Mass.)—Fiction. I. Title.
  PS3619.N537W47 2010
  813'.6—dc22   2009039826

Set in Adobe Garamond
Designed by Ginger Legato

Printed in the United States of America

For Rusty, Kenn, and Remy—
old friends and the new

ACKNOWLEDGMENTS

Love and so much more to LeeAnne, and to Mulder for helping me through another one.

Many thanks also to Ginjer Buchanan, Cameron Dufty, Christopher Golden, Sheila Walker, Dave Kraus, Mike Mignola, Christine Mignola, Katie Mignola, Lisa Clancy, Pete Donaldson, Mom and Dad Sniegoski, Mom and Dad Fogg, David Carroll, Ken Curtis, Kim and Abby, Jon and Flo, Pat and Bob, Timothy Cole, and the followers of Delilah down at Cole's Comics in Lynn.

And a very special thanks to James and Liesa Mignogna.

WHERE ANGELS
FEAR TO TREAD

PROLOGUE

Vietnam, 2004

Everybody loved her.
And when they didn't, she made them.

Delilah sat in the passenger seat of the old Jeep in a central Vietnam valley—the Cat's Tooth Mountain barely visible through the thick canopy of lush vegetation—and waited for a sign.

Large, buzzing insects flew about her head, but only for as long as she allowed them. A single thought to cease the annoying behavior was enough to send the simple life-forms back into the emerald green forest, although many chose to linger about the bullet-riddled corpses of the holy men lying on the ground at the entrance to the ancient vine-covered temple.

She closed her eyes and breathed in the smells of this primordial location, the heady aroma of humid earth mingling with the thick scent of nearby coffee plantations. But it did little to calm her excitement.

The waiting was always the most excruciating part.

How many other faraway locations had she and her followers visited in their search for the prize? Delilah had lost count many years before, but she never gave up hope that the next unexplored cave system, forgotten temple, long-buried city, or forsaken church would offer what she so desperately sought.

The sound of gunshots from within the temple had stopped only moments before; the rapid-fire barks of death had temporarily silenced the voice of the jungle. But now, regaining its courage, it started to speak again in its primitive language of buzzing, howling, shrieking, and squawking.

And she continued to wait, watching for a sign from her followers, her eyes focused on the darkness of the temple's entrance.

Finally bored with just sitting, Delilah got out of the Jeep, her high-heeled black leather boots—inappropriate for any sort of jungle excursion—sinking into the damp, spongy earth, which was made even moister by the copious amounts of blood seeping from the bullet-riddled corpses.

It had been quite some time since one of their expeditions had been met with such adversity. She still remembered an Inuit village in the Canadian Arctic where their attempt at locating the object of her obsession had left a bloodbath in its wake, with little to show for their troubles except some lovely fox pelts that she'd had a Paris seamstress make into a coat.

She loved that coat but seldom had a chance to wear it.

Pity.

The way those villagers had fought, she'd thought for sure she had at long last been successful, but that wasn't the case. The Inuit tribesmen had fought with such fervor, and for what? It was as if they somehow sensed the ruthlessness of her search and how she would let nothing stand in the way of finding her prize.

It was an item she would kill again, and again, to find.

And she had killed many times more since that doomed Inuit village, but she was still no closer to finding it.

Until now, perhaps.

There was movement inside the entrance to the temple, the thick obsidian dark churning like black smoke billowing from a wet fire, as a lone figure emerged.

The man's name was Seldon Blondelle, and he was an excellent Hound, a person gifted with an extraordinary sensitivity to objects of preternatural origins. It was his job to help her find what she so desperately sought.

"Yes, Mr. Blondelle?" she prompted, holding her breath.

Blondelle was thin—horribly emaciated—but that was to be expected, as he hadn't eaten in weeks. The man took his job as her personal Hound very seriously, although as an extra incentive she'd made him promise not to eat until he had found her prize.

He could barely stand, and swarms of hungry insects buzzed about his gaunt face as if drawn by his nearness to death. Stumbling, he leaned heavily against the stone frame of the doorway, licking dry and cracked lips with a dark, swollen tongue.

"It's here," he managed, his voice an awful croak.

His words were like magic, and she felt a vitality flow through her, the likes of which she hadn't experienced in centuries.

"It's here," Delilah repeated, heading toward him, walking atop the corpses as if they were little more than rubbish strewn in her path.

Nothing would keep her from the item.

Blondelle raised a trembling hand as she climbed the three stone steps to the temple landing.

"Please." He beckoned.

She knew what he wanted; the sound of his rumbling stomach was almost as annoying as the incessant hum of the jungle bugs.

"You've done well, Mr. Blondelle," she told him with a rewarding smile. "You have earned the right to eat again."

The man's eyes closed and he started to sob. "I can eat," he said in a trembling hiss as he pushed himself off the wall, heading unsteadily down the steps toward the Jeep and the food supplies stored in the back of the vehicle.

There was a sound like the crack of a bullwhip, instantaneously followed by a flash from within the darkness of the temple entrance. Delilah spun around to see Blondelle fall forward, the back of his head opened up to the jungle by a well-placed bullet.

She turned again to the entrance to see one of the Vietnamese holy men cautiously emerging, chattering in his foreign tongue as he aimed a pistol, ready to gun her down.

"Don't you dare point that thing at me," Delilah raged.

The man instantly dropped the weapon to his side. She could see he was struggling to fight her, to usurp her will, but those who were capable of such a feat were few and far between.

She remembered the days when she would have played with the man first, maybe forced him to pluck out his own eyes and crush them between his teeth, before ordering him to kill himself by smashing his head repeatedly against the ground.

But that was a Delilah with little purpose—a Delilah drunk on the cruelty of the world and the accursed one who'd made it that way.

"Shoot yourself dead," she instructed the man, who immediately placed the gun beneath his chin and fired, the top of his head erupting in a plume of crimson.

She stepped over the man's still-twitching legs and eased herself into the cool darkness of the temple entrance, allowing her eyes to adjust.

More gunfire shattered the fragile silence within the temple, and she pressed herself firmly against the vine-covered stone wall, assessing its location. The shots were coming from somewhere down the corridor. She charged the hall's length to find another doorway, and stairs descending into a larger chamber.

Bullets chewed across the wall to her left as she reached the bottom of the steps, which opened into a temple of some kind, a primitive place of ceremony, lit by flickering candlelight.

A hand grabbed her wrist firmly, yanking her to cover behind a pillar as more bullets mercilessly tore through the stone where she'd just been standing.

"What are you doing down here?" Mathias demanded. "I told Blondelle to make you wait in the Jeep until we secured the area."

"The Hound is dead," Delilah said.

"All the more reason you should have stayed put," her head of security growled.

She was tempted to tell him to shut his mouth, and he would never have spoken again, but this wasn't the time. "Is it true?" she asked instead, attempting to keep her excitement in check. "Is it here?"

"Blondelle believed it was," the man answered as the members of his security team continued to shoot at the priests defending their temple.

Delilah peered around the pillar to catch a glimpse of the holy men, but a spray of automatic gunfire threw a cloud of powdered stone into her face, obscuring her vision.

"Damn them!" she shrieked, digging at her eyes.

"Are you all right?" Mathias asked, genuine concern in his voice. Mathias loved her more than his own life, and he would have given her the world if she asked for it.

But she didn't want the world.

Yet.

"I'm fine." She impatiently waved off his worried ministrations. "Just put a stop to this before—"

"What's *this*?" Mathias interrupted, peeking out from behind the ceiling support.

One of the priests, his thin body adorned in robes of deep scarlet and yellow, had emerged from cover, wildly firing a handgun as he made his way to the ancient altar.

"What's he doing?" Delilah demanded, her eyes still watering from the dust.

"I don't know," Mathias replied, trying to get off a shot, but opposing gunfire continued to pin him and Delilah to their places behind the pillar.

Delilah waited for an opportunity between gunshots, then again stuck out her head. The priest was crouched before a small, curtained shrine on the altar. She watched as he pulled a disposable lighter from beneath his colorful robes and lit a dangling fuse that snaked out from beneath the curtain.

"What's he doing?" she asked again, starting to stand. "What is he doing?" she repeated, louder still.

Delilah stepped out from behind the safety of their cover.

"Delilah!" Mathias called out, reaching to pull her back, but she evaded his hands as she stalked out into the open.

He screamed her name again, while his team members continued to fire at their opponents in an attempt to protect her.

She grunted in pain as a bullet punched into her shoulder, but she did not stop. The scent of her blood mingled with the damp, stagnant air and the acrid smell of gunfire, and she used it as fuel to push herself on.

The priest saw her coming and withdrew a ceremonial dagger from beneath his robes, positioning himself in front of the curtain and the hissing fuse. His eyes told her he was willing to die rather than let her have what the curtain hid.

From the corner of her eye, she caught movement from the shadows around her, and she knew she must act. She hated to abuse her gifts, fearful that each use sent a tremor out into the ether, alerting her enemies to her whereabouts. But there were times when it simply could not be avoided.

"Stop shooting!" she screamed, her voice echoing off the stone walls.

And the barking of the guns ceased instantaneously.

"Stay where you are."

The old priest managed to turn slightly toward the shrine, drawing Delilah's attention to the still-burning fuse, which had almost reached the pale yellow curtain.

"You there," she ordered the priest, "stop that fuse now."

For a moment he seemed to be fighting her, and she considered giving the order again, but it wasn't necessary.

With tears in his eyes, the old priest finally crouched down, grabbing the sizzling fuse between two fingers and halting its progress. Slowly he stood and turned back toward her, as if awaiting her next desire.

Delilah breathed a sigh of relief, then took a moment to examine her shoulder. It hurt like hell and was bleeding profusely, but she would heal. She always did.

It was all part of the curse.

She looked around at the other holy men who had been defending the temple. They all watched with the same fearful expression that graced the face of the old man who stood before her.

She climbed the two stone steps onto the altar platform.

"Mistress," Mathias called out. Hearing him, she turned around to see her security head and his team watching her with eager eyes. "Be careful," he said.

His concern for her safety was touching, but after all this time, she found herself throwing caution to the wind.

Eye to eye with the holy man, she grinned widely. "What were you trying to hide from me?" she asked playfully.

The man could not help himself, and the words spilled from his mouth in his native tongue.

He still blocked her path, and she reached out with her good arm to roughly push him aside. Delilah could feel it now. She knew she was in the presence of something . . .

Something divine.

Forgetting the pain in her shoulder, she reached out, pulling apart the curtains and letting out a squeal of pleasure when she saw it. She could barely contain the intensity of her feelings as she gazed upon the sculpture.

It appeared to have been made of metal, crudely fashioned

into the shape of a sitting infant, its short, chubby arms outstretched as if in welcome.

Delilah reached out and grasped the statue.

The pain was both immediate and excruciating.

It was as if she'd tried to embrace the sun.

She fell back, leaving behind her hands, burned to nothing more than black, crumbling ash. She rolled upon the altar, resisting the urge to scream and using the charred stumps of her arms to push herself awkwardly to her knees. The pain was all-consuming, but she could already feel her limbs beginning to grow back.

The priest was smiling at her agony.

"Mathias, come to me," she managed, swaying to the song of her pain, forcing herself back from the brink of unconsciousness.

She felt Mathias behind her. "Help me to stand," she ordered, and he did as she asked.

He held her about the waist as she turned toward the holy man. The priest was now chattering—praying, she imagined.

It would do him little good.

"Open it," she spat, looking toward the metal idol upon the altar.

The priest's chatter ceased, but he did not move.

She gave the order a second time.

"Open it."

The man cried out in pain and lurched toward the altar. Thick, dark blood dripped from his ears, an unpleasant aftereffect for those who dared oppose her commands.

The priest's face was a mask of struggle even as his hands reached for the iron infant.

"That's it," Delilah encouraged, watching his every move, trying to distract herself from the agony of her limbs growing back. Flesh and blood, arteries, veins, muscle, and bone, all coming back at once in a symphony of pain played specifically for her.

The priest's hand hovered near the infant statue's bulbous stomach, trembling in the humid, tropical heat as if cold.

"Do as you're told and I'll make the pain stop," she whispered. "It's as simple as that."

Blood was oozing from his ears, running down his neck. He started to pray again and pulled his hands away.

The other faithful called to him from around the chamber, perhaps believing they could lend him some of their strength, hoping he would be able to defy her commands.

"Open it!" she bellowed, her voice booming horribly in the stone confines of the underground room.

The priest moaned.

"I'll make the pain go away," she said in a more controlled voice, although her own pain was quite incredible. "Open it and give me what I want. It's quite easy."

"Mistress, my men and I could . . . ," Mathias began, but she silenced him with a glance. The priest would open the idol; that was how it had to be.

The priest was gasping for breath, thick, dark blood continuing to flow from his ears. Stiffly, he raised a hand toward the statue's belly, his index finger beginning to glow, and rubbed the idol's protruding stomach.

Delilah watched in utter fascination, her newly formed skeletal hands flexing and unflexing. A hole—a keyhole—had appeared in the infant's belly, and her anticipation grew to a near-uncontrollable level.

The priest turned his tearstained face toward her, snarling as she stepped closer.

"Do it," she hissed, knowing that the old Vietnamese man was experiencing pain beyond measure. But it could be nothing compared to what she had endured throughout her long, long life.

He inserted his still-glowing index finger into the dark hole.

There was a sharp click, and a vertical seam appeared down the center of the idol.

This is it, she thought. The moment she'd waited centuries for was finally here. What had pulled her from a living death of her own making was about to be revealed.

She reached out with arms of exposed muscle and tendon, on the verge of tears. "Open it."

The priest started to twitch and groan. Finally, releasing a scream that seemed to come from somewhere in the depths of his soul, he pried the statue apart.

It was as if all the stars in the galaxy were inside the belly of that metal infant and as if the eyes of the Heavens were all looking at Delilah . . . looking at their new mistress.

Her pain was suddenly gone.

Tears streamed from her eyes as the priest slowly withdrew the idol's wondrous contents.

It hummed and pulsed and sang as it rested in the palms of his hands. He too was staring at it, her wonderful prize, his mouth moving soundlessly.

"Please," she said quietly, holding out her own hands, the pink of recently grown skin glistening wetly in the object's radiance.

And then she saw the look upon the old man's face, and she knew everything was about to go horribly wrong.

"Give it to me!" she demanded, hoping the command would finally break him, leaving him quivering and wishing for death upon the altar floor, but it seemed to do nothing.

Her prize had given him the strength to defy her.

The old man simply laughed as he tossed the object into the air, and, like a dove released from the confines of its cage, it flew up toward the ceiling of the chamber, exploding in a flash of blinding brilliance.

And then it was gone.

"You bastard," Delilah screamed in fury, charging toward the old man.

He just stood there, a look of serenity and calm upon his lined face, even though he surely knew what was about to happen.

"You selfish, selfish bastard!"

She grabbed him by the back of his neck with a hand still tender and fresh, pulling him to her.

Pulling him toward her eager lips.

They joined in a kiss; she felt him begin to struggle, but it was all for naught.

With this kiss she would feed upon his life and his soul, and leave very little behind for the insects of this damnable jungle to dine upon.

The old man flailed wildly, attempting to scream, but her lips blocked the scream's escape, and she fed upon that as well, savoring the deliciousness of his terror, as everything that defined him as a man—as a living, breathing human being—was sucked away.

It took only a moment to steal the old man's life. Then, unlocking her lips from the withered remains, she allowed the dried, brittle shell of the priest to fall to the floor of the altar, where it disintegrated into a choking cloud of heavy, gray dust.

Mathias coughed, waving a hand before his face. "Mistress"—he coughed again—"I'm so sorry."

The priest's life force coursed through her body, speeding her recovery. Her arms had completely re-formed, though they were quite pale; nothing a few days on the Riviera wouldn't cure.

Delilah stepped down from the altar, Mathias holding her hand so she would not fall.

Standing in the center of the chamber, she looked around at the other priests, still held in her thrall, terror etched upon their faces.

"He could have let me have it," she announced. "And it would have changed everything."

She turned away from their fear-twisted features, heading across the stone floor toward the stairs that would take her out of the underground chamber.

"Delilah?" Mathias called.

She stopped, turning a cold gaze to him.

"What should we do with them?" he asked, motioning toward the temple priests.

"Use your imagination," she said with a wave of her hand, and then ascended from the bowels of the Vietnamese temple, the sound of gunfire at her back.

CHAPTER ONE

Boston, now

Remy Chandler watched the older woman as she sat across from him, sipping her gin—no, her *Tanqueray*—and tonic from a short brown straw.

She'd been quite specific with the waitress.

He was trying to figure out what it was exactly that he didn't like about her.

She leaned forward, placing her glass precisely in the center of the cardboard coaster in front of her. "My grandmother, God rest her soul, used to have two Tanqueray and tonics every day," Mrs. Grantmore said, straightening the coaster. "She said they helped her keep her wits about her. She was ninety-eight when she finally passed."

It was obvious that Remy was supposed to be impressed.

"Isn't ninety-eight the new eighty-five?" he joked, taking a sip of his soda water with lime.

Mrs. Grantmore's daughter, Olivia, sitting quietly beside her mother on the love seat in the lobby bar of the Westin Copley Place hotel, chuckled before taking a drink of her Diet Coke.

Remy liked Olivia. She seemed like a sweet kid.

"I wouldn't know," Mrs. Grantmore said dismissively, reaching for her drink and bringing it to her mouth, careful not to drip any of the condensation from the glass onto her white silk blouse.

Remy crossed his ankle over his knee, pulling the cuff of his dark jeans over the tongue of his brown loafer.

This meeting was exactly what he had expected, and one he would have preferred to have had at his office. Having it at the Westin, out in the open, was uncomfortable, especially with Olivia present.

"So . . . ," Remy began, faking cheerfulness. He leaned forward in the overstuffed chair and placed his drink on the glass-topped table before him. "You're probably wondering about my findings." He grabbed the folder from the seat beside him and opened it.

Mrs. Grantmore turned to look at her daughter as she returned her glass to the coaster.

"Of course, Mr. Chandler. I'm sure you're a very busy man. Go on. Tell us what you've found."

Olivia, who had been silently staring into the bubbles of her soft drink, looked up, making eye contact with him.

He tried to assuage her fears with a comforting smile.

"You asked me to look into the background of one James Wardley," he said, looking down at the file.

Mrs. Grantmore reached over and took her daughter's hand. The look Olivia flashed her made it clear the gesture was not appreciated.

"Go ahead, Mr. Chandler. What did you learn?"

Remy shrugged. "To be honest, not a whole lot."

He watched as the older woman's features momentarily tightened, her stare becoming more intense.

Olivia looked as though a huge weight had been lifted from her shoulders.

"You found nothing out of the ordinary?"

"Nothing," Remy said, continuing the litany of his findings. "James Wardley of Lynn, Massachusetts, born August 16, 1988, to Harriet and Robert Wardley. Attended Lynn Classical High

School, graduating in 2006 at the top of his class. Enrolled at Northeastern University, currently majoring in electrical engineering and—"

"There was nothing . . . out of sorts . . . say, a criminal history?" Mrs. Grantmore interrupted.

Remy slowly shook his head. "Not really. There was something about a party and some underage drinking, but no charges were ever filed."

He closed the file and met the older woman's eyes. She was speechless. Obviously it wasn't the result she was looking for.

"See, Mother?" Olivia said, still clutching her mother's hand. "There's nothing for you to worry about. James is a good boy."

Silently Mrs. Grantmore removed her hand from her daughter's.

"I seem to be developing a rather bad headache," the older woman said. "Probably the humidity and this air-conditioning." Her handbag was on the floor at her feet and she bent forward, plucking out a wallet. Fishing inside for a moment, she found a twenty-dollar bill and handed it to Olivia.

"Would you be a dear and buy me a bottle of Tylenol from the gift shop?" she asked, a forced smile upon her strained features.

"Mother, you promised to let this go if I agreed to . . ."

"Please, Olivia," her mother snapped. "Go to the gift shop."

The pretty young woman rose from her seat, briefly glancing at Remy with pleading eyes before making her way across the hotel lobby toward the gift shop.

As soon as Olivia was out of earshot, Mrs. Grantmore turned back to Remy.

"A regular model citizen," she said sarcastically, picking up her drink and taking a gulp from the glass, this time forgoing the straw.

"As your daughter said," Remy answered, "he's a good boy. You should be glad."

"Glad, Mr. Chandler?" she scoffed. "It's obvious you don't have children."

Remy felt himself immediately rankle. Having children had always been a sensitive issue in his long, otherwise happy marriage to Madeline. No matter how much she had said that she understood they couldn't have a family, he had always believed a part of her resented him for it. Because she was human, and he . . . *wasn't*, he had deprived her—*them*—of something special.

But it didn't matter now, because she was gone. And at that moment, he realized that was the first time he'd thought of her that afternoon.

And it bothered him.

"No, I don't have children," he replied tightly. "But I think if I did have a young, attractive, intelligent, and respectful daughter like Olivia, I would be quite happy to see her dating someone with similar characteristics and not the local crack dealer."

Mrs. Grantmore used the stirrer in her drink to move the ice around.

"No, not the local crack dealer, but close enough."

Remy couldn't believe what he was hearing.

"What about the boy's father?" she asked. "One of the other investigators mentioned that his father might have had some trouble with the law."

"One of the other investigators?" Remy felt his pulse quicken.

"Well, you're certainly not the first I've hired since Olivia told me she was dating," the conniving woman scoffed. "Did you look into the father's background?"

It took all of Remy's strength to remain calm and professional.

But he could feel *it* stirring inside him.

The power of the Seraphim had been much more active and more difficult to silence of late. If he let his guard down, even just a bit, he could only imagine what the power of Heaven would do to the woman.

"His father did some time in a juvenile detention center for car theft more than twenty years ago, but he hasn't been in any kind of trouble since," Remy said. "But I don't see what that has to do with—"

"That's good," she said, ignoring him. "We can work with that; maybe make some connection to genetics."

"Genetics?" Remy started to laugh in disbelief. If he hadn't, he wasn't quite sure what he—what the angelic nature he had squirreled away inside him—might have done.

For an instant he imagined the fires of Heaven, leaping from the tips of his blackened fingers and consuming the woman's hateful flesh.

"This might seem funny to you, Mr. Chandler, but I assure you it is not," Mrs. Grantmore said with obvious annoyance. "My daughter is the most important thing in my life. Everything my husband and I have worked so hard to acquire will someday belong to her. . . ."

"And to someone you deem worthy," Remy completed, not bothering to hide his disgust.

"The key word is *worthy*," Mrs. Grantmore agreed. She finished her Tanqueray and tonic, slamming the ice-filled glass down with enough force to rattle the tabletop. "I'm not about to allow some worthless piece of riffraff to use my daughter—"

"Mother."

Olivia had returned, although neither Remy nor Mrs. Grantmore had noticed her approach, so wrapped up were they in their . . . *discussion*.

The older woman took a deep breath and composed herself. "Did you find the Tylenol?" she asked.

Her daughter let the bag containing the bottle of pills drop into her mother's lap.

"Thank you, dear."

Remy wasn't sure how much the young woman had heard, but the look upon her face told him it was enough.

"I think we're finished here," Mrs. Grantmore stated, shoving the bag into her purse.

And Remy couldn't have agreed more. For a brief instant he imagined the woman on her knees, begging forgiveness from the frightening visage of what he truly was, golden armor glistening, powerful wings beating the air as they held his mighty form aloft.

A soldier of God.

Seraphim.

But no matter how his true nature fought him, that wasn't who he was anymore.

"Thank you for your time, Mr. Chandler," the woman said stiffly, offering her hand as they stood.

"You're welcome," Remy said, taking and quickly releasing her hand, yet again resisting the urge to end her hateful existence in a searing release of Heaven's fire. "I'll send you my final invoice before week's end."

Without comment, the woman bent to gather her things, and Remy turned to her daughter.

"It was very nice meeting you, Olivia," he said, holding out his hand.

She took it with a small smile.

"I'm truly sorry about this," he told her as his gaze drifted to a displeased Mrs. Grantmore.

"As am I, Mr. Chandler," Olivia said, releasing his hand.

Remy left the two women then, feeling Mrs. Grantmore's eyes burning into his back as he walked toward the stairs, certain in the knowledge that it would take much more than Tylenol to kill the disease that grew inside her.

* * *

Outside the Westin, it was hot and humid, but how else would Boston be in August?

A quick glance at his watch showed Remy that if he didn't hurry, he would be late for his early dinner date with his friend Steven Mulvehill. Not that it really mattered; the homicide detective was never on time anyway.

Remy walked up Dartmouth Street toward Beacon, not a little concerned about his reaction toward Mrs. Grantmore. It was taking less and less these days to rouse the angelic nature he had worked so hard to contain. A sign of the times, most definitely, he mused as he stopped to let a cab pass that would certainly have run him down if he'd stepped in front of it.

And what then? he thought. *Would the Seraphim have emerged to smite the vehicle and its driver?*

A few years ago, a thought like that would have been just plain foolish. But now, since the death of his beloved wife, he couldn't be so sure. Everything had changed—in the earthly world, as well as in the unearthly.

He looked around him. Things looked the same, but the difference was there, an undercurrent. Whether they knew it or not—the pretzel man, the student, the teller at the bank stepping out for a quick cigarette break—the world was different.

And not in a good way.

Remy's own world had begun to change dramatically when his wife first became ill. From there it was as if a row of cosmic dominoes had begun to fall, with the disappearance of the Angel of Death and then the narrow averting of the Apocalypse, the nearly unbearable pain of Madeline's death, the return of Lucifer Morningstar to Hell, and the loss of Francis, the former Guardian angel who had been Remy's friend and frequent comrade in arms.

And it was just the beginning; of this Remy was sure.

He turned down Beacon Street, and the disturbing realization of how dramatically different things were suddenly became a reality when he caught sight of the bedraggled form of Steven Mulvehill waiting in front of the restaurant.

On time.

And the world became that much stranger a place.

The restaurant was pricey, even for an early dinner, but Mulvehill had a gift certificate he'd gotten from another detective whose wife had developed a wheat allergy and, according to Mulvehill, couldn't go out to eat anymore.

Remy was pretty sure there was more to the story; there always was when it came to things surrounding Mulvehill, but he didn't feel the need to dig any further. A free dinner was a free dinner, and he would leave it at that.

"Working today?" Mulvehill asked, reaching for his glass of water, in which a fresh lemon slice floated amongst the ice.

Remy popped another french fry into his mouth, nodding while he chewed.

"More of the weird shit?" Mulvehill asked, leaning forward to pick up the second half of an amazingly large hot pastrami sandwich that he had slathered with dark mustard.

Remy was having a cheeseburger, and, like the fries, it was excellent. He didn't have to eat; his sustenance came from the life energies around him, but eating had become one of his biggest pleasures and he wouldn't give it up for anything.

"Nope, nothing weird this time," he said, picking up his burger. "Just a very wealthy woman looking to put the kibosh on her daughter's relationship."

"That bitch," Mulvehill snarled, wiping his mustard-covered hands on the cloth napkin. Remy noticed that some of the dark condiment had dribbled onto his friend's tie, but there were so many other stains there already, it wasn't worth mentioning. "Did you set her straight? No, wait—did you get paid, and then set her straight?"

"Final bill hasn't gone out yet, but it will," Remy said around a large bite of burger. He hesitated a moment, then continued.

"She really pushed my buttons; I had to stifle the urge to fry her where she sat," he said, not looking at his friend. He pulled a slice of red onion from his sandwich and stuffed it into his mouth.

Mulvehill was strangely silent, and Remy looked up. The homicide detective knew all of Remy's secrets, and he was the only one Remy could share this with—now that Maddie was gone. He knew Mulvehill often wished he didn't know what he did, but that cat had been let out of the bag some time ago.

And besides, it always led to really interesting conversations.

"Seriously?" Mulvehill finally asked. "You really wanted to burn her alive with your angel superpowers?"

Remy halfheartedly nodded, shrugging his shoulders as he tried to explain. "It wasn't really me per se, but, y'know, the part of me that . . . you know."

Mulvehill slowly nodded. "Yeah, I know, but damn. Remind me never to piss you off unless we're near a fire extinguisher or a lake or something." He picked up a half-eaten pickle spear from his plate and took a bite.

"I'd never burn you alive," Remy said. He set what was left of his burger on his plate. "With all the booze you drink, you'd probably go off like some great big, fleshy Molotov cocktail."

"Oh, you're a fucking riot," Mulvehill said sarcastically. He reached for his water and held up the glass. "See, water." He took a drink.

"Only because you're on duty," Remy teased. "If you were off today, we'd probably need another three gift certificates to handle the bar bill."

"See if I invite you out on my dime again," the homicide cop said, going back to his mustard-drenched sandwich.

"It's a gift certificate," Remy reminded him.

"Yeah, that I could have used with any number of hot babes trying to become the next Mrs. Mulvehill."

Remy laughed, leaning back in his chair. "Any number of babes?" he repeated. He pulled a few more fries from his plate. "That's good."

"What, you don't think I'm desirable?" Mulvehill asked with a smile, a giant gob of brown mustard oozing down his chin.

"If we weren't in a public place, I'd take you now, you gorgeous hunk of man," Remy said.

They both laughed, then turned their attentions toward finishing their meals.

"Did you really want to burn her?" Mulvehill asked suddenly, breaking their silence. "Seriously?"

Remy looked up into his friend's worried gaze. He couldn't lie to him. "Yeah, I did," he answered quietly. He took the napkin from his lap and wiped his mouth.

"I have to say that isn't such a good thing."

Remy agreed. "No, and it worries me. Since Madeline . . . I feel myself drifting. . . . Not all the time, but sometimes, when certain things push a button."

Mulvehill noisily chewed the last of his pastrami sandwich and wiped the grease and mustard from his face. "The next well-done corpse I find in the city, I'm looking for you, pal," he said.

Remy gripped his water glass, staring at the ice and lemon slice. "It scares me."

His friend remained quiet. No snarky comeback; it wasn't the time.

"I'm afraid of the day when I can't . . . when I don't want to keep it inside anymore."

"Is that a possibility?" Mulvehill asked.

"Could be." Remy shrugged. "Probably not right now, but there could come a time when I won't have the things around me that keep me anchored to this world."

"Like Maddie," Mulvehill said quietly.

Remy silently nodded. "She was the most amazing thing in my life here, but now there's just this giant void where she used to be." He could feel a darkened mood descending on him, as it had a tendency to do when he thought too hard about things connected to his fragile humanity.

"I know what your problem is," Mulvehill said, tossing his napkin onto the tabletop. "I should've given you the gift certificate."

Remy looked across the table at his friend. "Should've given me the gift certificate? What the hell are you talking about?"

"You could've used it for a date," Mulvehill said. "You could've taken somebody out for a nice dinner and maybe found a new anchor—not that anybody could ever replace Maddie. I'm just saying it might help."

Remy had to laugh. "You think I should date?" he asked incredulously.

"Yeah, why not?" Mulvehill asked. "What was the name of that woman you told me about?" He snapped his fingers. "The waitress . . . you know who I mean."

"Linda," Remy said, focusing on the water in his glass again.

"Yeah, Linda. Why not go out with her?"

It was all so very complicated. Remy had met Linda Somerset through Francis. During the Great War in Heaven, Francis had chosen the wrong side, but then saw the error of his ways and was desperate to make amends. The Almighty had given him the duty of watching over one of the passages to the Hell prison of Tartarus, which just so happened to be in the basement of the apartment building that the Guardian angel owned on Newbury Street.

The last time Remy saw Francis, he had been badly wounded in the effort to prevent the Morningstar's catastrophic return to

Hell. Remy still held out hope that somehow Francis had managed to survive.

Although as time passed, it was becoming less and less likely.

Francis had been obsessed with Linda Somerset, even though she knew nothing of his interest. Remy had spoken to the attractive waitress at Newbury Street's Piazza restaurant a few times since Francis' disappearance, and he could understand his friend's fixation.

There was definitely something about Linda Somerset.

"I'd rather not talk about it," Remy said, hoping, but doubting, that would be the end of the discussion.

Their waiter approached the table. "Are you gentlemen finished?" he asked, reaching for their plates.

"Could you wrap that last piece of burger in some foil for me?" Remy asked the well-groomed Hispanic man who had introduced himself as Harry.

Harry smiled. "You must have a dog?" he asked, lifting the plate from the table.

"No, he's gonna have that as a snack later," Mulvehill offered. "He's really cheap."

"Will you shut up," Remy snarled. "Yes, I do, and if I don't bring him something, I'm going to be in trouble."

"No problem," Harry said. "Any coffee or dessert?"

They both declined, Mulvehill sticking out his belly and patting it as a sign that he was sated.

The waiter said he'd be back with Remy's food, and the check, excusing himself as he left with their dirty plates.

"So, why not?" Mulvehill started up again

"I said I don't want to talk about it," Remy said, trying not to become upset with his friend. He did not want to even think about burning his best friend alive. "It's far too early for me to even be thinking about things like this; Madeline hasn't even been gone six months."

"Stop right there," Mulvehill said. "I don't mean to be cold or heartless, but you just said the magic words."

Remy tilted his head inquisitively to one side, as he'd so often seen Marlowe, his four-year-old Labrador retriever, do.

"Madeline's gone, Remy," the detective said. "I know how you felt about her—I loved her too—but if her being gone and your being lonely mean you're going to start losing your shit and frying people every time you get annoyed, maybe you should think about the benefits of some female companionship."

Mulvehill's words were like a kick to the teeth, and Remy really didn't know how to react.

"You're not pissed that I said that, right?" Mulvehill asked cautiously as Harry returned to the table with their check and Remy's leftovers wrapped in foil.

"No," Remy lied.

"You're not gonna cook my ass?" he asked, pulling the wrinkled gift certificate from the inside pocket of his sports jacket and placing it in the leather folder with the check and an equally wrinkled twenty-dollar bill.

At first Remy didn't answer.

"You heard what I said about the dangerous levels of alcohol in your body."

"Screw you. Are you mad at me or not?"

"I'm not mad. I just don't want to talk about this anymore," Remy said, slowly getting up from his seat.

"You said Maddie's been gone for less than six months, and I bet it's been the longest almost six months of your life, hasn't it?" the normally unemotional man said, gripping Remy's elbow. "I hate to see you like this and then to hear you say things about losing control. It just gets me thinking that . . ."

"I'm all right, Steven," Remy said, forcing a smile. "Really, I'm all right. I think this case just brought out my bad side, but it's done now, and I can get back to my naturally cheerful self."

He felt his friend studying him, searching for a sign, a crack in the armor. Remy started for the door so Mulvehill couldn't look closer.

"Hey, Chandler," his friend called.

Remy turned slowly.

The homicide detective was holding the piece of foil-wrapped hamburger.

"You taking this or do you want to be on your dog's shit list?"

Remy returned to take the package from Mulvehill.

If there was one shit list he couldn't bear to be on, it was Marlowe's.

Marlowe paced excitedly in the backseat of Remy's Corolla.

"*Rabbits.*" Remy heard the dog muttering beneath his breath in the guttural language of his breed. "*Rabbits, rabbits, rabbits.*"

"And maybe squirrels," Remy contributed, looking at the dog's reaction in his rearview mirror.

"*Maybe squirrels,*" Marlowe repeated. "*Rabbits; maybe squirrels.*"

Remy had returned to his Pinckney Street home, strangely agitated after his dinner with Steven Mulvehill. His friend had definitely touched on a particularly sensitive nerve.

Putting his signal on, Remy took a right into the parking lot of Mount Auburn Cemetery. He had the pick of the lot and eased into a space in a nice patch of shade thrown by an oak tree.

His wife had been gone for nearly six months and he still felt the magnitude of her passing each and every day. The idea that he could push aside her memory, and the love he still felt for her, was unthinkable.

So why was it that deep down, he knew his friend was probably right?

Marlowe was panting like a runaway freight train as he turned off the car's engine and opened the door to a blast of August heat.

"All right, all right," Remy said, opening the passenger-side rear door.

Marlowe leapt out, immediately placing his nose to the ground and beginning to track his prey.

"Anything?" Remy asked.

"*Rabbits; maybe squirrels,*" Marlowe reported quite seriously.

"Thought so," Remy answered.

There was no one in sight, so he let Marlowe roam. He followed his dog through the metal gateway onto the winding path that led through one of the prettiest cemeteries in the Greater Boston area. Marlowe continued the hunt, nose moving along the ground, and off the path to the grassy areas around the trees and grave markers.

"Hey!" Remy called.

The Labrador stopped and lifted his head.

"No peeing on the headstones," Remy reminded him.

"*No pee,*" Marlowe grumbled.

It was certainly hot, but there was a hint of a cooling breeze from the north, a harbinger of less-stifling weather, and perhaps even some much-needed rain, the angel thought.

The vast lawns surrounding the grave sites were dappled with dried, brown patches of grass, and even the trees had that parched, withered look with branches hanging low.

But things couldn't have been more different at Madeline's plot.

The green around her grave site was lush, dark, and healthy, with wildflowers more vibrant than all the colors of the rainbow surrounding her concrete marker as if in celebration. This was how it was year-round, a special gift to her memory—a thank-you from the Angel of Death, Israfil, to Remy, for his help in preventing the angel from triggering the Apocalypse.

Remy approached the grave as he normally did, feeling the same pangs of sadness then that he'd had during his very first visit.

"Hey, beautiful," he said, reading her name on the stone, while admiring some of the more unusual blooms that flourished there. He was pretty sure that most of the flowers weren't even native to this hemisphere, but here they were, growing just for her.

"How're things?" he asked, kneeling upon the grave. There were some weeds growing up amongst the flowers, and he reached down, plucking them from the always-fertile ground.

Remy knew his wife wasn't actually there anymore.

He knew full well that when she had passed, her remaining life energies had immediately left her body and returned to the source of power in the universe that made all things. The stuff of creation; Madeline was in the sun and the stars, the trees and the grass; a part of everything that flew, crawled, swam, slithered, ran, and walked upon the surface of the earth.

Yes, Madeline as he remembered her wasn't there anymore, but he liked to come to this place of beauty to honor her memory. It was a monument to the amazing person she had been and to the special love they had shared.

Remy found himself pondering Mulvehill's words. They'd struck a chord deep within him.

It wasn't as though he'd never had the thought himself. Remy knew he was lonely, and in moments of weakness, had briefly considered the what-ifs of seeking companionship. But his thoughts would always return to Madeline and how it all felt like some sort of horrible betrayal to her memory.

That was why he had come today, just the thought that Steven Mulvehill might be right sending him to his wife's grave site for penance.

"There could never be another you," he used to tell her, and he remembered the smile that would appear on her face. It still had the same effect on him, even if it was only from memory.

His stomach sort of dropped, as though he were on an elevator suddenly starting down to the next floor, and then he smiled, recalling how lucky he had been to have had her in his life.

But now she was gone, leaving behind a sucking void of loneliness that seemed impossible to fill.

And did he truly want to?

That was the question, and the reason he was so disturbed by Mulvehill's observation that it might be time to let go of the past and look to the future.

"If I can't have you, do I want anybody else?" he asked the grave, not expecting an answer.

He rose to his feet, brushing some stray blades of grass and dirt from the front of his jeans, and looked to see where Marlowe had gotten to. He could see the dog off in the distance, circling the base of an oak tree, and called to him. The dog glanced threateningly up the tree, then gave a single bark, a warning to a squirrel that next time it wouldn't be so lucky, before bounding across the cemetery toward Remy.

"Did you give that squirrel the business?" Remy asked the Labrador as he lovingly patted his head.

The dog panted furiously, lapping up the affection.

"*Gave business,*" Marlowe agreed, his thick pink tongue lolling with the heat.

"I think it's time to go," Remy told him, and the dog agreed, turning toward the trail back to the parking lot and the air-conditioned car.

"Aren't you going to say good-bye to Madeline?" Remy asked the back of the animal.

"*Not there,*" Marlowe said, not even turning around. "*Madeline gone.*"

Madeline gone.

*   *   *

They returned to Beacon Hill only a little late for Marlowe's supper, but the dog nevertheless wasted no time in letting Remy know.

"I don't remember your ever being this demanding," Remy said. He picked up Marlowe's water bowl and rinsed it before refilling it with fresh water. "Is this some new teenage phase you're going through?"

"*Hungry*," the dog said, his tail wagging.

"You're always hungry," Remy responded, pulling a plastic container filled with food out of a lower cabinet. Using a metal measuring cup, he dumped a full scoop of the nugget-sized food into another metal dish.

"This stuff looks delicious," Remy said jokingly, giving the bowl a shake. The contents rattled enticingly.

Marlowe's eyes were locked on the bowl as Remy crossed the kitchen to set it down beside the water.

"Go to it," he said, stepping back as the hungry Labrador charged the bowl and immediately began to eat.

"Don't forget to chew," Remy warned. They'd had some problems with this in the past, usually on the living room carpet or in Remy's bed.

"Is it all right if I have a moment to myself now?" he asked the animal.

The dog ignored him, chowing down on the tasty morsels that filled his bowl.

"I guess that's a yes," Remy said. He reached down and thumped the dog's side with his hand, before turning toward the kitchen doorway.

And then he noticed the flashing red light of his answering machine on the counter.

"Huh," he said, having a hard time remembering the last time he'd had a message on his landline, never mind receiving a call. Most of his calls these days came over his cell, or the office phone.

He stopped and pushed the PLAY button.

You have one new message, the machine told him in a clipped, mechanical voice, over the sound of Marlowe's slurping at his water bowl.

At first there was the hiss of silence, and for a second Remy thought it might be a hang-up, but then a woman began to speak.

"Um, hi . . ." There was another pause, the woman grumbling something beneath her breath that Remy couldn't make out.

He leaned closer to the machine.

"Yeah, ummm, this message is for Remy Chandler. . . . I'm calling because . . ."

Again she paused, and he listened as she whispered to herself, "How do I say this without your thinking I'm crazy?"

Marlowe had joined him, wiping his face, still wet from his drink, on the side of Remy's leg.

Thank you very much, Marlowe, he wanted to tell the dog, but he was still listening to the message.

"I'm calling to ask . . . Why am I calling?" She sounded frustrated, and perhaps a little confused. "I was calling to ask . . . I was calling to ask if you had a big black dog," she finally said.

Remy quickly glanced at Marlowe, who was looking up at him with that patented Labrador smile and tail wag.

"Oh my God, I can't believe I did this," she finally said and, without another word, ended the call.

End of message, his machine then told him with a high-pitched beep.

"Okay," he said to himself, and then to the dog standing beside him, "What the hell was that all about?"

But Marlowe didn't have any answers either.

CHAPTER TWO

Clifton Poole took a deep breath, then slowly exhaled, awaiting the effects of the drug combination he'd just taken.

It was a special cocktail of barbiturates and antidepressants made just for him after years of trial and error. It was the only thing that would silence the voices.

Everything in the world had a voice—psychic impressions left by contact with living beings—and Poole could hear them all, whether he wanted to or not, which was why he so enjoyed his special medication, and the numbing bliss it provided him, no matter how short.

He lay naked in the windowless room of his country estate in Lincolnshire, England, surrounded by nothing. Built to his own specifications, the room was only cold plaster walls and ceiling and a wooden floor. No more than three people were involved with its design and construction, and the materials had come from local merchants.

The voices that radiated from this room were minimal, and the drugs readily dulled them, allowing him to slip into sweet, restful oblivion, without too much of the usual commotion.

Poole felt himself drifting down, down, down, into the darkness of the abyss, the prattling voices growing softer and less defined by the second.

He was just about to succumb to the embrace of his beloved mistress, oblivion, when he noticed the pulse of color through the lids of his closed eyes. He tried to ignore the yellow flash that was trying to pull him from his rest.

But he opened his eyes instead.

The room clamored to tell its story, as over the single, wooden door, a yellow bulb flashed for his attention.

Look at me. I come from a factory in China where . . .

He watched the light continue to flash, praying it would stop, but it didn't. He sighed, blocking out the voices, and climbed awkwardly to his bare feet.

"This had better be good," he slurred as he stumbled numbly to the door and opened it to find his valet, Broughton, standing on the other side, white handkerchief pressed to a bleeding nose.

"There's someone here to see you," Broughton said, his voice sounding nasal.

"Tell him I'm busy." Poole started to pull the door closed, but Broughton's foot blocked it.

"No, sir," the man said, a disquieting look in his eyes. "You must see this fellow now." The valet took the handkerchief away from his nose, allowing the blood to flow freely. "He's quite insistent."

The voices from the hallway were louder now, buzzing, insistent that he listen, even though he'd heard their stories millions of times, and would continue to do so as long he was alive, or sober. He desperately wanted his rest and was tempted to refuse Broughton, but the look in his valet's eyes—and the blood streaming from his nose—told him that might not be wise.

"Give me my robe," Poole finally ordered, stumbling out of the special room.

Broughton handed his employer a terry cloth robe.

"Make a very strong pot of coffee," Poole instructed as he slipped his pale, naked form into the warmth of the thick white bathrobe. It too tried to tell him how it had come to exist, and Poole shook his head violently to dislodge the images.

Broughton bowed slightly, handkerchief again pressed to his nose, and turned to leave.

"Who is it?" Poole asked suddenly, holding the ends of the terry cloth belt in each hand.

"Excuse me, sir?" The valet turned back to him.

"Who's the visitor?" Poole asked. "What's his name?"

"Mathias, sir," Broughton said. "A Mr. Mathias from America."

"American," Poole grunted, cinching the belt tightly about his waist. "Bloody hell."

Mathias hated to be away from his mistress, and hoped this bit of business wouldn't take long.

He glanced down at the knuckles of his right hand, and the hint of blood that stained them. Nothing could stop him from seeing Poole.

Delilah needed him, and she would have him.

He got up from his chair in the elaborate den of the English country estate and walked to one of the large windows, looking out on what appeared to be miles of lush green grass and blossoming trees. Peacocks roamed the grounds, letting loose their strangely haunting call as they strutted about.

Mathias wondered how they would taste roasted on a spit over an open fire, the image bringing a smile to his face.

He turned back to the study, taking note of its ancient statuary and heavy, wood-framed glass cases filled with all manner of priceless artifacts, from jeweled goblets to bracelets made of gold.

Objects of great worth, no doubt found by Poole using his

unique ability, Mathias wagered. But did this man have the talent required to find what his mistress most desired?

"Admiring my baubles?" asked a voice from behind him, a voice Mathias immediately found annoying.

He turned to look at the man standing in the doorway to the study. He was thin, and dressed in an expensive cream-colored suit, his white shirt unbuttoned to display a pale, hairless chest.

"Just a few of my private acquisitions, ones I couldn't bear to part with," the man said, stepping farther into the room. "I'm Clifton Poole, and you must be Mr. Mathias."

Mathias smiled coldly, walking toward the man, hand extended. "Just Mathias."

"I'm sorry, but I don't shake hands," Poole said nervously. "I hope you understand."

Mathias moved with the quickness of a cobra snatching the man's spindly, cold appendage in his.

"No, I hope *you* understand," he said, holding tightly to Poole's hand.

If what Mathias understood about Clifton Poole's unique ability was true, the man was able to read psychic impressions from anything he touched, a strange mixture of psychometry and remote viewing, a kind of voice Poole could use to track items of great wealth and power.

Poole was a Hound of the highest esteem and someone Delilah believed could assist her.

Poole fell to his knees, his pale features almost gray, reminding Mathias of meat left to spoil in the hot summer sun.

He wondered what Poole was seeing . . . experiencing. Mathias had most certainly led an interesting life, a professional soldier since the age of eighteen, eventually leaving service to his country and committing his extensive talents to the highest bidder. The life of a mercenary had been his pleasure, but he hadn't really known the true meaning of the word until he had found *her*.

A powerful mixture of lust, fear, love, and awe flushed through his body as it always did with the thought of his beloved Delilah.

The Hound was crying, weakly attempting to pull his hand away, but Mathias continued to hold fast.

"What do you see?" Mathias asked, taking a certain amount of pleasure from the man's discomfort.

"Please," Poole begged through streaming eyes, "please let me go."

"Do you see her?" Mathias asked urgently. "She is my world. . . . Nothing matters except her happiness. Do you see, Clifton Poole?"

"You . . . you gave it to her." Poole's voice was strained, barely able to speak the words. "You gave her your soul."

Mathias at last released Poole's hand, and the Hound slumped to the floor of the study, whimpering.

"Yes, I did give her my soul," Mathias said with a smile. He held his hand out, gazing at the strange scars on the back of it, the marks that she had given him, marks to show that he belonged to her. They were of two lips, a kiss, burned into the flesh of his hand. He wore the red, raised scars proudly. "And why not? I wasn't using it anyway."

Poole managed to crawl to a cabinet and used it to haul himself up from the ground. "What do you want?" he asked weakly, turning toward Mathias, the sound of fear in his voice.

Mathias liked that sound; fear was good, an excellent motivator.

"My mistress has need of your talents," he said, "and is willing to pay quite handsomely for them."

The Hound shook his head. "I couldn't possibly—"

Mathias lunged forward and drove his fist down through the

front of the case next to Poole, sending fragments of glass flying into the air and falling into the case.

"And that is why she sent me," he said. His knuckles were bleeding as he fished around inside the case for a beautifully intricate gold bracelet he had spied earlier. "I don't take no for an answer."

Mathias removed the bracelet, slipping it onto his wrist. "I think she'll like this," he said with a smile.

The study door opened and Poole's valet entered, carrying a silver serving tray with coffee. He came to an abrupt stop when he saw his employer and the glass on the floor around him.

"Broughton . . ." Poole beckoned pathetically.

"Bring that in here," Mathias instructed Broughton, ignoring Poole. He motioned the servant toward a nearby table. "I think a cup of coffee would be just the thing before we begin our journey." He turned toward the Hound. "Don't you agree, Mr. Poole?"

And Mathias smiled as Poole slowly nodded, a look of utter resignation on his pale, sickly features.

It was when she slept deeply that she remembered them.

Their faces flashed by her dreaming eyes, breaking what remained of a shattered heart into razor-sharp slivers of sorrow. The pain was excruciating, but it was also her fuel—the fuel that fed the fires of her rage.

They were her husbands and her children, her countless attempts at a normal, peaceful existence.

But *He* would not let her have that.

No matter how much she begged or prayed to be forgiven, He would eventually take notice of her happiness and steal it away with a swipe of His hand. She should have learned by now, but perhaps that was part of the curse as well—the belief that maybe, this time, she would be forgiven her trespasses and allowed to love with all her heart.

She remembered them, their beautiful faces haunting her from the past; she also remembered how they had died. From natural disaster to debilitating disease, one by one by one they were taken from her, leaving her only the memory of what she'd had, and the deep, burning pain of her loss.

She wanted to die, but He would not allow that either.

Although with each loved one lost, a piece of her humanity did die, and it had been a very long time since she'd last thought of herself as truly human.

In her dream, the children were crying for her, for their mother, a symphony of sorrow. She wanted to hush them, to hold them to her bosom, and tell them that soon they could stop crying.

That soon she would end the curse.

And they would all be together again.

Delilah awoke, not with a start, or a scream, or a cry dancing upon her lips. She awoke perfectly calm, a sense of satisfaction growing in her breast.

Mathias had returned; she could feel him, his sense of anticipation.

She stretched languidly upon the four-poster bed, then rose and slipped into a robe of Chinese silk. She pulled open her double bedroom doors just as Mathias drew near.

There was no question of whether or not he had succeeded in his mission.

For those who loved Delilah would rather die than fail her.

Her first impression wasn't the best.

A frail, silly-looking man in a dirty white suit, he was sitting on the balcony of her home, which overlooked the Bicol River in the Philippines, while sipping from a tumbler of whiskey.

"Mr. Poole?" she asked, stepping out through the open doors. The diaphanous material of her long dress floated in the humid breeze blowing from the river. "I'm so happy you came."

Mathias followed close behind her like the obedient dog he was, and the sight of him made Poole begin to tremble, the ice in his whiskey tinkling like bells.

"I had no choice," Poole said in an attempt at defiance.

Delilah clucked. "Oh, don't be like that." She seemed to float across the balcony and onto the divan across from him. Mathias remained standing, hands clasped behind his back, as if awaiting his next command.

"I have need of your special skills," Delilah continued.

A boy came from the house carrying a crystal pitcher filled with ice water and lemons. There was a tall glass on the table in front of Delilah, and he filled it without making eye contact.

"Thank you, Maynard," she said, taking a sip of the cold water. "Mr. Poole, would you like more whiskey?"

"I'm fine," he said, staring angrily into his glass.

Delilah motioned the boy away, and he left them alone.

Back to business.

"You need me," Poole said with a laugh, before bringing the whiskey to his mouth. "What if I refuse?"

Delilah said nothing, mixing the ice and lemon in her glass with a long, delicate finger.

"You'll have this one here take me out into the jungle and put a bullet in the back of my skull?"

"Heaven forbid," Delilah said, in mock offense. "You're free to go at any time . . . after you hear my offer."

Poole gulped his whiskey, refusing to look at her.

"And what is your offer?" he asked, finally looking into her eyes, as if the whiskey had given him courage.

"Help me find what I'm looking for and I will make you a very wealthy man," she said. "It's quite simple really."

"I'm already a wealthy man," he replied.

"Oh, Mr. Poole." Delilah smiled. "Wealth can be measured in so many ways."

She held the man's gaze, working her magic upon him. He was like a fish on the end of a line, being slowly drawn to her.

"You will have whatever you need to find my prize. . . . Every resource will be at your disposal. Isn't that right, Mathias?" she asked.

The warrior behind her nodded. "Anything . . . just ask."

Poole smiled. "Anything?" he repeated, finishing off what remained of his drink. "How about some more of this?"

"Of course," Delilah said, about to call for Maynard.

"I want him to get it," Poole interrupted, holding out his glass to Mathias.

Mathias glared at him.

"You did say anything," he said, giving the tumbler a little shake, making the ice jingle merrily.

"Yes, we did," Delilah agreed. "Mathias, if you would be so kind."

Mathias stepped forward to snatch the glass from the man's hand, quickly turning and disappearing into the house.

Alone, Delilah and Poole smiled at each other.

"Does that mean you accept my offer?" Delilah asked.

"How could I resist?" Poole said with a giggle. "I've always wanted my own bloody island."

Delilah laughed with the vile little man, making him believe he actually had some power in this situation. She much preferred when they came to her willingly. "Only an island, Mr. Poole? You're thinking far too small."

They shared another laugh as Mathias returned with a tray,

carrying an ice bucket, Poole's glass, and a bottle of whiskey. He set it down on a small table beside Poole.

"Just a little ice, please," Poole prodded.

The look on Mathias' face told Delilah there was nothing he would have liked better than to kill the English Hound with his own two hands. But ever the good soldier, her warrior carefully placed a handful of cubes into the glass and then filled it with whiskey.

"Thanks ever so much," Poole said as he took the glass from Mathias.

"Is that all?" Mathias asked, his words as sharp as a knife blade.

"For now," Poole replied, motioning Mathias back to his position behind Delilah's divan.

"So, what are you looking for?" Poole asked, taking a drink of his whiskey.

"Right to the point," Delilah said. "I think we're going to get along just fine, Mr. Poole." She turned her head slightly toward Mathias.

Immediately he left the balcony, returning just a few moments later with the iron statue they had taken from the Vietnamese temple, before detonating the explosives that had reduced the holy place to so much rubble. He cradled the metal infant in his arms, carrying it as carefully as he would have one of her many children.

"What is that?" Poole asked, his speech somewhat thick as the whiskey began to take effect.

Delilah flowed from the divan, meeting Mathias in the center of the balcony.

"A vessel," she said, staring at the statue. No matter how many times she looked upon it, it never ceased to infatuate her. Sometimes, late at night, when she fought to keep sleep from claiming her, she swore she could hear it crying.

"A vessel for what?" Poole asked.

"Give it to him," Delilah instructed, and Mathias slowly moved closer.

"No, wait," Poole cried nervously. He tried to set his drink down on the nearby table, but it crashed to the floor.

"This vessel once contained my prize, Mr. Poole."

The Hound was trying to move away. She was sure he could hear the vessel . . . hear it as it whispered its secrets to him.

Mathias placed the infant-shaped container at the man's feet.

"Please," Poole begged. His face had become bright red, and his body shook spastically. "Take it away."

"Touch it, Mr. Poole," Delilah commanded, using her talent to bend his will to hers.

Unable to resist her, the Hound leaned forward, fingers splayed to touch the child. He screamed as his fingertips brushed the sides of the infant's head. He tried to pull away, but the power of the vessel drew him back. He slid from his chair, dropping to his knees, running his hands over the tarnished metal body. His eyes had rolled back in his head, and he was murmuring indistinctly as tears stained his face.

His probing fingers found the hidden latch, splitting the metal child open, allowing him access to where Delilah's prize had rested for centuries.

Poole gasped, his breath catching in his throat.

"Control, Mr. Poole," Delilah barked.

Her commanding words seemed to have an effect as his eyes rolled forward, and he seemed to be trying to focus on the smooth, concave surface inside the vessel.

He reached out a shaking hand, but quickly pulled it back, as if afraid he might be burned. "I—I can't," he sobbed pathetically, a trail of mucus running from his nose. "Please, I just want to . . ."

Delilah was growing impatient. She wanted her answers now.

"You will, Mr. Poole," she snarled, reaching out to grab hold of his wrist, forcing his hand down into the open body of the vessel.

The Hound immediately began to scream and scream. . . .

And Delilah wasn't sure if he was ever going to stop.

CHAPTER THREE

Remy knew it was going to be one of those days.

"It's hot as Hell in there," the man from McNulty Heating and Cooling warned as he held open the front door to Remy's office building.

He was short and a little fat. The front of his light blue shirt was stained with grease, his dark navy work pants powdered with dust.

"Let me guess," Remy said, passing through the foyer. "The air-conditioning is broken."

The repairman laughed. "You must be the detective." He pointed at the building registry hanging on the wall in the lobby.

"Bingo! Any idea when it'll be fixed?" Remy asked, more out of curiosity than anything. He really wasn't affected by temperature, be it hot or cold.

The McNulty guy smiled, shaking his head. "Haven't a clue. We're gonna have to order some parts—could take a few days."

Another McNulty employee, a disgruntled look on his face, came up from the building's basement.

"What's the verdict?" the first asked.

"Put a fuckin' bullet in it," he grunted. "Gonna need a whole new unit." He kept right on walking through the doorway and out to a van parked in front of the building.

"There you have it," Remy's new friend said with a shrug.

"Guess so." Remy turned toward the stairs.

"What, you're still going up?" the repairman asked from the doorway.

"Yeah, probably push some papers around and take an early lunch."

"Better you than me," the man said, letting the door close as he left to join his partner. "It's gonna be hot as Hell up there."

Remy continued up the stairs to his office, letting the man's words bounce around inside his skull. He was tempted to explain that Hell was actually a place of extremes—of both intense heat and numbing cold—but he doubted the repairman would have really much cared, and then of course, he would want to know how Remy knew so much about the infernal realm.

Why, I was just there on business, he imagined saying.

He chuckled out loud and unlocked his office door. But still he couldn't help wondering what was happening in Hell. After usurping Heaven's power there, the Son of the Morning had begun to reshape the realm. What had once been prison to those who had followed him in his rebellion against Heaven was slowly becoming Lucifer's twisted version of the Eternal Realm. And how exactly did Heaven plan on dealing with that?

Remy shook his head. Those were matters of the damned and the divine, with humanity caught square in the middle.

He stepped into his office and realized the air-conditioning repairman had been right. It was stifling in the room. He closed the door and went directly to the window, opening it wide in the hope of catching a breeze to air out the stale, musty smell.

Then he checked his phone for messages and, finding none, decided to spend the morning working on invoices and paying some bills. But first there was a mighty need for coffee.

He had just filled the machine and set the carafe to collect the elixir of life, when there came a knock at the door and a woman cautiously entered the office.

"Hi," Remy said cheerfully, moving toward her in greeting. "May I help you?"

The woman was wearing a dungaree jacket and skirt, and a bright red T-shirt. She was about five foot six, with bleached blond hair, and looked at first to be in her late thirties, although as Remy drew closer, he realized her eyes didn't seem as old as she appeared.

The woman closed the door behind her, nervously moving her bag from one shoulder to the other.

"Umm," she said, uncertainty in her tone. "You're Remy Chandler, right? The private investigator?"

"Yes, I am," Remy said, smiling kindly. The woman looked about to snap. "Is there something I can do for you, Ms. . . . ?"

"York," the woman replied, her sandaled feet scuffing across the hardwood floor as she stepped farther into the room and extended her hand toward him. "Deryn York."

Remy shook the woman's warm and clammy hand.

"Why don't you have a seat, Ms. York." He directed her toward the chair in front of his desk, then headed back for the coffeepot.

"Coffee?" he asked her. "I've just made it."

"Yes, thank you," she said, pulling at the front of her skirt so it just about touched her knees.

Remy realized he had only one clean mug, the other one being sort of dusty.

"Let me just rinse this out," he said, going to the tiny bathroom across the room. "It's really warm out there today," he said, raising his voice over the water in the sink.

"Yeah," she answered, "hot as Hell."

Y'know, Hell is a place of extremes. . . .

"It certainly is," he replied instead as he left the bathroom. "How do you like your coffee?"

"Oh, just sugar, please."

"How many?" he asked, pouring her a cup, and placing it on the edge of the desk in front of her. He went around his desk and opened the center drawer where he'd recently seen a few packets.

"Do you have six?" she asked.

"Six?"

She smiled self-consciously and shrugged. "I like it really sweet."

Remy counted the packets in his drawer. "I only have five," he told her.

"That's fine," she said. "Five should be good."

He set down the sugar packets. "Here you go," he said.

"Thank you." She immediately ripped open the packets one after another, pouring their contents into the dark brown liquid.

"So, Ms. York," Remy said, sitting down in his chair and taking a sip from his mug with the picture of a black Labrador retriever, "what can I do for you?"

She sipped her own coffee and made a face. Obviously it wasn't sweet enough.

"I called your home last night," she said, setting the mug carefully down on the edge of his desk, "but I didn't leave a name . . . or much of a message really." She laughed nervously.

"I thought that might have been you," Remy said.

"Yeah, I'm sorry. I really didn't know what to say, and I had no intention of even coming here, but . . ."

"But here you are," Remy finished for her.

"Exactly," she responded. "You're all I have left . . . my last resort."

"Okay then." Remy grabbed a pad of paper and a pen. "What's brought you here, Deryn York?"

She took another sip of coffee, perhaps to fortify herself, before starting to speak.

"My daughter," she said, her eyes becoming misty. "My daughter, Zoe."

"All right," Remy encouraged her. "Take your time and tell me what happened." He was trying to make her feel comfortable; the tension was spilling off her in waves. "Are you from this area?"

Deryn shook her head. "Originally I'm from South Carolina, but we moved to Florida about five years ago."

"You and your daughter?" he probed.

"And my husband," she added, reaching for the coffee again. "We've since separated, but I can't seem to get rid of him. He insisted on coming here with Zoe and me, even though I didn't want him to."

"So you've moved here from Florida?"

"Not permanently," she quickly corrected. "I hate the cold, but I heard the best doctors are here, so I didn't really have a choice. As soon as they figure out what's wrong with Zoe, we'll go right back home."

Remy nodded, taking a drink of his coffee. "Your daughter is sick then?"

Deryn stared down into the contents of her mug. "The doctors in Florida say she's probably autistic," she explained quietly, then looked up at Remy. "But Carl wanted to be sure, and he said the best doctors are here. He's from here originally."

"Where were you taking her?"

"Franciscan Hospital for Children." She stopped, reaching down into her bag and removing a pack of cigarettes. Without even asking Remy if it was okay, she placed one between her lips and lit it with a disposable lighter.

"I can't believe how fucking stupid I was," she said, dropping the lighter and package of smokes back into her bag. "Oh, is this all right?" she asked, suddenly conscious of what she was doing.

"It's fine," Remy said, not wanting to upset her. They were

finally getting someplace, and he didn't want to cancel the momentum. "Why do you say you were stupid?"

"Because I trusted him," she said angrily. "I let my guard down." Deryn feverishly puffed on the cigarette, forming a toxic cloud around her head in the too-warm office. "I wasn't feeling well, so I stayed at the hotel and let Carl take Zoe to an appointment. And that's the last time I saw them. It's been six days." Deryn choked back a sob, bringing a hand to her mouth.

"There hasn't been any contact with Carl since he took Zoe?" Remy asked.

"No," she said miserably, finishing the smoke and dropping the butt into her coffee mug where it hissed faintly.

"Have you contacted the police?"

"Yes, once I realized what the son of a bitch had done. There's a warrant out for his arrest."

"And you have no idea where he might have taken your daughter?"

"I don't have a clue."

Remy stood and grabbed his mug. "Would you like another cup? I can rinse yours out."

"No, no thanks," she said with a nervous shake of her head. "I'm good."

Remy refilled his cup and returned to his desk. "So tell me about your relationship with Carl," he began. "Was it an amicable split or . . ."

"We only stayed together as long as we did because of Zoe," Deryn explained. "We thought a baby would help us, but with her being different and all . . ." Her voice trailed off and she looked as though she had the weight of the world upon her shoulders.

"Does Carl have any history of violence?" Remy asked. "He wouldn't want to cause Zoe any harm, would he?"

"Oh no," she said quickly. "Carl really is basically a good guy.

We both had kind of screwed-up childhoods, but we managed to get beyond that. We were good parents, Mr. Chandler."

"Except that Carl has taken your daughter."

"Yeah," she said, her voice cracking with emotion. "But maybe if I had paid better attention, this could all have been avoided."

"Ms. York, you can't beat yourself up about—"

"I need to show you something, Mr. Chandler," Deryn interrupted, pulling her bag up onto her lap.

Remy leaned forward, curious, as she withdrew a handful of folded pieces of construction paper from inside the bag. Carefully she unfolded them, looking at each before handing them to Remy.

He looked at the first. It was obviously a child's drawing, done in crayon, crudely depicting a little girl and a man leaving what appeared to be a hospital. The next picture was of the same girl and man, only they were in a car. The man was in the front seat, driving, while the child stared out the back window, yellow circles beneath her eyes—probably falling tears, Remy guessed.

"Zoe did these?" he asked, looking up at Deryn.

She nodded. "About three weeks ago."

He was looking at the drawing again when the woman's words permeated his brain. "Three weeks ago?" he repeated. "So your husband must have been preparing her for this?" He waited as Deryn shook her head no.

"She drew those pictures without any knowledge of what her father was going to do," the woman explained. "But she knew he was going to take her, Mr. Chandler, just like she knew I would be coming to see you."

Deryn leaned forward and handed him one last drawing.

Remy's eyes widened in surprise as he studied it. Zoe had drawn a childlike depiction of the front entrance to his brownstone, a person standing in front with a black dog on a leash. He was certain the person was himself—the feathered wings were a dead giveaway—and, moreover, floating in the air, written in a small child's handwriting, were his address and telephone number.

Mathias stopped the Range Rover halfway down the dirt path, just close enough to see the bungalow ahead.

Poole had eventually proven his worth, using information he derived by touching the Vietnamese vessel, as well as extensive maps of the entire world. According to the Hound, Delilah's prize would be found here, in Palatka, Florida, of all places.

It wasn't exactly a place that Mathias imagined finding an object that could quite easily change the course of the world, but perhaps that was the point—no ancient temples surrounded by worshippers ready to die in its defense; instead, a run-down bungalow in the backwaters of Florida.

Ingenious.

He removed the Glock pistol from the holster underneath his arm and chambered a round.

"Are we ready?" he asked the other four men on his team.

They grunted their responses as each prepared his own weapons. Febonio, Yelverton, and Wallace, in the backseat, put rounds in the chambers of their hand weapons, while Cole, in the front passenger seat, flipped off the safety of his Mac 10 semiautomatic machine gun.

Mathias hoped it would be enough. They had no idea what they were walking into.

"Let's go," he said, turning off the engine and stepping out into the tropical heat.

Mathias led the way up the rocky dirt path. A mutt tied to a rusting swing in a backyard overrun with weeds began to bark ferociously at their approach, and Mathias was tempted to put a bullet in the mangy beast. But they had to appear harmless; no sense in alerting those inside of potential danger.

As they neared the falling-down porch, he motioned his men to step back out of the line of sight and walked up the four cracked concrete steps to the front door. He could hear the sounds of a television from inside.

He took a quick glance over his shoulder to be sure his team was in position, then rapped loudly on the dented, rusted aluminum door.

Mathias waited, listening to the sounds from inside. The volume on the television went down, and that was his cue to knock again.

Now he could hear muffled voices coming from inside—a man, a woman, and at least one child. The door suddenly opened a crack, and half a face peered out, glaring at him over a short length of chain.

"Yeah?"

Mathias could smell the stink of beer wafting from the man's breath. "Hi," he said with his biggest, fakest, nice-guy smile. "Is this thirty-seven Nautical Way?" he asked, reading from a wrinkled piece of scrap paper he pulled from his jacket pocket.

"Who wants to know?" the man asked.

He could hear the woman in the background whispering. A child started to cry, and she instantly barked for it to shut up.

A mother after his own heart.

"I'm from Destination Delivery, and I have a certified letter for thirty-seven Nautical," Mathias said, pretending to reach inside his jacket for the envelope.

"What is it?" the man demanded.

"I don't know, but if you want to sign for it, you can see for yourself," Mathias said, wearing his mask of harmlessness.

The door slammed closed and Mathias could hear the man and woman talking again. Then came the sound of the chain being moved and the door opened wide to reveal a scruffy middle-aged man wearing shorts and a sweat-stained T-shirt, a filthy NASCAR hat perched atop his head, with long straggly hair like straw creeping out from beneath.

"I'm the resident," he said.

He held out a filthy hand, but instead of holding an envelope, Mathias had withdrawn his Glock, which he was pointing at the man's face.

"Sorry," he said with a sneer. "Guess I don't have a certified letter after all, but I do have this loaded gun."

The man's hands flew into the air. "What the fuck!" he exclaimed, slowly backing away from the door.

Mathias gestured for Febonio and Wallace to follow him inside, leaving Cole and Yelverton to watch the perimeter.

The woman immediately began to screech as Mathias closed the door behind him with his foot.

"What the fuck do you want? Get the fuck out of here!" she hollered. The child was crying all the louder now; a little boy or girl—Mathias couldn't tell—no older than two.

Febonio pointed his weapon at the child clutching at its mother's leg and brought a nicotine-stained finger to his lips. "Shhhhhhhhhhhhhhhhhh."

"Listen, I don't know what you want, but if you see it, take it," the man said. "We don't even live here."

Mathias was taken aback. "You don't live here?"

"Naw," the man said. "Friends of my old lady here do. . . . They asked us to watch the place while they're away."

Mathias had been in places of unnatural power before, and this didn't feel like one of them. Had Poole screwed up? he wondered. He looked around. The place was certainly nothing special from what he could see.

Wallace came around a corner, finished with checking the place out.

"Anything out of the ordinary?" Mathias asked.

The man shook his blocky head. "Looks like a fucking pigsty to me."

"What do you want?" the woman asked again, her voice shaking with fear and anger. She had picked up the crying child and was cradling it in her arms.

Mathias ignored the question, pulling his phone from his pocket. He had other things to concern himself with right now, such as the possibility of disappointing his mistress.

She didn't like to be disappointed, and he so hated to be the one to give her bad news.

Delilah was waiting for the phone to ring.

She sat in the backseat of another Range Rover, trying not to stare at the phone on the seat between her and Clifton Poole. But no matter where she looked, her eyes always returned to the phone lying silently beside her.

If only Poole could be so silent.

The Hound muttered incessantly, rocking back and forth, still clutching the infant-shaped vessel that had once contained her prize. Ever since she had forced him to lay his hands upon it, he had refused to let it go.

Poole had been driven nearly mad by his contact with the vessel, but he still seemed to be useful. Between bouts of screaming and crying, he had been able to tell that the object, which had been stored within the container of metal, was very aware that they, or rather *she*, was looking for it, and was doing everything in its power to hide its trail.

But Poole was good, very good, and was able to lift a reading even though the object's vast amount of power threatened to utterly destroy his mind.

Delilah hoped he would live long enough to receive the funds that were owed him for his services. He certainly was earning them.

He had demanded maps, and she had obliged him, laying map after map of the entire charted world down upon the floor before him. And after some time, and a great deal of pain, the Hound had found what he believed to be the location of her precious heart's desire, and it had brought them here, to the United States.

To Palatka, Florida.

The phone suddenly rang and she gasped, picking it up and quickly placing it against her ear.

"Did you find it?" she asked immediately.

"Not exactly," Mathias replied, and Delilah felt the world drop out from beneath her.

"What do you mean, not exactly?" she snarled, glaring at Poole. She was tempted to order him to stop breathing; that would certainly fix him for his incompetence.

"Perhaps you should come inside," Mathias suggested. "And bring Poole along."

Delilah broke the connection, letting the phone drop from her hand.

"Poole," she said.

The man immediately stiffened, his gaze slowly turning toward her.

"You're coming with me," she commanded.

The driver was already out of the truck and opening her door to the sweltering Florida air.

Poole followed, still clutching the metal container forged in the shape of a child, still mumbling beneath his breath, as he trailed his mistress up the overgrown path to the dilapidated house.

*   *   *

Mathias averted his gaze.

"I'm sorry, mistress," he said.

Delilah strode into the room, her eyes scanning the paltry location.

A woman held a child in her arms, placating the little boy with animal cracker after animal cracker. "Who are you people?" the mother demanded. "Is this about the weed Ron sold? Because if it is . . ."

"Janie, shut your fucking yap," the filthy man said, scowling.

"Be quiet," Delilah snapped, and Ron was compelled to shut his mouth at once. She then looked back to the woman.

The child smiled warmly, offering Delilah one of his half-eaten treats.

She approached the mother and child, her anger and disappointment partially dissipating with the child's attention.

"I used to have a little boy just your age," she told the little one, reaching out to stroke the side of his head. "He died of pox while I cradled his tiny body in my arms," Delilah continued, remembering in a violent slash of recollection the death of one of her sons.

Janie twisted her child away from Delilah's affections, her eyes filled with a mother's rage. "Don't you touch him."

Delilah remembered that rage. She had used it to fuel her survival through the ages.

And there was so much of it, so much pain.

She often wondered how much damage her pain would do if it were somehow turned into a weapon and unleashed upon the world.

"Have Poole come in," she said, turning away and focusing on Mathias.

Her head of security went to the door and opened it. "Bring the Hound," he said.

Yelverton dragged the wild-eyed man through the doorway.

He looked around, his head bobbing as his entire body began to twitch.

"What the fuck's wrong with him?" Ron asked.

The little boy started to laugh, clapping his cookie-covered hands together as Poole dropped violently to the floor, the vessel clattering from his grasp.

Mathias moved to haul the man up, but Delilah stopped him.

"Leave him," she commanded, watching as Poole thrashed and bucked upon the floor.

"Maybe we should call 911 or something," Ron offered, fear in his eyes. "Looks like the poor bastard's having a fit."

In a way the man was correct; Poole was indeed having some kind of fit as his body attempted to lock on to traces of Delilah's prize, and by his reaction, it had most definitely been here.

"What is it, Poole?" she asked, striding closer as he lay on the floor moaning, his hands reaching for the vessel.

"Hiding," the man croaked, dragging himself toward the metal container. "Trying so hard . . . trying so hard to mask its trail . . . but it was here. . . ."

His hands finally closed around the vessel, and he fought to stand.

"It was here," he screamed again, hurling himself across the house toward a cabinet in the corner. He smashed the panes of glass in the cabinet door, scattering the gaudy knickknacks displayed inside.

"It was here," he said again, and again, his eyes scanning the contents of the cabinet.

It had become deathly silent in the room; all eyes were riveted on the crazy man as he stood before the cabinet. Holding the vessel beneath one arm, he reached inside and fumbled about.

"It was here."

He stumbled backward, his eyes darting here and there.

"I can . . . I can hear it. . . . I can . . ."

His eyes fell upon a drawer just below the cabinet door. He reached out and yanked it open. There was all manner of refuse inside, from take-out menus to old calendars, but that wasn't what the Hound was searching for.

It wasn't what was speaking to him.

And then the man became very still, his hand deep inside the drawer.

"What is it, Poole?" Delilah asked. "Did you find something?"

He turned toward her, an insane look upon his pale features. Slowly he withdrew his hand, clutching a colorful pamphlet.

"There it is," he said over and over again, his body slumping as he held out the paper. "There it is."

Delilah strode toward him and took it. It was an informational flyer about Franciscan Hospital for Children in Boston.

"Do you know what this is?" Delilah turned to the woman holding the child.

"It's the hospital where Deryn and Carl took their kid," Janie said.

"Deryn and Carl," Delilah repeated.

"They're the ones who really live here," Ron said. "We're just house-sitting 'til they get back."

"And they're still in Boston?" Delilah asked.

Janie nodded. "Why? Who are you fucking people anyway?"

"Janie, shut up," Ron said, rising from his chair.

"Don't you fucking tell me to shut up," Janie shrieked. "I want to know who they think they are coming in here and pulling guns on me and my kid and . . ."

Their bickering annoyed Delilah, distracting her from the excitement of what she'd just learned.

"Both of you be quiet," she said, rubbing her brow with a perfectly manicured hand.

Janie and Ron were silent, and Delilah could see the deep, primal fear in their eyes as they struggled to understand why they suddenly couldn't speak.

"Much better," Delilah said, turning her attention back to the pamphlet. "So Deryn and Carl are in Boston, and they've taken their child here . . . and my prize?"

Poole nodded. "Yes, it's there. It's there with the child."

She then looked at her soldiers, who watched her with cautious eyes. "This is good," she said with a wide smile that was returned by each of the mercenaries. She showed them the pamphlet. "This is where I'll be going next," she added.

She glanced back at Ron and Janie, and their little boy smiled at her. Her heart practically melted. She turned and held out her hands to him, and he did the same, leaning forward in his mother's arms.

Janie instantly reacted, pulling her child back.

This made Delilah angry.

"Give him to me," she commanded.

And though it was apparently excruciating to do so, Janie handed the baby boy to her.

The child was laughing, playing with the gold chains that hung around Delilah's neck. She had no idea what his name was, but she really didn't care. It didn't matter anymore. She'd decided to keep him and give him an entirely new name.

"I think I'll call you Maximilian," she said, bouncing the boy in her arms. "Max . . . Do you like that name?"

Janie let out an animal-like moan, throwing herself toward Delilah and her child.

"Come no closer," Delilah bellowed, stopping the woman in midstride.

"I'm going to give him a better life," she explained. "A much better existence than anything you and that hopeless wretch of a father could provide for him."

The woman's face twisted as she struggled to speak.

"Go ahead," Delilah said. "You can thank me if you like."

"You fucking bitch," Janie screamed from the very depths of her soul. "Give me back my son."

How ungrateful and rude, Delilah thought.

"Your old mother has quite the filthy mouth, doesn't she, Max," Delilah said as the child continued to squeal happily, grabbing at her chains.

"I think it's time for Ron to put himself to good use," she said, her cold gaze falling upon the man in the NASCAR hat.

"Kill her," Delilah said with a sly smile. "And don't tell me you've never wanted to."

The weak-willed were always the easiest to manipulate. Ron didn't even hesitate. He lunged forward and wrapped his strong hands around Janie's throat.

"That's it," Delilah said, bouncing the child who was now watching his father kill his mother. "This is how Daddy shows how much he loves your old mommy," she said in a soft voice. She kissed the top of Max's head as Ron drove a thrashing Janie to the floor of the living room.

Ron was moaning now, trying to stop himself, but he had a better chance of holding back a tidal wave than trying to defy Delilah.

"Are we ready to go to Boston?" she asked the baby in her sweetest voice. The child cooed excitedly, arms flapping, as Delilah glanced at Mathias and headed for the door.

She stopped as she heard a pitiful cry behind her, then turned to see a pathetic Ron, kneeling beside the strangled body of his wife, his cheeks flushed from the exertion of murder.

"No," he managed, reaching out for his child.

She smiled at him, holding the baby she called Max all the closer. "He's mine now," she said, kissing the side of the child's head. "And when we're gone, I want you to burn this place." She looked about the disheveled interior with a scowl, then turned and headed out the door that Mathias held open. "Burn it to the ground."

She was singing a Mesopotamian lullaby to her new baby when the house at the end of the path exploded, fingers of fire and thick black smoke reaching up into the sky in a futile attempt to blot out the bright Florida sun.

CHAPTER FOUR

"Will you help me, Mr. Chandler?"

Remy heard Deryn York's plea again, echoing through his mind as he took a right into the visitor lot of Franciscan Hospital for Children, pulling into the first empty space he could find.

How could he resist? This case reeked of the bizarre; one of those weird ones that Mulvehill loved to give him shit about. The missing child was drawing pictures of herself being taken by her father weeks before it happened, never mind the fact that she had drawn him as an angel, and Marlowe, and had even managed to get down his telephone number and address.

There wasn't a chance he would have turned this one away.

He pulled a wallet photo of a six-year-old girl in an Elmo sweater from his shirt pocket and gazed at it. According to Ms. York, it was taken at Sears last Christmas, but Zoe's sad, vacant stare was a sharp contrast to the usual childlike excitement of the season.

What are you really looking at? he wondered.

Then placing the photo back in his pocket, he headed toward the hospital's main entrance in the still-sweltering heat.

The automatic doors slid open with a hiss, and a cold blast of air-conditioned air flowed out to greet him. He stepped into the small lobby just as an ear-piercing scream filled the air.

To his right, in the reception area, Remy caught sight of two very nervous-looking parents with a little boy about Zoe's age. They were trying to coax him deeper into the hospital, but the child's body was rigid as he rocked rapidly back and forth, and every time they placed a hand on his shoulder, he began to scream and flail wildly.

Remy slowed his pace as he passed by and caught the child's eye. Almost immediately the little boy settled down.

It was a strange fact that many physically or mentally challenged humans seemed to possess a unique gift of sight, as if their disabilities in the natural world somehow made them more sensitive to the unnatural. Very often they were able to glimpse the other side, and those who lived just beyond the veil.

This little boy could see Remy for what he truly was.

Angel.

And he seemed to like what he saw.

Taking advantage of the sudden calm, the boy's parents hustled him by, his gaze tracking Remy as they passed.

Remy smiled, then turned to the reception window.

"May I help you?" a receptionist asked, sliding back a glass pane and looking at him with unblinking, laser beam eyes.

"Good morning," he said, flipping open his wallet and showing her his identification. "My name is Remy Chandler. I'm a private investigator working a missing person's case, and I was hoping to speak with Dr. Parsons."

The woman's glasses hung on a chain around her neck, and she placed them on her face so she could scrutinize his license. "Missing person?" she asked.

"Yes, a little girl, Zoe Saylor. I believe she is, or was, a patient of Dr. Parsons'."

The receptionist removed her glasses and gazed up at Remy. "I'm sorry, Mr. Chandler, but the laws of patient confidentiality won't allow us to acknowledge that a child has or has not received care at this hospital."

"Yes, I'm aware of that, but the child's mother did call Dr. Parsons this morning. . . ."

"I'm sorry, Mr. Chandler," she said with a dismissive smile, handing back his identification. "Have a nice day." Then she slid the window closed as she reached for the trilling phone.

That was it; Remy was dismissed. It was as if he were suddenly invisible, and that gave him an idea.

Remy stepped back, as if he planned to leave. Then, glancing around to be sure no one was watching, he willed himself unseen. It was an angelic talent that had proven quite useful over his many years, but it bothered him to use it. Anything that fed the power of the force he kept locked inside him was never a good thing.

Remy walked past the reception desk toward a bank of elevators, where he found the hospital directory. Dr. Parsons' office was on the first floor, so he headed down the corridor where he had seen the parents take their child, perusing the names over the doors until he found PARSONS.

The door was ajar, and he peered inside to find a middle-aged African American man with graying hair sitting at his desk looking over a file. Willing himself visible, Remy tapped his knuckle upon the door.

"Yes?" the man asked, looking over the top of a pair of bifocals balanced precariously on the tip of his nose.

"Dr. Parsons, I'm Remy Chandler," Remy began as he pushed open the door to stand fully in the doorway. "I'm a private investigator." He pulled out his wallet again and showed the man his identification.

"Mr. Chandler, you've already been told we can't speak to you," the man said with a hint of irritation.

"I guess news travels fast around here," Remy chuckled. "Look, I have only a couple of very simple questions. Your patient's confidentiality won't be affected, I promise. Besides, Zoe

Saylor's mother did call to give her permission for you to speak with me."

Parsons closed the file and stood. "A telephone call is not good enough, Mr. Chandler. We must have the parent's permission in writing. Now, if you'll excuse me, I'm late for a consultation." He turned to one of three filing cabinets against the wall near his desk and stuffed the file into the second drawer.

"I just need to know if Zoe's father was acting strangely on the day you last saw her or if he said anything out of the ordinary to anyone on your staff. Please, Dr. Parsons, even the smallest piece of information could be helpful," Remy begged.

The doctor slammed the file drawer closed, then grasped Remy's arm by the elbow and guided him toward the door. "If you'd like, I can ask security to escort you out," he said tightly.

Not wanting to cause a scene, Remy simply thanked the doctor for his time and headed down the hall. As soon as he was certain the doctor wasn't watching him, he willed himself invisible again and walked back to the office.

Dr. Parsons had gone, so he quickly let himself inside and went directly to the file cabinets. Zoe's file was in the top drawer of the last file cabinet. Pulling it out, he carried it to the doctor's desk and began to thumb through the surprisingly thick file.

He found page after page of test results, therapy evaluations, and dated doctor's notes, none of which proved helpful. But then in the back of the file, he found something familiar—childish drawings in crayon. Zoe certainly did like to draw.

Remy flipped through the illustrations, searching for something, anything, he could consider a clue. And then he found it—a crude drawing of a brown-skinned man dressed in what seemed to be green scrubs. Above the figure, the name Frank was scrawled in a child's hand.

Frank was in quite a few of the later drawings as well, and in one, he was even in the car with Zoe and her father.

Remy went back to the beginning of the file and began to search for any mention of Frank. He found it. Frank Downes was an occupational therapy assistant who had frequently worked with Zoe.

Remy closed the file and returned it to the cabinet.

He'd found his first good lead; now it was time to find Frank.

Carl Saylor's daughter was an angel.

He glanced over at the little girl, sitting in the front passenger seat of his 2000 Chevy Cavalier as they drove south on I-95, on their way to . . .

Where? Where were they going? He wasn't entirely sure.

Carl knew he shouldn't have taken her, but it had felt right.

He'd *had* to do it.

Zoe stared straight ahead through the windshield. She was staring into the future; that was what Carl liked to believe.

He reached across the seat and lovingly patted her bare leg.

"How's my girl?" he asked cheerfully.

She'd been so quiet—even more than usual—since leaving the hospital. He thought she might be missing her mother, but who could tell?

Who knew what was going on inside her pretty little head? If she wasn't sitting and staring, she was drawing. He'd had to take away the paper and crayons or that would have been all she did. The doctors at Franciscan Children's had said they should try to force her to interact with them, with the world around her, and not let her escape into her head, which was where she went when she drew.

Now her hands lay limply on the seat at her side, fingers twitching, as if eager to hold crayons again.

Carl remembered how he'd felt when he and Deryn had first

realized there was something wrong with their little girl. At first there was disbelief, then sadness, and then came the anger—lots and lots of anger.

It had been murder on their marriage; like salt eating away at a piece of metal. They'd been so good together, but with the baby being sick . . .

He honestly believed that they were being punished; that a higher power had struck at them for the sins of their past, even though that sinful past had been so long before. But the offended higher power obviously hadn't forgotten and had been waiting for the perfect time to illustrate its displeasure with their indiscretions.

In the early days, Carl and Deryn had been strong. They'd thought nothing could hurt them, and that just showed how stupid they had really been.

The forces they'd offended had found the one thing that could shake them to their core, striking at their pride and joy, their little girl, and marking her with this affliction.

So Carl had made himself a promise. He would do anything to make his little girl well, even if it meant making amends with an angry higher power. He glanced at Zoe again; she hadn't even reacted to his touch.

Thy will be done.

Remy eventually found Frank in the hospital's cafeteria.

He'd gone by the therapy department, this time posing as a friend of Frank's, and learned that he was on his break.

He grabbed a cup of coffee, which tasted as though it had been made with the finest dishwater, and then caught sight of a man wearing green scrubs. Could he be Frank? He was sitting by himself, reading from a pamphlet and sipping from a bottle of water.

"Excuse me," Remy said, leaning in to be heard over the clatter of the lunchroom. "Frank Downes?"

Zoe had captured the man's likeness pretty well, especially his protruding ears.

The black man looked at him with cautious eyes. "Who wants to know?"

"My name is Remy Chandler," he said, pulling out a chair and flashing his identification. "I'm a private investigator, working a missing person's case. I was hoping you could help me."

"I don't know anybody who's missing," Frank said, screwing the cap back onto his water bottle.

Remy had removed the plastic cover on his coffee, hoping that somehow that would make it taste better. It didn't.

"A little girl named Zoe Saylor, and her dad, Carl," Remy said, sipping the foul fluid.

The man's eyes narrowed. "I don't think I know them," he said quickly, shaking his head. "Should I?"

Remy shrugged. "I thought you might. Zoe drew an awful lot of pictures of you, and your name was in her therapy notes."

Frank smiled nervously, pushing back his chair as he stood.

"Mister, I see a lot of kids here every day," he said. "Lotta pictures too. Sorry I can't be more help."

And that was that.

Remy watched as Frank left the cafeteria; he knew full well the man knew more than he was sharing.

Frank was hiding something. Now all Remy had to do was figure out what it was.

There was a Starbucks not far from Franciscan Hospital for Children, and Remy took a brief respite from his detective duties to grab himself a decent cup of coffee.

He sat in his car, the AC running against the August heat,

while he sipped his coffee and mulled over his options. He figured Frank was probably his best, so he decided to wait until the therapy assistant's shift ended, then follow him.

He found a parking spot on the street where he could easily see the comings and goings of the hospital, then used the time in the car alone to check his messages. Deryn York had called twice. He thought about calling her back but decided he'd wait to see if his suspicions about Frank paid off. Instead, he called Ashley, his neighbor and Marlowe's longtime dogsitter. He wasn't sure how long he'd be out, and he knew Marlowe would be frantic if his supper was late. They were lucky to have Ashley. She was always willing to help out, treating Marlowe as if he were her own dog. But Remy also knew the teenager would be off to college soon, and then what would he do? Well, that was a worry for another time. For now, Ashley agreed to feed and walk Marlowe tonight, allowing Remy to settle in and wait for Frank.

It was nearly four o'clock, and Remy was beginning to think he might have somehow missed Frank, when he caught sight of the man leaving the building, backpack slung over his shoulder. He was talking animatedly with a female coworker, who was clearly not interested in whatever Frank was saying. She nodded her head and tried to inch away, and finally, Frank pulled a flyer from his backpack and handed it to her. She took it, then quickly headed off toward the parking lot. Frank called something out to her, gave her a final wave, and turned toward the street.

Remy waited a few moments, then got out of his car, following the therapy assistant on foot as he sauntered down Warren Street toward Cambridge. Thankfully, the streets in this area bustled with people, providing Remy with enough cover to remain unnoticed, without having to use his angelic power.

He watched as Frank picked up his mail at the post office, then stopped to buy scratch tickets and a six-pack of Corona at a small Korean market. Finally he walked up the front steps of an apartment building on Saunders Street.

Remy stopped in front of a building a few doors down and watched Frank fumble through his backpack for a set of keys. He felt a wave of disappointment wash over him. There certainly didn't seem to be anything suspicious about this man's actions; he worked, and went home. He'd probably microwave a frozen dinner and watch the news while he downed a few beers. Then he'd doze in his favorite chair until it was time to go to bed, before waking up in the morning to do it all over again.

Sighing, Remy was just about to leave Frank to his night, when he caught sight of four men emerging from a black Range Rover parked across the street from Frank's building.

They headed straight toward Frank, quickly climbing the steps and coming up behind him just as he unlocked the door. Frank turned toward them, an expression of surprise, then fear, on his face as one of the men grabbed his elbow and pushed him through the door.

This was what made Remy's job interesting.

Life was always tossing him curveballs, and he had no choice but to swing.

CHAPTER FIVE

Remy quickly climbed the steps to the front door of the apartment building. He peered through the glass, but the lobby was empty. Frank and his friends must have already gone to the therapy assistant's apartment.

On the wall to Remy's left was an intercom system with a listing of the last names and apartment numbers of the building's residents. F. Downes was in number 306.

Remy ran his finger down the length of buzzers, pretty sure that at least one person would answer.

"Yes?" a woman asked after a bit of squawking feedback.

"UPS," Remy said, lowering his voice.

The front door buzzed as another voice asked who was there.

Ignoring it, Remy pushed through the door and headed up the stairs in the lobby. On the second-floor landing, a woman in a bathrobe asked him if he had seen a UPS man in the lobby, and Remy told her he was on the way up. He continued up himself, listening to the sounds of the building—his hearing was good, inhumanly so—a television tuned to a newscast, an animal snoring, a microwave announcing that dinner was ready. . . .

There it is, he thought as he reached the third floor. *The sounds of a struggle.* And it was coming from number 306.

Standing on the threadbare runner outside 306, Remy

knocked on the door, and the sounds of violence inside came to a sudden stop.

"Guys, it's me," Remy called, placing his mouth close to the door.

He heard sounds of movement inside and placed his thumb over the peephole. "C'mon, let me in," he said.

The door opened a crack and Remy stared into the eyes of one of the intruders. "Who the fuck are you?" he snarled.

"Is Frank home?" Remy asked with a smile.

"Get the fuck out of here," the man replied, getting ready to close the door.

"Now, is that any way to answer the door?" Remy said as he slammed his shoulder into the door, pushing the man backward and forcing himself inside. "What if I were from Publishers Clearing House?"

He quickly scanned the room.

Frank was down, lying on his side in the middle of the tiny kitchen floor, two toppled dinette chairs near him. Blood stained the front of his green scrubs top, making it look dark and wet; more seeped onto the linoleum in a crimson pool beneath him.

The four attackers were eerily silent, their eyes slack, void of emotion.

Then the closest lunged at Remy with a snarl. He reacted in kind, putting everything he had into a punch. The man's face snapped to the left and he stumbled to the side. Remy drove the heel of his shoe into the guy's knee and was greeted with a wet snapping sound as the man screamed and crashed to the floor.

Two headed for Remy next, one of them brandishing a blood-stained knife. Remy could feel his heart hammering in his chest, hot blood pumping through his veins, as the angelic nature trapped within him shrieked to be free.

He dove to the right, grabbing one of the overturned chairs, using it to parry the knifeman's thrusts. Remy lifted the chair and brought it down on the man's outstretched arm. The knife clattered to the floor. He quickly kicked it away, then slammed the chair against the side of the second attacker's face.

He turned to see that knifeman had found his blade and drove a knee into the man's groin as he bent to pick it up. With a wheezing groan, the guy went down like a ton of bricks. But Remy was suddenly grabbed around the throat from behind—the man he'd hit with the chair had recovered.

Remy struggled, and the two crashed through the kitchen into the small den. Their legs struck a cheap coffee table, shattering it as they tumbled to the floor against a worn leather couch. The shock of the impact loosened his attacker's grip, and Remy managed to free himself, picking up a piece of the broken table and using it as a club. The man raised his arm to block the blows, then kicked Remy in the stomach, knocking him back into the kitchen.

His true essence wailed, demanding to be unleashed.

And he continued to ignore it, scrambling to stand as soon as he hit the floor.

Three of the attackers were trying to escape and he lunged toward them, but something grabbed his ankle and he tripped, crashing to the floor. He rolled onto his back to find knifeman, a balding man with a fat, red face, still holding his ankle in a vise-like grip. Infuriated, Remy lashed out, kicking the man in the face and knocking him back, his head bouncing off the kitchen floor and rendering him unconscious.

Remy jumped to his feet and spun toward the door, but the others were gone, the sounds of their feet on the stairs floating through the open door.

He took a deep breath and went to Frank.

The man was lying in a shivering ball on the floor, and at once Remy could see he was too late. The aura of death was wrapped around Frank like a comfy blanket.

Remy knelt beside him, careful to avoid the still-spreading puddle of crimson.

"You," Frank slurred as Remy lifted his head, resting it in the crook of his arm.

"It's all right, Frank," Remy said. "Relax. Everything is going to be fine."

Most would have thought he was lying to soothe the dying man, but it was true. Soon there would be no worries, no pain, as the powerful force that was Frank's immortal soul returned to the source of all life in the universe.

But before he was gone, Remy had questions that needed answering.

"Who were they, Frank?" he urged. "Why did they attack you?"

Frank's eyes had started to close, but as Remy spoke, they slowly opened. "They wanted to know about Zoe . . . and Carl."

A chill vibrated down Remy's spine.

"Carl and Zoe?" Remy asked. "What did they want with them?"

"Want them," Frank grunted. He tried to move, but his face twisted in pain and he began to convulse. It wouldn't be long now.

"Parsons," Frank said weakly. He reached up, grasping Remy's biceps.

"Dr. Parsons? What does he . . ."

"Told them," Frank gasped. "Told them where . . . where I lived. . . ."

"Were Carl and Zoe here, Frank?"

"Gone now . . . left . . . left this morning. They must know . . . ," he said, his voice growing weaker. "Know how special . . ."

"Who's special, Frank?" Remy urged.

"The child . . . little Zoe."

Even through his pain, Frank smiled at the mention of the

child's name. Then Remy felt the man's grip on his arm suddenly strengthen.

"Scared," he managed, his eyes looking up into Remy's.

Remy pulled him closer. "Don't be, Frank." He loosened the mask of humanity he wore and allowed Frank to see him for what he really was.

The last thing he would see before he passed from this world.

The aura surrounding Frank was completely black now, and his hand slipped from Remy's arm, dropping to the floor.

The Angel of Death appeared in a flicker of time before them, taking what was his, before moving on to the next to feel his touch.

A part of Remy was annoyed that Israfil hadn't even acknowledged his presence. Even a simple *Hey, how's it going?* would have been nice, for if it hadn't been for Remy, Israfil would have triggered the Apocalypse and brought about the end of the world.

But then again, angels with that magnitude of power and responsibility often had very short memories.

At least that was what Remy liked to tell himself.

Gently, Remy laid Frank's head upon the kitchen floor. Israfil had taken what had defined the man as a human being, leaving only a husk behind.

Remy remembered trying to explain that to Mulvehill during one of their late-night drinking binges on the rooftop patio of his Beacon Hill home. He thought the candy bar and wrapper analogy had worked best.

He stood and stared down at Frank's lifeless features. Now only the wrapper remained.

His thoughts were suddenly interrupted by the sound of a

moan from behind him. He turned to find the remaining creep gradually making his way back to consciousness. Remy planned on questioning the guy before calling the police, but first he wanted to have a quick look around Frank's apartment. If Carl and Zoe had been here, perhaps they had left something that could shed some light on where they might have gone.

Remy walked into the small den and scanned the debris left from his struggle with Frank's killers. He bent down and picked up some old copies of the *Boston Herald*, revealing some crumb-covered plates and an empty juice box, a sure sign that a child had been here.

He tossed the papers on the couch, then lifted up the largest piece of the broken coffee table, leaning it against the wall. He knelt on the area rug, poking through the pile of animated movies and princess coloring books, until something red caught his eye.

He reached out and picked it up. It was a flyer advertising a place of worship called the Church of His Holy Abundance. Remy had never heard of the place, but that didn't really surprise him—religions were popping up and dying all the time. This pamphlet was unusual though; some of the symbols drawn around its border were strangely old.

He folded the flyer, placed it in his pocket, and continued to rifle through the piles of debris. He found more pamphlets and information the church had mailed to Frank, and then something familiar.

"What've we got here?" he asked aloud, pulling the sheets of construction paper from beneath some more dirty plates.

Remy stared at a drawing, unmistakably done by Zoe's hand. At first he didn't understand what he was looking at, and then suddenly it dawned on him. The picture was of a man, kneeling on the ground, and of another man behind him, carrying a knife.

"Oh shit," Remy said, and spun around to find that the knife-man was conscious again and bearing down upon him.

Knife descending.

The blade dropped in a silver arc, slicing through Remy's shoulder as he tried to move out of the way.

With a grunt of pain, he pushed backward, away from his attacker, but the man had murder on his mind.

He threw himself at Remy, falling upon him, the knife raised again. Remy grabbed his attacker's wrist as the weapon dove toward his throat, and was momentarily distracted by a strange mark on the back of the man's hand. It resembled a pair of pursed lips.

Then the Seraphim inside him howled its fury.

And in a moment of startled weakness, Remy let slip the leash of control. The power of Heaven surged forward with a roar; the angel warrior that he was rejoiced.

He squeezed the man's wrist with all his divine might, feeling the bones crack beneath his grip. The man screamed in agony and tried to pull away, but the Seraphim would have none of that. Remy drew the man closer, inhaling his fear-tainted scent with a growl.

Immediately his angelic essence recoiled, a convulsive reflex that caused him to hurl the man away and across the room. Remy began to cough, as if his lungs had been filled with some sort of corrosive gas, a foul taste coating the inside of his mouth making him gag.

Remy struggled to rein in the angelic nature and force it back deep inside him where it belonged. Through watering eyes, he glanced up to see the last of the attackers escaping through the open door.

"Shit," Remy managed, slowly climbing to his feet.

He tried to piece together what had just happened. It had something to do with his attacker's scent. Something was different. . . . Something was missing . . . and in its place was only the poisonous stench of loss and despair.

And then it hit him.

It was what set humanity apart from all lesser things.

The thing that most separated the human from the angelic.

The man was missing his soul.

Remy had to get out of there.

He started through the kitchen toward the door, and his foot kicked something across the room. It was a wallet. He leaned down, picked it up, and opened it. The driver's license inside belonged to his red-faced attacker, Derrick Bohadock, forty-six years old, from Michigan.

Remy committed the name to memory, then dropped the wallet on the floor and left Frank's apartment, willing himself unseen as he closed the door behind him, just in case the struggles inside the apartment had attracted attention from the neighbors.

He was a few blocks away before he allowed himself to be seen again. He removed his phone from the holder attached to his belt and dialed an all-too-familiar number.

"Mulvehill," announced a weary voice on the other end of the line.

"You are so sexy when you answer the phone like that," Remy said.

"I don't know what it is," the detective replied. "Sexiness just oozes from my pores; makes me feel bad for the poor bastards out there who don't have a fraction of what I've got." He barely stifled a belch before continuing. "Excuse me; that'll teach me to have leftover Chinese for lunch. What can I do for you?"

"Got a murder," Remy said.

"Finally, something to do. What's the story?"

"The victim is—was—Frank Downes, a therapy assistant at Franciscan Children's."

"And what did Mr. Downes have to do with you?"

"A person of interest in a case I'm working on," Remy explained. "Looks like someone else found him interesting too, only that someone murdered him."

"Any idea who that somebody might be?"

"There were four of them. I tried to help him, but I was too late. Although one of them did leave his wallet behind—Derrick Bohadock of Novi, Michigan."

He didn't mention that the man apparently had no soul, putting this investigation heavily into that weird-shit category that Mulvehill liked to give Remy so much trouble about.

"Are you on the scene?" Mulvehill asked.

"No, I'm on my way back to the hospital to follow up on a few more things."

"Try not to get anybody else killed," Mulvehill cautioned.

"I'll do my best," Remy answered. "Come by the house tonight. I'll fill you in, and if you're good, there might even be a bottle of Jameson in the freezer."

"Will there be loose women?"

"Sorry," Remy said. "No loose women."

"Good, more Jameson for us."

CHAPTER SIX

Zoe was furiously drawing, her thumb stuck in the corner of her mouth.

Carl returned to the table and dropped a colorful Happy Meal box down in front of her. "Here ya go," he said. "Time to put your crayons away and eat your hamburger."

She dropped her red crayon and picked up the black, as if he had never spoken.

"Zoe, you can finish that later," Carl said firmly as he sat down across from her.

The child continued her work, her face close to the paper, scrutinizing every line she drew.

"All right." Carl had had enough. "That's it for now." He reached across, pulling the paper out from beneath her moving crayon, and she continued to color upon the tabletop.

"Hey!" he warned. "Stop that."

She seemed to realize what her father had done and set the crayon down beside the others, growing very still.

"You can finish this after you've eaten," Carl repeated as he moved to set the paper down on the far side of the table. But something caught his eye and he stopped, staring at the drawing.

It was of a black man lying on the ground, a puddle of bright red circling his body.

"What's this supposed to be?" Carl asked the little girl, feeling a chill suddenly vibrate up his spine.

"Frank's dead," Zoe muttered as she began to rock forward and backward, forward and backward. . . . "Frank's dead.

"Frank's dead."

Over and over again.

The sun was on its way down, but the heat still remained, a relentless humidity that made the air feel solid with moisture.

Remy headed back to the hospital, his mind filled with questions. Were Frank's other attackers missing their souls as well? What was so important about Zoe and Carl that they'd be willing to murder to find them?

And what exactly did Dr. Parsons have to do with four soulless men, an autistic child, and her father?

Remy wasn't in the mood to be questioned, and so, having learned his lesson earlier in the day, he willed himself unseen as he stepped into the hospital lobby. The lovely receptionist, who had been immune to his charm that morning, was gone, replaced by another who was answering the phones with the same almost robotic efficiency.

The traffic in the hallways was considerably lighter at this hour, and Remy had no problem getting to Dr. Parsons' office. The door was open a crack, and he could hear talking from within as he approached. Peering inside, he could see the doctor talking on his cell, standing at his desk, the top of which looked as if a bomb had gone off, scattering papers everywhere.

The conversation sounded intense, and Remy could hear panic creeping into the physician's voice.

"I told you I'm trying," he was saying, nearly frantic. He fell silent, obviously listening to the voice on the other end of the line.

Remy could just about make out the hum of that voice, buzzing in the doctor's ear like a fly trapped between a screen and a storm window. He couldn't make out what it was saying, but it didn't sound the least bit pleased.

"I'm sorry," Parsons said with a pathetic whine. "Just give me another chance . . . please." He sounded ready to cry.

Then he began to paw through the papers on his desk. "I have some right here," he said, picking up a piece of construction paper with drawings on it.

One of Zoe's drawings.

"I'm trying to figure it out, but . . ."

The buzzing from the other side of the phone grew louder, more intense.

The expression on the doctor's face became pained, and he dropped down into his office chair.

"Please, just give me a chance. . . . Please. . . ."

And suddenly, as if in a fit of rage and despair, Parsons threw the cell phone against the nearby wall. He was sobbing as he pulled open a side drawer of his desk and removed a pair of scissors, trying to saw through the flesh of his wrist with one of the blades.

Remy instantly pushed open the door, strode across the office, and snatched the scissors from Parsons' hand. "I don't think you want to do that," he said, tossing the scissors to the floor.

Parsons stared at him for a moment, his face damp with tears. "I've tried so hard for her," he finally sobbed, covering his face with his hands, shaking his head as he cried.

And that was when Remy noticed the mark on the doctor's neck, a dark patch on the cocoa-colored flesh—shaped like a pair of pursed lips.

He called upon his angelic nature again, allowing his human senses to become something more. He sniffed at the air around the wailing doctor, taking the scent of the man into his lungs. He could smell his soul, but there was something not quite right about it.

It was damaged, traumatized.

"Get ahold of yourself," Remy said, moving around the desk and placing a hand on the doctor's shoulder.

Parsons lifted his head and looked at Remy. "I . . . don't know what to do," he said, turning his attention back to the desk. He began to shuffle through a pile of Zoe's drawings, looking at one colorful piece after another.

"They're supposed to help me," he said. "They're supposed to tell me how to find them."

"The girl and her father?" Remy asked.

"Yes," the doctor replied. "The answers are here, I'm sure of it, but I can't figure it out."

He was crying again, his teardrops staining the corners of the child's drawings.

"Is that why you sent those men to Frank's place?" Remy asked. "Did you tell them Frank would know where they were?"

Parsons looked up again, his eyes red and wet.

"I didn't want to disappoint her," he said, his voice quivering, and as he spoke he reached up to touch the mark staining the flesh of his neck. "I promised her. . . ."

"Who?" Remy asked. "Who did you promise?"

The man crumbled, sobbing and shaking.

"I can't," Parsons said, suddenly standing. "I can't do this anymore."

He lurched across the room, grabbing his suit jacket from the coatrack behind his door, and headed out into the hall.

Remy felt as if he were standing in a minefield, at first not quite sure how to proceed. Then he figured he had probably gotten as much as he could from the doctor; the man was an emotional wreck. He turned his attention to the desk and picked up Zoe's drawings. *Maybe I can find something that Parsons wasn't able to*, he thought, folding them up and placing them beneath his arm.

Remy left the office. Dr. Parsons was nowhere in sight, so he headed for the lobby and left the building, his mind once again ablaze with questions.

He was halfway to the street and his car when the sounds of commotion distracted him. He turned back to the hospital and saw people running toward the side of the building. Someone called out an order to dial 911; another voice screamed, "He fell off the roof!"

Before he even realized what he was doing, Remy was moving with the crowd as sirens filled the air with their banshee wails.

Still clutching the child's strangely portentous drawings, he made it to the edge of the gathering. A number of people were kneeling around something on the ground. And as one of them slowly rose to his feet, his form no longer obscuring Remy's view of a broken, bleeding body, he knew the victim wasn't some poor soul who had accidentally plummeted to his death, but someone who had been in the depths of remorse, so painful that the only way to relieve it was to end his worthless existence.

But by the look on Dr. Parsons' face, frozen in death, not even that had been enough to free him from his agony.

Remy sat on his rooftop patio with his closest human friend, a glass of Irish whiskey in his hand as he gazed out over the buildings of Beacon Hill to the Esplanade, almost visible through the hazy fog.

His mind wandered as he allowed the first few sips of Jameson to affect him. And as his thoughts strolled the night, and his mental guards fell, he could hear the prayers of the devoted and desperate all across the city.

The cacophony of voices filled his head to bursting, and he

immediately pulled himself back, blocking out the petitions to a higher authority.

"What is it?" Mulvehill asked, reaching for the chilled bottle of whiskey in the center of the circular table. He slid the bottle over and then reached for the ice bucket, filling his glass with more cubes. It was so humid that the ice seemed to melt as quickly as he dropped it into his glass.

Remy took a sip from his drink and set it down on the table-top. "I let my mind wander too far," he said. "Sometimes that's not such a good thing."

"Huh," Mulvehill said, filling his glass for a third time. "Thinking about stuff you don't want to think about?"

"Sometimes," Remy said, his eyes drawn to the city view again. "But if I'm not careful, I also hear things I don't want to hear."

"You're hearing voices now?" Mulvehill asked. He leaned back in his chair, resting his sweating tumbler on his rounded paunch of a belly. He picked up his already-lit cigarette and had a puff.

"Prayers," Remy said, swirling the liquid in his glass, making the ice tinkle like chimes. "I can hear the requests of all kinds of folks looking for a little divine intervention."

"Jesus," Mulvehill said, leaning his head against the back of the plastic chair and blowing smoke into the air. "That must get a little much."

Remy nodded. "It does, which is why most of the time I try to tune it out, but every once in a while I let my guard down and the solicitations come rolling in."

"What are they asking for . . . ? Like, to make sick family members well, or for the bank not to foreclose on their houses and stuff?"

Remy nodded. "Sometimes, and sometimes they want God to help them get a new bike, or a puppy."

"I prayed for a bike once," Mulvehill said, then took a large gulp of his whiskey.

Remy glanced over at his friend. "Did you get it?"

"Naw." He shook his head. "I guess the Almighty figured I needed some new school uniforms more than a bike."

"The Almighty is very much into school uniforms," Remy said, confirming his friend's beliefs.

They both laughed then, mellowing out from the effects of their drinks.

"So nobody's really listening then," Mulvehill said, fishing another cigarette from the pack lying on the table.

Remy thought for a moment, not sure how to respond.

"No, not really," he finally said, turning his attention to his friend. "It's just sort of a hit-or-miss thing as to when someone's listening . . . and whether they decide to do anything about what they hear."

"Sounds complicated." Mulvehill finished what remained in his glass and reached across the table for more.

"Yeah," Remy agreed, his thoughts drifting in the direction of ancient times, when he'd first left Paradise to make the world of man his home. "It always was."

Mulvehill helped himself to some more ice, and yet another splash of whiskey. "More?" He held the bottle out to Remy.

"You know I prayed you'd ask me that," Remy said, sliding his glass within reach.

Mulvehill obliged him with ice and booze.

"And I decided to answer."

The homicide cop slid the glass back to the angel.

"So, Frank Downes," Mulvehill began, settling back in his chair.

"Very dead," Remy added.

"He certainly was," Mulvehill agreed. "And what exactly did you have to do with his untimely demise?"

"Absolutely nothing," Remy explained. "I asked him some questions about a missing person's case I'm working on, and when he wasn't forthcoming with the info, I followed him to see if he'd lead me to a clue."

"Okay." Mulvehill nodded. "So how did he end up murdered?"

"We finally ended up at his building and I was going to call it quits for the night, but then four guys decided they needed something from Frank too, only they forced themselves into his apartment."

"And you decided to check this situation out, instead of calling law enforcement," Mulvehill suggested, waving his lit cigarette around.

"I wasn't sure what was going down, so I decided to go it alone," Remy agreed. "I probably should have given the PD a call."

"Yeah, you probably should have." Mulvehill had some more whiskey. "You didn't happen to use that UPS trick to get into the building, did you?"

"I most certainly did," Remy said.

"Thought so." His friend nodded. "Lady on the second floor said she thought she was getting a delivery but saw an unfamiliar guy heading up the stairs."

"That would have been me," Remy said.

"No shit."

Remy chuckled. "Anything on the guy who dropped his wallet? What was his name . . . Bohadock?"

"Derrick Bohadock. Reported missing last month by his wife of sixteen years. Supposedly disappeared on his way home from a business trip to the Philippines."

"Really?" Remy took a sip from his drink. "Kind of odd that he would show up as part of a kill squad in Boston, don't you think?"

"It is kinda funny."

"He had a strange mark on the back of his hand," Remy said, rubbing the back of his own. "Lip marks . . . as if left by a kiss."

"Like a tattoo?" Mulvehill questioned.

"I only got a quick glimpse of it, but it seemed more like a burn . . . a brand maybe. And that doctor who supposedly sent these guys after Frank had one on his neck." Remy pointed to an area below his ear.

"The one who took a swan dive off the roof of Franciscan Hospital for Children?" Mulvehill asked. "I suppose you were questioning him about this missing persons case too?"

"Yeah, I was," Remy acknowledged.

"You realize I should probably arrest you right now on suspicion of murder," Mulvehill said, setting down his empty glass.

"There isn't a jail around that could hold me, copper," Remy said in a pathetic attempt at an Edward G. Robinson imitation.

"Hey, that's pretty good," Mulvehill said. "I didn't know you could do Katharine Hepburn."

"Go screw yourself," Remy said with a laugh.

"Didn't she say that to Henry Fonda in *On Golden Pond*?"

They were both laughing now. It was times like these when it all made sense to Remy; why he stayed upon the planet wearing a guise of humanity. He'd never had a friend like Mulvehill in Heaven, and Katharine Hepburn jokes were completely out of the question.

"So this case you're working on," Mulvehill began as their laughter died down.

"Yeah?" Remy asked. The ice in his glass had melted to nothing, and he drained some of the liquid and tiny pieces of cold into his mouth.

"I'm guessing it's another one of *those* cases," he said, putting air quotations around the word *those*.

"I wasn't completely sure at first," Remy said, "but the more I poke around, the stranger it becomes."

"I think it's you," Mulvehill said. "If somebody else were investigating this case . . ."

"Katharine Hepburn?"

"Especially Katharine Hepburn. If she were investigating this case, it would be so normal, it'd be boring."

"Maybe, but then again, maybe not," Remy said. "We live in interesting times now, my friend."

"What're you, Confucius now? Face it, you attract weird like a magnet." The homicide detective stood and stretched. "I gotta get outta here," he said, glancing at his watch and then snatching up his pack of cigarettes from the table. "Duty calls in less than four hours."

"It's not my fault, you know," Remy told him. "I've told you how the world has changed since that business with the Apocalypse and—"

"And I don't want to hear it," Mulvehill interrupted, throwing up a hand. "The less I know, the more surprised I can continue to be when this shit gets weirder."

"Suit yourself," Remy told him.

They were heading toward the stairs that would take them back into Remy's building, when Marlowe made an appearance in the doorway, a stuffed monkey clutched in his mouth.

His tail was wagging furiously.

"Well, look who it is," Mulvehill said as Marlowe trotted to him for an ear scratch. "A little late for the party, aren't you?"

The dog tried to answer, but the stuffed animal in his mouth was making it impossible to understand him.

"If you're going to talk, you're gonna have to drop the monkey," Remy told him.

Marlowe dropped the monkey to the floor of the deck. "*New toy*," he said excitedly, swatting at it with his paw.

"That isn't new," Remy said. "It's just been lost behind the couch."

"*New*," the dog said, not convinced.

"He thinks the toy is new because he hasn't seen it in a while," Remy explained to Mulvehill.

"So he thinks it's new." Mulvehill shrugged. He bent down and picked up the monkey, giving it a shake in Marlowe's face. "Where's the harm in that? Why do you have to spoil everything for us?"

Marlowe pulled the toy from Mulvehill's hand and shook it vigorously.

"Spoil everything?" Remy asked, surprised. "What have I spoiled?"

"In my reality, the world is a perfectly normal place that plays by all the tried and true rules, and in Marlowe's, that's a brand-new monkey toy."

Remy tried not to say anything, but as they headed down the stairs, he couldn't hold back any longer. "Whatever makes you happy," he said. "Even if it isn't true."

Halfway down the steps, Mulvehill turned and without missing a beat said, "In the immortal words of Katharine Hepburn, go screw."

After Mulvehill left, Remy spent some time playing with Marlowe and his "new" monkey toy, until the Labrador got bored and retired to the love seat, leaving the detective to settle into his office and review his latest case.

Deryn had called three more times; once at the office, once on his cell, and the final time on his home phone in the kitchen. He could understand her anxiousness for answers; at this point, he was feeling a bit like that himself. He would call her in the morning, but he would leave out the stuff about missing souls and murder; no need to get her worked up until it was absolutely necessary.

He reclined in his office chair, swiveling it from side to side and letting his mind wander. This was the perfect time to do just that; late enough that the sounds of the city had died down to a little less than a murmur. Marlowe was sound asleep, as was just about everyone else he knew, and since he didn't need to sleep, he could think.

A father had apparently abducted his autistic daughter, the two of them hitting the road to who knew where. The child appeared to have a strange artistic gift that allowed her to draw things before they happened.

Remy paused in his musings to retrieve the drawings he had taken from Dr. Parsons' office and those that Deryn had left with him. He hadn't had a chance to look closely at the ones from the hospital, but now that he did, he found they were harder to decipher, a bit more abstract. There were lots of pictures of multiple structures; houses, they seemed to be, set in the woods. However, one particularly eerie drawing caught his attention. It depicted people growing out of the ground like a crop of corn.

"What's that about?" Remy muttered.

He finally decided he just didn't have enough information to be able to correctly interpret the drawings, so he set them aside and turned his attention to the pamphlets he had found in Frank's apartment.

"The Church of His Holy Abundance," he read aloud, his eyes scanning the strange markings that adorned the cover. There was not a crucifix, cross, or dove to be found, but there were some odd symbols and crude drawings of some very funky fish.

Remy knew these symbols and images were very old, and the more he stared at them, the more he felt his true nature begin to stir. He briefly entertained the idea of paying the church a visit—according to the pamphlet, they had an address in Somerville—but then he decided maybe he should find out more about the religion itself first. He'd already gotten into enough trouble for one day.

Besides, he knew just the right person to talk to.

Leaning forward in his chair, he slid the overly stuffed Rolodex toward him and found the number he was looking for.

It had been a few months since he'd last spoken to the man, even longer since he'd seen him, and Remy knew he'd have to suffer through a ration of shit because of it.

But then what else did he expect from a retired Catholic priest? They could use guilt as deftly as a surgeon wielded a scalpel.

Remy glanced at the clock on the wall, eager to move into the next phase of his investigation, but it was still pretty early in the morning and he didn't want to risk waking the good father. So he sat, listening to the sounds of his home, and waited for the world to rouse itself from slumber.

Remy had much to do before his visit to the priest. He had to feed Marlowe, take him for his walk, drink a pot of Dunkin' Donuts coffee, shower, dress, and because of whom he was planning to visit, he had to stop at Mike's Pastries in the North End for a box of Italian cookies.

It was well past ten when he finally headed to Roslindale to see the priest he hoped would be able to shed some light on the Church of His Holy Abundance.

Father Darren Coughlin was one of the Vatican's top experts in ancient and modern religions, including various cults both long extinct and recently emerged. He had retired in 1995, returning to Massachusetts to live with his brother in the Roslindale home where he'd grown up. Father Coughlin's brother had died in 2002, but the priest continued to live in the house, doing research and special jobs for his Vatican masters, as well as the

lowly private investigator from time to time. His only require-
ment was that he be paid with cookies from the North End's fa-
mous pastry shop.

Remy squeezed his Corolla into Father Coughlin's tiny drive-
way, behind the unused Ford that had been sitting there for years,
and had to fight off the drooping branches of the neighbor's overgrown willow tree as he exited his car. He carried the white box
of cookies across the small expanse of brown grass and up the
steps of the old Dutch Colonial.

He rang the bell and waited. Even through the closed front
door, he could smell the strong odor of cigarette smoke.

After a few minutes, the door opened to reveal the tall, almost
cadaverous form of the retired priest, an unfiltered Camel dangling from the corner of his mouth. His hair was snow-white,
although faint traces of a faded yellow could still be seen in certain lights.

The old priest, looking over the tops of wire-framed glasses
that had slid to the end of his ruddy nose, pushed open the screen
door and reached for the white pastry box.

"Thanks for coming by," he said, snatching the box from Remy's hands, then quickly closing the door.

The priest was laughing, a laugh that turned into a lovely wet
cough, thanks to years of smoking the unfiltered cigarettes.

"All right," Remy said, playing along. He started back down
the stairs with a wave. "I'll be seeing you."

The old priest came back out, motioning Remy inside. "Get
your ass in here," he said in between coughing jags, the bouncing
cigarette flinging ash into the air.

"That sounds good," Remy said as the old man patted his
back, pushing him into the house. "Did you run the marathon
this year?"

That just made the priest laugh and cough all the harder as he
followed Remy inside, closing the door behind them.

As usual, the place was immaculate, not a piece of dust or clutter to be found, but that didn't change the reek of cigarettes.

"Come into my office," Coughlin said, moving past Remy, down the short corridor to the kitchen. "Coffee?" he asked, going to the stove, where an old-fashioned metal pot had just finished brewing.

"Most definitely," Remy said, taking a seat at the small dinette set in the corner.

He watched the retired priest pour two huge mugs of the dark brown, almost black, liquid. Coughlin referred to his brew as rocket fuel, and Remy did not argue. The stuff would put hair on areas that never knew hair before.

The priest carefully walked toward the table, a mug in each hand. Even though retired, he still wore the black suit of the priesthood, white collar and all. "Once a priest in the Catholic faith, always a priest until the day you breathe your last," he always said.

He set the mugs on the table, then retrieved the box of cookies he'd left on the stove, wasting no time in breaking the string that held it closed.

"Let's see what we have here," the old-timer muttered through the cloud of smoke that trailed from the burning Camel still protruding from the corner of his mouth. "Ah," he said, perusing the contents, "nothing you'd like. Guess I'll have to eat them all myself."

"And spoil your girlish figure?" Remy said. "It would be a sin."

The old man went to a cabinet over the sink and returned with a plate. He reached into the box and placed a handful of cookies on the plate.

"There," he said, stepping back from the colorful display. "Picasso couldn't have done better."

He pushed the box to the other side of the table and sat down.

"Drink your coffee before it gets cold," he ordered Remy as he took the remains of the cigarette from his mouth, snuffing it out in an ashtray in the center of the table.

Remy picked up his mug and took a sip. The stuff was stronger than usual, but that was fine by him.

"A little bit of the Holy Spirit?" the old man asked.

Remy shook his head. "No, this is fine, thanks."

"Your loss," Coughlin said. He removed a metal flask from the pocket of his black jacket, unscrewed the top, and poured a splash of Irish whiskey into his coffee. Then he moved his hand in front of the mug, blessing it before lifting it to his mouth.

"Amen," he said just before taking a slurping sip.

Remy chuckled as he reached for one of the cookies.

"You would take that one," the old priest muttered, reaching for one as well.

"Do you want it?" Remy asked, holding the cookie out to him.

"Go ahead," the old man said. "And I hope you choke."

"As charming as always," Remy said, popping the cookie into his mouth and following it with a sip of rocket fuel.

He had never told the priest what was beneath his disguise of humanity, but he had always suspected the old man knew there was something not quite normal about him. Father Coughlin would never pry; he was always very respectful of Remy's privacy, and for that the detective was grateful. Eventually, he probably would tell Coughlin the truth, but not today.

"So, to what do I owe this visit?" the priest was asking through a mouthful of pink cookie. "It's been what . . . a year since I've seen you?"

"Last time I was here, you threw me out and told me never to darken your doorstep again," Remy replied with a smirk.

"And since when does anybody listen to a poor old priest?" Coughlin said, reaching for another treat.

"I always listen to my church elders," Remy said.

"Do your clients buy that bullshit?" the priest asked as he took a gulp of coffee.

"Completely," Remy answered. "That's how I make the big bucks."

They both laughed, ate most of the cookies, and finished off the pot of coffee before moving on to more serious things.

"You had a loss recently, didn't you?" Coughlin asked, making reference to Madeline's death.

Remy nodded, staring into his cup. The old priest knew about the relationship, but didn't understand the complexity. Most believed that Madeline was Remy's mother, not his wife and the love of his life.

"I'm very sorry for your loss, brother," Coughlin said, and reached out to grab Remy's arm, squeezing it in a powerful grip. "May the Lord God have mercy on her soul."

"Thank you," Remy said, looking into the priest's wise and caring eyes. "It's been hard."

"It always is. No matter how old we are, it's never easy to lose someone we love."

Remy remained silent, and then Father Coughlin was out of his seat again. "How about another pot?" he asked, breaking the tension as he headed for the stove.

"I'm good, Father," Remy said. "I don't want to be floating out of here."

"Well, I might as well make a fresh pot anyway." The old man rummaged around in a cabinet and pulled out a can of coffee. "What else do I have to do these days?" he asked as he prepared another pot. "Most of the time I'm just sitting around, waiting for somebody to visit me." He turned his head slightly, looking at Remy from the corner of his eye.

"You got me," he said. "I should come by more often."

"Damn right you should," the priest scolded. "The only time I see you is when you need something."

The old priest loved to complain, and Remy doubted the old-timer had had a boring day since supposedly retiring. From what he understood, the Vatican kept him quite busy with the research and cataloguing of ancient religious beliefs and practices.

"Which brings me to why I'm here today," Remy said.

"See?" Coughlin turned the pot on to percolate and slowly returned to the table.

Remy removed the folded flyer from his back pocket, straightening it out as he spoke. "What do you know about the Church of His Holy Abundance?"

"The Church of His Holy Abundance," Coughlin repeated, taking the pamphlet from him. "Sounds vaguely familiar, but I can't remember why . . . probably something I read in passing." He studied the flyer. "Somerville, huh?"

"Yeah, I was thinking of checking it out, but thought I'd talk to you first. See what you knew."

"Sorry I can't help you," the old priest said, taking his seat, and another cookie. "This for a case you're working?"

"Yeah, missing person . . . a little girl."

Father Coughlin picked up the pamphlet and studied the cover again. "Hmm, this is pretty odd," he commented after a moment.

"The symbols?" Remy asked. "Thought you'd have something to say about them."

"Yeah, really old stuff . . . ancient Sumerian, I think."

"That old?" Remy responded. He was a bit rusty on his ancient writings.

"It's a little strange seeing them on something like this," Coughlin said. "Can I keep this?" he asked, holding up the flyer.

"Sure," Remy told him. "Just give me the heads-up on anything you find out."

"No problem," the priest said, his attention already back on the symbols. Remy could practically smell the plastic burning as the old priest started to lose himself in the new distraction.

He stood and slid his chair back under the table. "I should probably get rolling."

Coughlin grunted a response before looking up. "Did you say something?"

"I'm leaving," Remy said with a laugh.

"Sure you don't want to stay for another cup?" the priest asked him. "I've got a few Italian cookies left that some stranger dropped off."

"I get the hint," Remy said as he headed down the hall to the front door. "I'll visit more often."

"You're going to have to," Coughlin said, following him with a twinkle in his eye. "How else are you going to know what I've found out?" He held up the pamphlet.

"Got me there," Remy said. "Give me a call as soon as you've got something, no matter how small. We'll settle what I owe you next time I come."

"Two boxes from Mike's ought to cover it," the priest said.

"With prices like that," Remy complained, "no wonder I only visit once a year."

He opened the door and stepped out onto the porch, turning back for a final wave to the priest, but the old man was already heading back to the kitchen, the ancient markings on a church pamphlet providing him with the kind of mystery that piqued his voracious curiosity.

CHAPTER SEVEN

Katie Allen had been chosen.

At least that was what her sponsor had told her.

She sat nervously on the sofa in the sparse living room of Pastor Zachariah's home and waited to be called.

Elijah, her sponsor to the Church of His Holy Abundance, had said that the pastor was very sick, and that only very special novices were granted an audience with the holy man.

Her stomach gurgled noisily from a combination of nerves and hunger. Placing a hand on her belly and feeling the vibrations, she tried to remember the last time she'd eaten. She'd had a bag of chips and a Coke at the bus station before meeting Elijah.

He'd approached her as she was waiting for her bus. He'd said she had the look of somebody very important and promised her that would be true if she agreed to go with him to the compound.

There was something about Elijah and the way he spoke. Katie could smell a creep from a mile away, but Elijah wasn't that at all. He hadn't even tried to touch her the entire ride, and when she'd asked him why, he'd just smiled that very special smile of his and said it wasn't his place.

If only her stepfather had been so polite, she thought with a chill. Maybe she wouldn't have been at the bus station, looking for a place where she wouldn't be afraid.

And Elijah had promised her that; all she had to do was become a member of the church.

The Church of His Holy Abundance.

She looked around the room. It reminded her of a furniture store display—nothing out of place, unlived in.

But Elijah did say the pastor had been sick.

She'd arrived at the church compound with five others Elijah had found along the way—all lost souls that were now found; at least that was what he'd called them.

Katie smiled. She found it kind of special to be called a lost soul, and even more so to think she had been chosen. Of the six who had arrived together, only she had been picked to meet the pastor. Her travel companions had been paired up and led away with other members of the church.

There was a mirror over a fireplace that looked as though it had never entertained a fire, and she got up from the couch to stand in the middle of the room, staring at her reflection.

Was she special? She couldn't really see it.

The kids at school had always called her fat, and as she looked at herself in the mirror now, she had to agree that she was a little overweight. But it didn't matter anymore.

Because she was chosen.

She ran her fingers through her short blond hair and wished she'd had a chance to wash up before meeting the pastor. She had that travel funk about her, and she hoped the church leader wouldn't be offended.

What if he doesn't agree with Elijah? she wondered, suddenly on the verge of panic. *What if he was wrong and I'm just like everybody else?*

Katie scrutinized herself again in the living room mirror and almost began to cry. The T-shirt she wore was stained from her time on the road, and her denim shorts were perhaps a little too revealing.

What was Elijah thinking? Katie wondered. What could he possibly have seen in her that made her different from all the others?

The sight of herself was enough to send her running from the pastor's home, but just as she was about to do so, she heard a door opening somewhere nearby and the sound of footsteps coming toward the living room.

"Elijah," she said, suddenly very self-conscious.

He smiled at her from the doorway. "Are you ready?" he asked, holding out his hand for her.

"Look at me," she said, tears welling in her eyes. "I can't meet a holy man looking like this."

Elijah chuckled softly and shook his head. "You're fine," he reassured her. "In fact, you're better than fine; you're perfect. And he wants to meet you."

"Are you sure?" she asked. "I smell kinda funky, and my clothes . . ."

"None of that matters to him," Elijah said.

He stepped farther into the room and gently took her hand in his. His touch was warm and calming, and she trusted him.

"C'mon," he said, pulling her from the living room. "We don't want to keep Pastor Zachariah waiting."

They walked hand in hand down the dark corridor of the ranch-style house, heading to the back where the bedrooms were. Elijah stopped in front of a door at the end of the hall and placed his hand on the knob.

"Are you ready?" he asked as he smiled that wonderful smile and opened the door into a room filled with darkness.

"I've told him all about you."

*   *   *

The thing wearing the skin of Pastor Zachariah lay upon the bed, feeling itself slipping away.

Its flesh was rotting, each cell exploding with decay, deep, bloody sores blossoming on the surface of its thin epidermis.

Shifting upon the hospital bed, it felt the rub and tug of the sheet, tearing the delicate skin like paper. It moaned in the darkness, the pain almost too much for the godly being to bear.

It hated this fragile form it had been caged in, but the alternative was even more distasteful. The deity recalled the void and how it had come so very close to no longer existing. No, it would endure this torment a thousandfold rather than experience the guarantee of oblivion.

To no longer be was something even a god feared.

The body that housed its omnipotence was a fragile thing, not anything like it had been promised when it was cajoled from the other side. Its followers had guaranteed undiluted devotion and a body of worship that would grow by leaps and bounds.

It had been so long since it had fed upon the prayers of the faithful, so it swam from the darkness, fighting the undertow of inexistence, and entered what it thought was a world that awaited its return.

The deity raised its trembling hands, looking upon its pasty, sore-covered flesh and malformed fingers.

Is this wreck of a form suitable to house a god?

It was not, but it could do nothing to alter the circumstances; nothing except prolong its physical torment, staving off the decay of this fragile human shell with sacrifice.

The first thing Katie noticed was how very dark it was.

"Hello?" she called out, blinking rapidly, trying to acclimate herself to the darkness.

She could just make out the red and green lights from various pieces of medical equipment positioned beside the pastor's bed, and she moved in that direction.

"Pastor Zachariah? My name is Katie Allen, and Elijah said you wanted to meet me?"

The second thing she noticed was the smell. Katie couldn't quite put her finger on it, but it caused the hair at the nape of her neck to bristle. She thought it might be the damp coolness blowing from the air conditioner that purred in the window, but she couldn't be sure.

"Come closer, child," said a voice that sounded incredibly old and weak. It seemed to come from the area of the darkened room where Katie imagined the pastor to be.

Her eyes had adjusted enough that she could make out the shape of the looming hospital bed, and of a figure lying beneath a blanket upon it.

Katie did as she was told, and that was when she noticed the third and most unusual thing.

With each footstep, she heard the rustling of plastic; the floor seemed to be covered with it.

At once her mind tried to explain it. The most logical thought was that it was a leak of some kind, perhaps from the ceiling, and the plastic was meant to protect the flooring. Then, of course, there was the consideration that maybe Pastor Zachariah was so sick, he couldn't control his bodily functions, and the plastic was there to keep . . . *stuff* off the floor.

Gross, Katie thought, although it would help explain the funky smell in the room.

She could sense Elijah behind her, and almost wanted to turn to him and ask, but she was distracted when the old voice, much closer now, began to speak to her again.

"Do you willingly give yourself to me, Katie Allen?" the voice croaked. "Do you bestow unto me your flesh, your blood, and your soul?"

She tripped on a fold in the plastic covering. "What?" she asked, almost losing her balance in the darkness. "I don't understand. . . ."

"Say yes," the old voice growled, sounding much stronger now. The bed creaked, and Katie could just make out the almost-human shape moving upon it.

"Yes," she said quickly, suddenly more afraid than she'd ever been in her life. She stopped and began to turn back toward Elijah.

The sudden blow to the back of her head was brutal, and she dropped heavily to her hands and knees, gasping, the synapses in her brain firing like fireworks on the Fourth of July. She clutched at the floor, the slick plastic sliding beneath her fingers.

"What happened?" she managed, her speech slurred, as if she were drunk. "Elijah, what . . . ?"

She struggled to stand, but the room was spinning and she felt herself falling to her side on the plastic-covered floor.

"Shall I hit her again?" she heard the sweet voice of Elijah ask.

Her vision blurred, but through the haze, she could see the young man standing over her. He was smacking something against the palm of his hand as he looked down on her.

"Help me," she begged, raising a hand to him.

"No, leave her be," the old voice responded to Elijah's question.

And then Katie could sense movement from nearby. She could hear the creak of the hospital bed . . . feel the thump of something heavy landing upon the floor . . . the sound of something moving . . . crawling across the plastic covering.

She tried to move, but the room continued to spin, the throbbing in her skull nearly blinding in its intensity. She was crying now, wanting to scream, but the pain . . .

Cold fingers from the darkness grabbed onto the flesh of her thighs, a hard, bony body pulling itself onto hers.

She tried to push it away, but it clung to her with unwavering tenacity. Katie screamed for Elijah to help her, but the handsome young man simply watched, his eyes glistening wetly in the darkness.

"Your flesh, your blood, your soul," Pastor Zachariah growled, his old, withered face floating above her own.

Katie Allen was suddenly too tired to fight the old man lying atop her, and she tried to prepare herself for what was to come.

But nothing could have prepared her for what followed.

The old man opened his mouth far wider than humanly possible. He lowered his head, taking a huge bite of the flesh on her neck.

And he began to feed.

On her flesh, her blood, and her soul.

CHAPTER EIGHT

Remy lay upon the bed that he'd once shared with the love of his life, and pretended to sleep.

He went through all the motions: removing his clothes, climbing beneath the covers, and closing his eyes.

But he didn't sleep; not really.

Remy had learned to send himself into a deep fugue state, a kind of healing, dreamlike place where his mind wandered to review and reexamine. Of course, he found himself thinking an awful lot about Madeline on these long, lonely nights.

It was torture to see her again, but at the same time it made him so very happy.

She was young in this place inside his head, young, beautiful, and healthy. It was how he liked to remember her . . . how she always appeared to him, even when time and the ravages of her illness sought to take away her beauty.

They were reclining in beach chairs, side by side in the sand as the sun slowly set and the tide inexorably drew closer. He wore a loose-fitting cotton shirt—unbuttoned—exposing his hairless chest, and shorts, while she wore that red one-piece swimsuit that had always flattered her figure, large-framed sunglasses, and an impossibly floppy hat.

She reached out and took his hand in hers; he turned to smile at her and couldn't help but laugh.

"What's so funny?" she asked, giving his hand a loving squeeze.

"Nothing," he said, still taking her all in. "It's just really good . . . ," he said, pausing as he felt himself fill with emotion. "It's just really good to see you."

"It's good to see you too," she said, and brought his hand to her mouth to kiss it.

They sat there like that for quite some time, listening to the sounds of the beach. They were alone here, and Remy relished every moment of having her near him again.

Even though she was only a product of his memories.

"The case is a strange one," she said, staring out at the approaching tide.

"What?" he asked, looking at his wife.

"The case you're working on," she said. "It's turned into another strange one, hasn't it?"

"Yeah." He stuck his bare feet beneath the cool, damp sand. "It has."

"What do you think it means?" she questioned. "The lip marks on the back of that man's hand and on the doctor's neck."

Remy shook his head. "I really don't know. It's not a tattoo. It's almost as if the flesh had been burned . . . burned by a kiss."

He looked across to see that she was staring at him, a dreamy smile on her beautiful face. "What?" he asked.

"Aren't you glad my kisses don't burn?" she said, leaning toward him.

Remy did the same, their faces almost meeting.

"Even if they did, I'd tolerate them," he said.

"Even if they hurt like hell?" she asked, pulling back slightly.

"Even if they hurt like hell," he said.

And they kissed, gently at first, but becoming more passionate the longer their lips touched.

"I think that one almost burned me," Remy said, the first to break the lock.

"We'd better try again, just to make sure," Madeline suggested.

And they kissed again, long and passionate, stopping only when she brought her hand to the side of his face, and unlocked her lips from his.

"You realize this is likely important, right?"

"Our kissing? Very important."

Remy leaned in to kiss her again, but this time Madeline pulled away from his advance.

"The lip marks," she stressed.

"Yeah," he said, "you're probably right."

"Probably? I'm offended."

"Guess I should look into those more closely," he said, his eyes back on the crashing surf that had moved that much closer.

"Yes, you should." She gave his hand another squeeze.

And as the sun disappeared beneath the horizon, they continued to sit, holding on to the special moment, not wanting it to end.

But knowing it would.

"I love you," he told her. This time he brought her hand to his lips. "And I always will."

"Of course you will," she said with a smile bright enough to replace the sun. "Now get to work. Zoe is depending on you."

And the darkness came, as it always did, and Remy was alone.

Remy opened his eyes and stared at the ceiling of his bedroom.

His hand had drifted to Madeline's side of the bed, lying there as if hoping to feel some evidence that she had been there, but it was cold.

He turned his head and glanced at the clock. It was a little past three a.m. He hadn't been resting any more than two hours, so now what? He had no desire to put himself back into the fugue state.

He lay there a moment longer, then sat up, throwing his legs over the side of the bed. He caught sight of Marlowe, on his side as if shot, sound asleep at the foot of the bed. Carefully he stood, not wanting to wake the dog. Quietly he retrieved a shirt from his closet, then slipped on some socks and a pair of pants.

The memory of his conversation with Madeline was fresh in his thoughts. She was right; he had to look into the origin of the lip marks, and what it had to do with the torment of a man's soul.

He was slipping into his loafers when he realized he was being watched, and looked up to see Marlowe staring, his dark brown eyes glistening in the darkness.

"Go back to sleep," Remy told him. "It's too early for you to be up."

"*You?*" Marlowe asked curiously.

"I have work to do," Remy said, going to his dresser for his wallet and keys. "When I get back, it'll be time for you to get up."

Remy rolled his eyes at the sound of the animal jumping from the bed.

Marlowe approached him, sticking his butt into the air as he stretched.

"*Go to work,*" the dog grumbled.

"No." Remy shook his head. "I'm going somewhere that might not be safe for dogs."

The dog looked at him with a curious tilt of his head.

"Normally, I would have sent Francis to do this, but . . ."

"*Francis gone*," the Labrador said, and Remy could hear sadness in his animal's voice.

"Yeah, Francis is gone, so now I have to do it."

The dog sat down at his feet, tail sweeping the floor.

"*Go*," he barked, staring intently at Remy.

Remy ignored him, leaving the bedroom and heading downstairs, Marlowe close on his heels.

"Do you need to go out before . . . ," he began, then stopped and turned to look at the dog.

Marlowe was sitting perfectly straight, as if waiting for the secret password.

"No," Remy said again. "You can't."

"*Go*," the dog grumbled again, his tail wagging all the faster.

Remy was about to put his foot down, but he had a sudden change of heart. "All right, do you really want to go?"

The Labrador yelped and sprang to his feet. His thick, muscular tail wagged so fast that it was practically a blur.

"Fine," Remy said, going to the kitchen counter for the dog's leash. "But you've got to promise me you'll stay out of trouble."

"*Promise*," the dog answered as Remy slipped the chain around his neck.

"Okay, let's go," Remy said, and Marlowe beat him to the front door. "But first we have to stop by Francis' house."

"*Francis gone*," Marlowe said, bounding into the predawn morning as Remy opened the outside door.

"Yeah," he said, following the dog down the steps. "Thanks for reminding me, again."

It was close to four in the morning, so Remy had no problem finding a parking space close to Francis' Newbury Street apartment building.

Since his friend's disappearance, the building had been under

Remy's care, but he'd allowed it to remain empty. There was just so much bizarre history connected with this building that Remy had thought it best to let it be for now, although he must have received twenty calls a week from various real estate firms practically begging to buy the building.

He didn't even bother to return the calls.

Remy climbed the stone steps and let himself into the building, the eager Labrador at his side. The air was tainted with the smell of mustiness and age. Marlowe immediately began to prowl the foyer, his nose pressed to the old rug.

Francis had lived in the basement apartment, and Remy went to the heavy wood door that would allow him access. He took a key from his pocket and undid the lock.

"Coming?" he called after Marlowe.

The Labrador had his nose wedged beneath an old steam radiator.

"*Mouse*," he grumbled as he pushed past Remy to go down the stairs into Francis' apartment. He always had to be first.

Remy followed, feeling a sense of melancholy as he stood at the foot of the stairs and looked around. He'd left it pretty much as he'd found it, almost a shrine to his friend.

Marlowe was sniffing around, following a trail through the living room and into the tiny kitchen.

"More mice?" Remy asked him.

The dog ignored the question, far too busy to be bothered.

Remy left the animal to his business and set about on his own particular chore.

Francis had something that Remy required.

Whenever one of his cases had taken a turn toward the bizarre, Francis had always been there to provide the intel from the supernatural community that prowled the streets of Boston, and just about every other major population center on the planet.

Francis had no problem at all dealing with these citizens of the weird, and Remy was more than happy to pay the former Guardian angel for his troubles. Remy hated to deal with the unearthly inhabitants; it served only to remind him of his own true, inhuman nature.

He stood in the center of the living room and placed his hands on his hips. "If I were a key, where would Francis put me?" he muttered aloud as he scanned the apartment.

In the far corner of the room was a large wooden wardrobe. That was where Francis kept his most prized possession—his weapons collection.

"As good a place as any," Remy said, pulling open the heavy wooden doors to reveal the arsenal stored within.

So much death in one place, the angel thought as he perused the collection. There were swords both long and short, knives from all over the world and time periods, handguns, rifles, shotguns, explosives.

Francis had certainly loved his weapons.

And if he had been going to store something away for safe keeping, this was where he would have put it.

There was a place called Methuselah's where the citizens of the weird liked to hang out, have a few drinks, maybe an appetizer or two.

It existed between the here and the there . . . the now and the then, and only members could get in, with a special key. Francis had been a member.

There were a number of small drawers inside the wardrobe, and Remy began to pull them open. One was filled with ammunition, while another, strangely enough, contained marbles. And then in a drawer that held only random scraps of paper with phone numbers scrawled on them, Remy found the key.

It resembled an old-fashioned skeleton key, but the magickal energies it contained made the tips of his fingers tingle as he picked it up.

Turning, he saw Marlowe standing in front of a closet that had once contained a powerful secret. At one time that closet was the doorway to Tartarus.

But now with the prison no more, and Lucifer in control of Hell, the closet was just a closet.

Or was it?

"*Pee*," Marlowe said, sniffing the hardwood floor in front of the door.

"You peed there, remember?"

Marlowe glanced at Remy with an almost-embarrassed look.

When Marlowe was last in Francis' apartment, the poor animal had caught a glimpse of Tartarus, one of the most horrible places in existence, and had lost control. Who could blame him?

Remy imagined Mulvehill would have reacted in very much the same way.

With a cautious eye, the dog watched him approach the door, and Marlowe backed slowly away, tail between his legs.

"It's all right," Remy reassured him. "That bad place isn't behind the door anymore. But with this key"—Remy held up the skeleton key he'd found—"it'll be a doorway to another place."

"*Bad place?*" Marlowe asked.

"Not really," Remy said. "There are people there I have to talk with."

Marlowe relaxed some, creeping closer.

"You ready?"

The Labrador stared at the door, the black fur around his neck bristling slightly.

Remy took the old-fashioned key and slid it into the lock. He could feel the magick pulsing through the key, and up his arm. It stirred the Seraphim inside, and the power of Heaven awakened.

Remy turned the key, the sound of the door's unlocking far

louder than it should have been. He gripped the knob, which had become unusually warm, and readied to turn it.

"Stay with me," he said to his dog as he opened the door.

And they stepped into another place.

Remy and Marlowe found themselves in a stone alley. It was as dark as pitch, the only source of light a red neon sign over a rounded wooden door at the end of the rock corridor—METHUSELAH'S, it announced.

Remy removed the key from the door, allowing it to close—and disappear as if it had never been there at all.

Marlowe woofed, sniffing at the wall, his tail wagging nervously.

"Don't worry," he reassured the animal, patting his flank. "It'll be there when it's time to go home."

They started down the stone passage toward the tavern at its end, their acute senses picking up the sounds of movement in the thick shadows on either side of them.

Marlowe started to stray, his nose twitching as he moved closer to the scrabbling sounds, but Remy was quick to draw him back.

"Stay with me, pal. I don't think you want to be messing with what's lurking in there."

Marlowe growled menacingly at the scratching noises and returned to his place at Remy's side as they approached Methuselah's front door.

Remy reached for the door handle, attempting to enter, but the door didn't budge.

"Shit," he muttered, trying again. "Don't tell me they're closed."

A wooden panel in the door suddenly slid open, and a fearsome face peered out at them.

"Hey," Remy said, "I'd like to come in."

Marlowe looked up at the face and began to bark.

"Shut up," Remy told him. He looked back to the face in the door. "Sorry, he gets a little excited sometimes."

The dark eyes from the door studied him, and Remy decided that what was on the other side of that door wasn't even remotely human.

"Do you have a key?" the creature asked, its voice a throaty rumble.

Remy held up the key.

The dark eyes stared at it, then shifted back to Remy.

"It is not your key," the beast said. "You cannot be admitted."

Remy rolled his eyes in exasperation. "I know whose key it was, but he's not around, and I have been awarded all of his possessions, making the key mine."

"And who are you?"

"I'm Remy Chandler."

The beast squinted, before two large nostrils appeared in the opening, a brass ring hanging between the two cavernous holes. The nostrils twitched, sniffing at the air around Remy.

"Who are you really?" the beast asked again.

Remy hesitated a moment. "I am Remiel of the Heavenly host Seraphim," he said reluctantly, his voice taking on the air of authority befitting one of his species.

The beast's eyes appeared in the opening again, and Remy expected the door to open.

"You still cannot come in."

"Why the hell not?" Remy asked incredulously. "I have a key that rightfully belongs to me. . . ."

"No dogs allowed," the creature growled, turning its gaze to Marlowe, who sat patiently at Remy's side.

Remy felt his ire on the rise and was about to cause a scene, when he heard another voice from inside the establishment. The wooden panel slid closed, but he could still hear two low and tremulous voices locked in heated conversation.

The voices suddenly went silent.

And then Remy heard the sounds of locks turning, and slowly the door opened with a high-pitched creak.

A huge figure stood silhouetted in the doorway, and all Remy could do was stare. He'd heard the stories, but this was the first time he had actually seen him.

The man stood at least seven feet tall and was apparently carved from dark gray stone. He wore a bright red vest and black slacks obviously made from a stretchy, durable material. *Methuselah* was stitched in cursive on the left side pocket of the golem's vest.

"Remy Chandler," the stone man said, his voice sounding like tectonic plates rubbing together.

"Hello, Methuselah," Remy said. "I like the new look."

Remy had heard that the old man's body, after living close to a thousand years, was starting to show some wear and tear, and he had been in the market for something new and more durable.

Apparently he'd done exactly what he'd set out to do.

"You like it?" Methuselah asked. "Crude, but effective. Come on in."

The stone man turned, and Remy was impressed; for a body made of rock, it moved with far more grace than he would have expected.

"Is it okay if Marlowe comes too?" Remy asked before passing through the door.

Methuselah squatted down, his great stone hand reaching out to gently pat the Labrador's head.

"Of course he can," he said with a rumble.

Marlowe, always the charmer, licked the rock man's face.

"*Salt*," the dog said in between licks. "*Taste salt.*"

Methuselah laughed, and it sounded like thunder in the distance. He and Marlowe then strolled into the tavern, best buddies, as Remy brought up the rear.

A minotaur stood just to the right of the door; the doorman—door*beast*—that had attempted to deny him entrance. It eyed him suspiciously.

"Guess he likes dogs." Remy shrugged as he passed.

The minotaur responded with a grunt, and a wet blast of air came from its flared nostrils.

"What can I get you?" Methuselah asked as he deftly navigated the bulky body of rock behind the bar. Remy sauntered up to one of the stools and sat, motioning for Marlowe to lie down on the wooden floor beside the chair.

"Scotch, neat," Remy said.

"Could've guessed that," the stone man said. "It's what your buddy always had."

Methuselah poured Remy a tumbler of golden liquid from a dusty bottle without any label, which could have been good, or very, very bad. Remy took note that most of the bottles behind the bar were minus any kind of labeling.

The bartender placed the glass before his customer. Not wasting any time, Remy picked up the glass and had a sip.

It was good, very, very good, probably some of the best Scotch he had ever tasted. He knew Francis had to keep coming back to this place for something other than the company.

Casually, Remy looked around. Methuselah's wasn't busy, but there were still enough clientele to make the journey worth his while.

Some appeared human, but he knew they weren't, while others—most of whom sat in the deep pockets of shadow around the bar—were the farthest thing from human he could imagine.

They were creatures of another time, beings that had passed from one reality to another.

They were myths and legends, and a few nightmares tossed in for good measure.

"Does your pooch want some water?" Methuselah asked.

Remy looked down to the floor. "Hey, Marlowe, do you want some water?"

"*Not thirsty*," the dog said, furiously sniffing at the wooden floor. Remy could only imagine the things that had been spilled there over the long lifetime of the bar.

Remy shook his head, bringing his glass to his mouth again. "He's not thirsty."

Methuselah leaned against the bar, staring at him with that big, almost expressionless stone face. It was hard to read a face like that.

"What's on your mind?" Remy asked.

"Nothing really," the ancient being said. "I always wondered when I'd see you in here."

"And here I am," Remy said, having some more of the amazing Scotch.

"And here you are," Methuselah repeated, his words sounding like a small avalanche.

The stone man picked up a rag and began wiping down the bar.

"Sorry about Francis," he said.

Remy shrugged. "He went out the way he wanted to."

Methuselah nodded. "I guess that's all we can hope for."

"I guess you're right." Remy sipped some more, denying the alcohol any effect over him. Steven would have sold his soul for a bottle of this stuff.

"So, what brings you in?" Methuselah asked, still wiping the wooden counter. "Can't be because you were up for a little socializing, seeing as you seldom mingle with your own kind."

Remy bristled. *His own kind.* He was as far from these . . . *beings* . . . as one could possibly be.

The Seraphim stirred, aroused by Remy's annoyance.

Or was he?

"I'm looking for information," Remy said, keeping his annoyance to a minimum.

A waitress who appeared perfectly normal came up to the bar and ordered a round for a table in the back. She seemed to be in her late thirties, attractive, but Remy knew not to look too closely in Methuselah's; the normal didn't often make it through the door.

Again Remy marveled at Methuselah's stone body as he mixed one drink after another; his dexterity was truly amazing.

The waitress had her drinks and was off again.

"Sorry about that," Methuselah said. "You were saying?"

"I'm looking for information," Remy stated flatly.

Methuselah picked up the dusty Scotch bottle and offered him another, but Remy passed, placing his hand over the tumbler's top.

"I'm good."

"Maybe I can help," the stone man said, placing the bottle back amongst many others behind the bar. "What are you looking for?"

"It's not much, but in this case I'm working, I've come across these strange marks . . . almost like a brand."

"What do they look like?" Methuselah asked.

"Lips," Remy stated. "It looks like these guys have been kissed by some pretty full lips that have left an indelible mark."

Remy stared at the silent bartender, attempting to read him, but as before, there was very little expression available on the stone face. He would have had better luck with one of the Easter Island heads.

"I've got nothing," Methuselah said finally, picking up the damp cloth and starting to wipe down the counter again.

And that was when Remy heard the commotion.

"You'd better go get your dog, Chandler," Methuselah said, and Remy spun around on his stool to see that Marlowe had found his way into one of the more foreboding corners of the room, and was currently attempting to have a discussion with a demonic entity about its appetizer—it looked like one of those big fried onions.

Of all the *things* in the bar, of course Marlowe had to bother that one.

Demons were foul; there was just no other way to describe them.

Knowledge of the dark entities was scarce, but some in the know believed they were a life-form that existed in the all-encompassing darkness before the Lord God turned on the lights, while others thought they were one of God's failed experiments, something that went really, really wrong.

Nonetheless, they existed, even after multiple attempts by various angelic hosts to wipe them out. And they waited in the shadows for their opportunity to bring darkness back to the world, in any form they could.

Like this one, for example, Remy thought as he slid from his stool and moved past the tables and chairs to get to the scene. *This one wants to cause problems by hurting my dog.*

Not a good idea.

The demon had stood up from its chair, its pale, moist flesh glistening in the candlelight from the table. The creature was completely hairless and glared at Marlowe with eyes like two red LEDs adrift in twin pools of darkness. Its mouth was pulled back in a snarl that could have been disgust, or rage, and its sharp yellow teeth were as rude as the rest of it.

Marlowe, on the other hand, was sitting before the demon's table, looking as pretty as could be, tail wagging happily—the perfect example of a good dog who deserved a piece, or two, or three, of somebody's onion appetizer. It was obvious that Marlowe really wasn't picking up on the hostility.

"Marlowe, no," Remy commanded.

The Labrador looked his way with that perfectly simple look, drool trailing from the sides of his grinning maw.

"You know it's not polite to beg," Remy scolded.

"*Food*," the dog woofed excitedly, looking back at the demon still standing by its table.

Pointed spines had begun to emerge from the demon's pale flesh, their tips, dangerously sharp, dripping with moisture.

"There's no need for that," Remy said to the demon, his voice booming.

Methuselah's became deathly quiet as all eyes turned to Remy and conversation stopped. Obviously they'd had no idea there would be entertainment this night.

The demon cocked its head strangely, studying Remy. It had no nose, but Remy could see some form of a sensory organ, pulsing beneath the wet skin that was pulled tight across the angular skull of its horrible face.

"You should pay better attention to your pet," the demon said. Its voice sounded as pleasant as fingernails being dragged down a blackboard.

"I know; I'm sorry about that," Remy said with as much honesty as he could muster.

The Seraphim was still awake, and it rose to the situation.

"Sometimes his belly gets the better of him," Remy said goodnaturedly. "We're sorry to have disturbed your meal."

He was about to call Marlowe away again, but the demon had other things in mind.

"This cur invaded my personal space," it screeched, turning its attention back to Marlowe, who had remained sitting, still staring at the untouched fried onion in the middle of the table. "I am within my rights to harm it."

And then the demon did a very bad thing. It extended its long, bony index finger, one of the dripping poison quills pointed directly at Marlowe's face.

And for that, the Seraphim emerged.

Remy's body erupted in light, the human flesh that he wore on the verge of being shed. Remy could barely restrain the divine power that had bubbled to the surface of his humanity, ready to cast it aside and lay waste to this loathsome being.

"Stay your hand, wretch," the angel Remiel ordered, the power of his words and the radiance of his presence causing the demon to cry out in pain. It dropped to the floor of the tavern, averting its sensitive eyes from the light of Heaven.

In the light cast by his angelic frame, Remy could see the reaction that his actions had caused. The patrons of Methuselah's looked upon him with expressions of fear and awe, the glory of his form forcing the shadows from every nook and cranny, and filling them with the Almighty's resplendent light.

And then he saw something that didn't seem to belong in a place such as this; in a far corner, now cleansed of concealing shadow, two fearsome angels of Heaven—of the Retriever host—tensed for conflict.

They were clad in the awesome armor of their class, and all Remy could think of was a stealth bomber, ready to lay waste to an enemy and its territories. Their eyes were cold, and their exposed flesh resembled the surface of glacial ice.

These were the personification of God's intensity, His desire to reclaim any and all that had been taken from Him.

Sensing the potential for escalating violence, Remy pulled back upon his holy essence, tucking it fitfully away before matters could get out of hand.

His flesh tingled like the aftereffects of a severe sunburn, but his humanity remained intact.

As his divine light was extinguished, the darkness wasted no time in rushing back to flood the secret corners, swallowing up the mysteries that had momentarily been exposed.

Why are Retrievers here? Remy wondered, but that was something he would have to think about later, and in another place.

He'd worn out his welcome at Methuselah's.

The patrons continued to watch him with equal parts fear and hostility. Marlowe, on the other hand, sat, completely unfazed by the activity around him, his eyes still fixed on the prize on the table.

"You know dogs can't have onions," Remy said, grabbing his collar and pulling him away.

The demon cowered on the floor, a foul-smelling fluid leaking from its moist, almost luminescent flesh.

"Never threaten a man's dog," Remy said to the trembling thing. Then, holding on to Marlowe's collar, Remy escorted the Labrador back to the bar where Methuselah watched.

"Sorry about that," Remy said, but the golem remained quiet. "What do I owe you for the Scotch?" Remy asked, using his free hand to fish his wallet from his back pocket.

Methuselah held up his blocky hand. "It's on the house," he said with a rumble of stone against stone.

"Thanks, I appreciate it," Remy said. He pulled a business card from his wallet and laid it on top of the superclean wooden bar.

The golem reached for it, delicately picking it up.

"If you should hear anything or think of anything about those marks I mentioned, give me a call."

Sliding the card inside his vest pocket, Methuselah nodded. "Will do."

Marlowe in tow, Remy started for the door, still feeling the eyes of the tavern upon him.

The minotaur stood up from its chair by the door, giving Remy the hairy eyeball as it opened the door for them.

"Sorry for the commotion," Remy said again, loud enough for Methuselah and the remaining patrons to hear.

And the minotaur slammed closed the heavy tavern door behind Remy and Marlowe with a good-riddance-to-bad-rubbish kind of grunt.

CHAPTER NINE

Delilah was exhausted from her travels, but she would not rest until the object was finally in her possession.

And if she could not rest, neither would those who served her.

Clifton Poole had been set up in his own room and given everything he could possibly need in order to lead them to her prize.

So far his attempts at divining its location had not borne the kind of results she had hoped for, and she prayed this morning would be different.

She strolled down the corridor of her new Boston home, high heels clicking upon the meticulously cared-for hardwood floors. She knew she was being followed and deliberately slowed her pace, then turned to confront a woman in a navy blue suit.

"Who are you?" she asked in a powerful voice that reverberated down the sprawling corridor.

"I'm so sorry for disturbing you," the woman said, cowering beneath Delilah's gaze. "I'm Ms. Burnett . . . Janice Burnett. . . . I . . . I brought you to this house."

Delilah smiled. "Of course, Ms. Burnett."

She looked up and down the corridor, at the beautiful religious murals painted on the walls. The estate, once owned by the

Archdiocese of Boston, had been put on the market to help pay restitution to the victims of the recent clerical sex abuse scandals.

Their loss was her gain.

"You've served me well," Delilah said to the young woman.

Ms. Burnett looked as though the weight of the planet had suddenly been lifted from her shoulders. "Oh, thank you," she said, tears beginning to flow from her eyes. "You don't know what that means to me."

But Delilah knew exactly what it meant; how special it was to serve her. All it had taken was one conversation with the Boston real estate agent for her to realize how much she had wanted to please Delilah.

Ms. Burnett rushed down the corridor and dropped to her knees in front of Delilah. "I . . . I didn't know if you were happy . . . if I had pleased you," she said, reaching for Delilah's ring-covered hand, lovingly kissing it.

Delilah pulled her hand away, startling the woman.

"I'm pleased," she said. "For now."

Burnett stared up at her with wide, desperate eyes.

"What else can I do for you?" she begged. "Ask me anything. . . . I'll do anything to . . ."

"Go," Delilah said with a wave of her hand. "I have other concerns that demand my fullest attention." She turned her back on the groveling woman and continued on down the hall to Poole's room.

She rapped loudly on his door with one of her rings. "Mr. Poole," she called out, pulling a key from the pocket of her slacks.

She opened the door and stepped inside.

The room was dark, and it stank of stale sweat and bodily waste.

Delilah fumbled on the wall to the right of the door, searching for the light switch. Finding it, she flipped it up, and a chandelier brilliantly illuminated the room.

Poole screamed, his naked body appearing pale and malnourished in the light as he hunched over his work upon the floor.

Had she given him permission to eat? Delilah couldn't remember, but that was the least of her concerns at the moment.

The Hound dipped his fingers into a bucket of his own waste and drew feverishly upon the hardwood floor.

She wrinkled her nose in disgust. "Mr. Poole," she announced, trying not to breathe in the foul aroma.

"I'm trying," he screamed.

His work was elaborate; a map, covering a good eighty percent of the floor inside the nearly barren room, and she was certain it would soon encompass even more than that.

"But when I get close . . ."

He started to scream, his body thrashing upon the floor as if electricity were being pumped through him. Then just as suddenly, he seemed to recover, crab walking across the floor to a stack of atlases and maps piled in the corner.

The metal child vessel, which had once contained the object of her desire, sat there as well, arms outstretched.

"Do you have anything, Mr. Poole?" she asked, fearing his answer.

He ignored her, scratching at his filthy genitalia, before snatching a road map from the floor and unfolding it to its fullest. He practically lay upon it, pressing his face to the elaborate cartography, as he muttered unintelligibly.

He reached out and dragged the empty vessel closer, holding it in his arms, as he studied the map, licking the metal container's head with a thickly coated tongue.

"Talk to me, Mr. Poole!" Delilah bellowed, flexing the muscles of her commanding ability.

Poole recoiled as if slapped, then fell backward to the floor.

She crossed the room, careful not to step upon the waste.

"It knows we're looking," Poole rushed to explain. "It knows we're looking and hides when I try to find it." He grabbed the sides of his head in pain and slowly began to rock. "It's putting . . . putting things inside me . . . inside my skull . . . trying to stop me. . . ."

"But you won't stop, will you, Mr. Poole?" Delilah asked him.

"No," he screamed, flecks of spit flying from his mouth. "I have to find it . . . find it for you . . . so . . . so you'll be happy."

"Exactly," she agreed.

Delilah tried not to think about how close she had been. If only they had moved just a little bit faster, they would have found the father and child in the city, but now they had gone.

And no one could tell her where they'd gone.

"So, to keep me happy, you will continue to search. . . . You will not sleep; you will not eat. . . . You will not piss or shit. You will not stop for a second. Do you understand me, Mr. Poole?"

The Hound twitched, trembling beneath her gaze.

"Well, what are we waiting for?" she asked with a predatory snarl.

Poole flopped about, scrabbling across the filth-covered floor on his hands and feet as he resumed his search.

Delilah strode from the room, locking the door behind her and turning to find Mathias waiting patiently.

"I hope for your sake you don't have any bad news," she warned.

Mathias averted his gaze. "No, my mistress, but I might have something you'll find pleasing."

Delilah was curious.

"Well?" she urged.

"It may not be exactly what you're looking for, but perhaps it could eventually bring us to that," the mercenary said.

"Get to the point, Mathias."

Mathias looked up, staring into her dark eyes.

"The child is with her father," he said. "He accompanied her to the hospital that morning."

She stepped closer, sensing something at the brink. "Get on with it," she hissed, motioning with her hand.

"The child is with the father," Mathias repeated.

Delilah loomed closer, her control nearly failing.

"The father," he said again, and she was about to reach out and pluck out his eyes when, suddenly, she understood what he was saying.

"She came to the city with both parents," Delilah said.

"And according to Parsons, the mother was calling repeatedly, trying to find them."

"They may have contacted her," Delilah said, trying to keep her excitement in check.

"Perhaps," Mathias said. "Who knows what we might learn if we were to speak to her?"

Images of the lives she had led, of the loves she had had, flashed through Delilah's mind. . . .

"Find her," she commanded.

The images reminded her of what she could have again, what could still be, if only . . .

"And bring her to me."

Marlowe was hungry, but then again, when wasn't he?

They'd managed to make it back from Methuselah's pretty much unscathed, but with very little to show for their efforts.

On the drive home, Remy tried to explain to the Labrador why it was a bad idea to try to get demons to give him food, but the dog just didn't understand. Why wouldn't everybody want to share their food with him? After all, he was Marlowe.

Remy couldn't argue with that kind of logic, so he let it drop.

They found a parking space on Irving Street and returned to the brownstone just as the early risers were starting to make their way downtown.

They were barely through the door when Marlowe demanded his breakfast, which he quickly scarfed down, followed by half an apple.

And that finally left Remy free and clear to shower and get ready for the day.

Methuselah's had left him feeling grimy. It wasn't the tavern per se, but what he had seen there, revealed when the shadows had been pulled away like a magician's trick.

Retrievers, and not the good, four-legged kind.

God's Retrievers.

Not good at all. All he could imagine was that the situation between Heaven and the newly reconfigured Hell was starting to heat up.

Clean and dressed, Remy headed back downstairs to find Marlowe fast asleep on the couch.

It was beginning to feel a little muggy inside, the hint of higher temperatures to come, so he put the air conditioners on for his pal, then went to the kitchen to start a pot of coffee for himself. He picked up his cell phone from the counter where he'd left it to charge and found he had missed a call from Father Coughlin.

He hit REDIAL, and the old priest picked up on the second ring.

"Hey, it's Remy," the angel said, taking his Little Britain mug from the dish rack and setting it down beside the coffee machine, which was still brewing.

"And where were you at such an early hour?" the priest asked curiously. "Out fighting crime, were we?"

"With my faithful four-legged sidekick," Remy affirmed. "There was much evil to be smitten this morning."

They both chuckled at that.

"So, do you have anything useful for me?"

The thick, delicious aroma of coffee permeated the kitchen, and Remy placed his hand on the handle of the carafe, impatient for it to finish. There was nothing he liked better than a fresh pot of coffee; it was a human vice he would not have been able to shed, even if he'd tried.

"I think I do," Coughlin said, and Remy could hear him shuffling papers around on the other end of the phone.

The coffee machine dripped, then gurgled its last as Remy pulled the carafe from beneath the filter and poured himself a full mug.

"Okay, those symbols on the flyer?"

"Yeah?" Remy prompted, taking a full swig of his first coffee of the day.

"They were most definitely Sumerian," the old priest said. "I faxed copies of the pamphlet over to an associate at the Vatican, and he confirmed it for me."

"Sort of odd, don't you think?" Remy asked.

"Most definitely," Coughlin answered. "Especially when you hear what the symbols were associated with. They're connected to an extremely rare, ancient sect that worshipped a deity called Dagon."

"Dagon," Remy repeated. "Wasn't he some sort of sea or fish god?"

"He was often depicted that way," the priest explained. "But in actuality, he was a god of fertility and the vivifying powers of nature and reproduction, of life and death."

Remy sipped his coffee, absorbing the information.

"So you're probably wondering how and why ancient symbols

connected to a seemingly forgotten Sumerian god found their way onto a pamphlet advertising a church in Somerville, and that would be a very good question."

"Hit me," Remy said, hearing the excitement in the old priest's voice.

"About ten years ago, a religious order sprang up rather unexpectedly in the southern regions of the country, specifically to worship Dagon. There were reports of child abuse and weapons hoarding, and eventually the ATF moved in with local police."

"Y'know, I seem to recall something about that. Weren't there mass suicides or something?" Remy asked.

"Yeah, it didn't end well for the church," Coughlin agreed. "The authorities found that the majority of parishioners, men, women, and children, had poisoned themselves." The old priest cleared his throat. "I have some pictures here from the Internet. It wasn't a very pleasant sight. From my understanding, the church's followers believed their suicide—their lives—would provide the power needed for their god to be reborn on this earth in a body that had been especially created for him."

"What, like Frankenstein?" Remy asked. He had finished his first cup of coffee and was moving on to the second.

"Nothing so crude," Coughlin said. "A couple had been chosen to conceive a child—a special child, blessed by the powers of the church family, and this child would be the vessel in which this deity could grow and prosper."

Remy felt a sick twinge in the pit of his belly.

"So I'm guessing this ritual never occurred."

"Supposedly it was in the midst of being performed when the authorities stormed the compound and put a stop to it. That couple were two of the only survivors, along with the church's mysterious pastor, who managed to evade arrest."

The feeling in Remy's stomach became worse, a horrible twisting sensation that meant things were about to go very wrong.

"The couple survived, huh?" Remy said.

"Yes, yes, they did. In the pictures I have here, they look so young, children themselves really."

"Do you happen to know names?" Remy asked, knowing full well he would come to regret the question.

"I don't see any last names," Coughlin said. "But their first names were Deryn and Carl."

It was as if the floor beneath his feet had suddenly dropped away, that descending-elevator feeling that made him want to hold on tight to something.

Deryn York and Carl Saylor.

Remy was going to need another cup of coffee.

Deryn York was staying at the Nightingale Motor Lodge in Brighton, about fifteen minutes from Franciscan Children's, if traffic was behaving.

Remy had called her from the road, telling her to expect him, and twenty minutes later, he was pulling into the lot of the run-down, stucco building. Deryn's room was around back, so he parked as close as he could and walked across the lot.

She opened the door before he had a chance to knock.

Remy entered the room and was practically overwhelmed with the stink of cigarette smoke.

"What is it, Mr. Chandler?" she asked, cigarette butt hanging from her mouth as she wrung her hands in nervousness.

"Remy," he corrected, attempting to put her at ease.

She took the cigarette from the corner of her mouth and pulled a chair from beneath the desk. "All right then, Remy. Please, sit down," she said, motioning to the chair as she plunked down on the queen-sized bed that was covered with a wrinkled floral bedspread.

"What about my little girl?"

Remy leaned forward in the chair and looked her straight in the eyes.

"What can you tell me about the Church of His Holy Abundance?"

She stared, slowly bringing the cigarette back up to her mouth. "Nothing," she said with a shake of her head. "Never heard of it."

"Are you sure?" Remy prodded. "Perhaps your husband mentioned it in passing?"

She shook her head again, releasing a choking cloud of smoke. "No, nothing," she said, squinting through the noxious fumes that surrounded her head. "Why? What's this all about Mr. . . . Remy?"

Remy thought for a moment. "I've been doing some poking into your past," he said finally.

She stared intensely, slowly bringing the cigarette back up to her eager mouth. "My past?" she questioned.

"The Church of Dagon," Remy said. "I know about what happened at the Church of Dagon."

"Fucking shit," she hissed, bouncing off the bed and practically hurling herself toward the dresser where an ashtray waited. "I—I can't fucking believe this," she stammered, stamping out her smoke.

"There was a therapy assistant at Franciscan Children's who had apparently befriended your husband and daughter. I talked with him briefly at the hospital, but when I went to his home to question him further, I discovered he had been murdered."

"Murdered?" she repeated with a gasp, both trembling hands going to her mouth as her eyes widened. "It's not Frank, is it? Please, tell me it's not fucking Frank."

"I'm sorry," Remy said quietly.

"Oh God, oh God, oh God," she repeated, grabbing her purse

from the dresser and pulling out a pack of cigarettes and a lighter. Immediately, she lit up.

"Seems there's some kind of connection between the church Frank belonged to and the one you and your husband . . ."

"That son of a bitch," she snarled. "I always knew he hadn't given up the old beliefs, even though he swore he had."

She started to pace, puffing on the cigarette as if she would die if she didn't.

"I thought he might've been slipping when he lost his job, and when we first learned how sick Zoe was, but he promised me it wasn't true. He knew how I felt about those . . . those freaks."

Remy stared and listened.

"That's what they were," she said to him forcefully. "Wanting to use my baby to stick some sort of . . . spirit inside her and . . ."

She threw her hands in the air in frustration.

"We were young and fucking stupid; what can I say," she explained. Her back was to him now as she stood in front of the double windows, their shades drawn to keep out the sun, and any nosy motel residents.

"So you think he might have gone back to his old beliefs?" Remy asked.

She picked a piece of tobacco off her tongue and flicked it away. "Yeah, he could have, especially if Frank was a member. I was sort of wondering where those two would go off to together sometimes. Seriously, with the way things were going, I don't think it would've taken much to push him back to the old ways."

A sudden knock at the door startled them, and Deryn looked at him. "It's housekeeping," she said, heading for the door. "I called for more toilet tissue just before you came."

The Seraphim inside Remy awakened in an instant, aroused

by something familiar, and Remy gasped, fighting the nearly overwhelming power that struggled to manifest as Deryn opened the door.

It wasn't housekeeping. Not unless they traveled in packs and stank of violence, desperation, and decay.

And not unless they were all missing their souls.

CHAPTER TEN

The pack of soulless beings spilled into the motel room, strangely silent in their attack.

Remy barely had time to react before they had Deryn on the floor, holding her down as one pulled plastic ties from a pocket and bound her hands behind her back, and another drew a hood over her head.

Remy threw himself in the fray, and they swarmed him like ants on a piece of bread. They drove him to the floor, but still he fought.

The Seraphim screeched and wailed to be unleashed, and this time Remy allowed his guard to drop, the essence of Heaven surging to the surface, only to be pushed away. It struggled wildly, but something was preventing its manifestation.

The soulless beings kicked and punched Remy mercilessly, driving him back to the floor every time he tried to stand. Through bleary eyes, he watched as Deryn was dragged from the room.

And then he saw a gray-haired man, standing just inside the door, smiling as he watched the ferocious beating.

The assault was relentless, and as they laid their hands upon him again and again, he caught sight of the mark they wore, his eyes taking in brief glimpses of a pair of lips caught in a flash of exposed flesh.

"Enough," a voice that sounded a million miles away called out, and the soulless ceased their abuse.

Remy managed to push himself up onto his knees, swaying as the cheap motel room's floor seemed to move beneath him. Through his unswollen eye, he looked into the barrel of a pistol aimed at his forehead.

The gray-haired man stared down its length, his thumb cocking back the hammer. Remy could sense—could *smell*—that this one's soul had been removed as well, but there was something about him, in his cold, unemotional stare, almost as if the absence of God's greatest gift were nothing important.

Maybe he had learned to live without a soul long before it had been taken.

Remy watched the man's finger begin to twitch upon the trigger, and summoned the strength to react. He reached up, grabbing hold of the barrel, and twisted it away just as the weapon discharged.

"Shit," the man cursed, lashing out at him with his foot and kicking Remy back to the floor. He chambered another round and aimed at Remy's face.

He was about to fire when a roar filled the room.

It was coming from outside, growing louder by the second, and giving Remy just enough of a distraction.

He rolled onto his belly as the sound outside the motel grew to a nearly deafening crescendo, his eyes drawn to the thick curtains that had been pulled across the large motel windows.

The window exploded in a cacophony of shattered glass and cinder block, as a four-wheel drive crashed through the wall.

The soulless screamed as they were scattered, the leader with his gun falling backward as shards of glass and broken cement blanketed the room.

A cloud of dust and dirt billowed through the air as the vehicle's doors opened and two people emerged.

Remy reached out to the small desk against the opposite wall, trying to pull himself to his feet. He watched in disbelief as a man and woman, exhibiting strength not usually attributed to humans, made short work of the soulless.

Limbs were broken and skulls shattered as the pair waded into the room, administering violence with cold efficiency.

Remy saw movement from the corner of his eye, catching sight of the gray-haired leader bolting from the room. He tried to pursue him, but his legs had become like rubber, and he stumbled forward, falling against the bed.

He quickly turned, trying to stay upright as the room spun, and came face-to-face with one of the pair. It was the man, his face large and square, adorned with a mustache and goatee, his hair shoulder length, the top a spiky mullet. Their eyes locked, and then the man drew back, driving a fist like a wrecking ball into Remy's face.

He fell back, fighting to remain conscious. He could feel himself being picked up, then tossed like a bag of dirty laundry into the back of the truck

He could hear sirens in the distance as he felt the truck back up.

Banshee wails that took him by the hand and showed him the way to the land of unconsciousness.

Carl Saylor had always thought of himself as a failure.

But as he drove his car up the winding dirt road, with little Zoe sitting in the seat beside him, he believed that now—finally—that was all about to change.

He'd never really been much good at anything. He was the middle child of three; his brother had been great in sports, and his sister had been top of her class in high school and college. Carl never really had much luck with sports, and school, no mat-

ter how hard he applied himself, was always just too damn difficult. Even after school, his failures had continued as he moved
from one low-paying job to another.

From an early age he knew where his path would take him.
Nowhere.

He stopped the car and peered through the windshield at a
rusted yellow gate. He'd followed the directions Frank had given
him, but he hadn't mentioned anything about a gate, and now
Carl wondered if he shouldn't have taken that right about two
miles back.

"Where are we, Daddy?" Zoe asked. She was rocking back
and forth. "Where are we, Daddy? Where are we, Daddy?" she
repeated again and again, not waiting for his answer.

"We're looking for that special place Frank told us about, remember?" Carl said, reaching across the seat to squeeze her bare
knee.

"Frank's dead," she said matter-of-factly. "Dead. Dead.
Dead."

"Don't say that, honey," he scolded. "It's not nice."

"It's not nice," she repeated, rocking faster. "It's not nice
Frank's dead."

Carl truly believed Frank had saved his life, removing him
from the path of failure and putting him on the highway to
redemption.

He'd thought that about Deryn too, at first. She'd seemed an
awful lot like him.

He glanced over at his little girl, mesmerized by her rocking.
He could see his ex in the shape of her face, in the blue of her
eyes.

Deryn was the first to hear about the church. Carl had never
been one for religion, but he loved Deryn as much as he loved
anything, and he went along to one of the meetings just to keep
her happy.

The Church of Dagon had welcomed them with open arms, giving them a place to stay when they'd had no other, and even inviting them for a special visit with the church's founder, Pastor Zachariah.

And suddenly their lives were changed. They were no longer failures. They were chosen, Pastor Zachariah had told them. The pastor's words were like a magic potion, and Carl and Deryn had thrown themselves into the church, body and soul, waiting for the time when they would be able to fulfill their special purpose.

Then Deryn became pregnant. All the plans began to fall into place, and their future never seemed clearer.

The pastor told them their baby would be the vessel for their god . . . Dagon. And the world would be changed forever.

Carl opened the door, letting a rush of moist, West Virginia heat into the coolness of the air-conditioned car.

"Stay right there," he told his daughter as he exited. She continued to rock to some silent tune that only she could hear.

He slammed the door closed and walked around the car, standing before the metal gate, craning his neck to see what lay beyond. It appeared to be more of the same, but he didn't want to believe he was lost.

Not again.

The closer it had come to the time for the ritual, the more doubt had filled Carl's mind. He'd known it was selfish, but he didn't want a god to live inside his baby. Carl wanted his baby to belong to him, and to Deryn, not to the church . . . not to the world.

And that was when he had taken a walk down the road to failure again, placing a series of phone calls to various state and federal agencies, suggesting wrongdoing at the isolated church compound.

He'd believed his attempts to rouse the suspicions of the authorities had failed as the night the god Dagon was to return to the world was upon them. All the church was to play a part in the ancient ritual, sacrificing their lives for the good of the world, for the good of their god.

Their lives would reach to the void, punching through the barrier that kept the Lord of Abundance separated from this reality.

The ritual had been well under way, the church brothers and sisters in the throes of death, when the authorities laid siege to the compound.

Carl hadn't taken his own poison as his wife lay there, waiting for the ritual to be completed and the god to take possession of the child—*their child*—growing in her belly. As the officials poured into the church, weapons drawn, he had looked into Pastor Zachariah's eyes and realized the holy man knew he was responsible.

The pastor had run, using the confusion and clouds of tear gas to escape prosecution.

Carl, Deryn, and the baby had been the only survivors, and Carl had believed he was the luckiest man alive.

But he'd been wrong.

Because of his betrayal, he was back on the path of failure, and things had gone from bad to worse.

Carl shook his head and returned to the car.

"C'mon, hon," he said, opening the passenger door and unbuckling Zoe's seat belt. "We're gonna go for a little walk and see what's up this road."

The child's hands were flailing. It had been quite a while since she'd last held a crayon.

"I'll get you some paper in a little while," he told her, taking one of her hands in his and leading her toward the rusted gate. Carl picked the child up and placed her on the other side, climbing beneath the metal obstruction to join her.

His life after the Church of Dagon had been exciting at first, as they were interviewed by the newspapers and television, but it seemed like no time at all before things had turned to misery. It had taken Deryn some time to get over their no longer having a special purpose, other than to be mother and father to their new baby.

She had eventually accepted that, but doubt ate at Carl every day. He had thought the move to Florida would help, but a change in temperature wasn't enough to convince him that what he had done was the right thing.

Zoe's being diagnosed with autism and his and Deryn's splitting up were punishment for what he had done, for allowing his selfishness to prevent the world from seeing something special.

But then he had met Frank and learned that the man's place of worship, the Church of His Holy Abundance, was an offshoot of the Church of Dagon. It was an opportunity for Carl to make amends.

"Let's go up here," he told his daughter, leading her up the rock and dirt path.

Frank had seen Zoe's drawings and taken them as a sign that Carl and his child had been delivered to him, that he would be the messenger, the one to return them to their god.

Carl had followed the man's directions to the West Virginia compound of the Church of His Holy Abundance to a tee, or at least believed he had, but now he was beginning to think that maybe he was, as he had been for so very long now . . .

Lost.

Rounding the corner, he saw that the rocky path continued.

Maybe a little bit farther, he thought, tugging on Zoe's hand. The child was bent over, her index finger moving in the dirt. As she drew, she made strange, explosive sounds, almost as if she were imitating gunshots.

"What are you doing?" he asked. "Why are you making those sounds?"

And as if on cue, the men with guns emerged from the high underbrush. There were six of them, dressed in military fatigues.

"You are trespassing on private property," one of them bellowed, aiming down the barrel of a semiautomatic rifle.

Carl immediately let go of his child's hand and put his own up.

"I'm sorry," he said, his eyes darting from one armed man to the next. "I didn't know. . . . I'm looking for a church and I think I'm lost."

"What kind of church?" the man asked, still staring down the length of his weapon.

"The Church—the Church of His Holy Abundance," Carl stammered. "I used to be a member—a long time ago. I want them to take me back—and to forgive me for what I did."

Carl was babbling, his voice quivering with fear and emotion.

The man who questioned him lowered his gun.

"You used to be a parishioner?" he asked.

Carl nodded. "When it was the Church of Dagon."

The mention of the old church got an immediate reaction.

"Lower your weapons," the man said, and the others did as they were told.

"Do you know of the church?" Carl asked nervously. "Is it close by?" His arms were starting to ache, so he cautiously lowered them.

A phone began to chirp. The man reached down to a pocket on the leg of his pants, retrieved the phone, and brought it to his mouth.

"Go ahead, base," he said.

"What's the problem up there?" a voice asked.

"Seems we have a lost sheep that has returned to the flock," the man said.

There was a pause. "A lost sheep, you say?" the voice asked finally. "Ask him his name."

"What's your name, sheep?" the man asked. He held out the phone.

"Carl. Carl Saylor."

The man brought the phone to his mouth again. "Did you get that?"

"I did," said the voice on the other end. "The Judas has come home."

The other men instantly raised their weapons, hate suddenly evident in their eyes.

"The Judas," the man with the phone said, and Carl thought there was a very good chance he was about to be killed.

But the voice from the phone spoke again.

"Bring the Judas to the compound," it said.

And Carl and his daughter were escorted up the road at gunpoint, but he was exactly where he wanted to be.

Lost, but now found.

The sun was going down, and the tide was rolling in.

Remy reclined in his beach chair; his entire body hurt.

"Are you all right?" she asked him.

He turned his head to see Madeline sitting there beside him, her silly beach hat still adorning her lovely head.

"I think I got my ass kicked pretty good," he said. Even talking hurt him. His jaw throbbed painfully with the beat of his heart, and the muscles in his neck and stomach were aching with even the thought of movement.

"What happened back there?" Madeline asked as a gust of

warm wind came off the ocean, nearly stealing away her hat. She gripped the brim, tilting her head down to ride out the breeze.

Flecks of sand irritated his eyes, but he stared ahead at the roiling ocean slowly making its way up the beach toward them, toward the end of their days together.

"I'm not sure really," he said. "The people who attacked me—they were missing their souls."

"That doesn't happen all that often, does it?"

"Not usually," he said with a shake of his head that hurt way more than it should. "Something has taken their souls and left them angry, destructive shells of what they once were. Without a soul, they'll just lose the will to live, and eventually waste away."

"What about their leader?" Madeline asked. "He didn't seem like he was going to be wasting away any time soon."

"No, he didn't," Remy said, remembering the gray-haired man's cold, lifeless eyes. "Something tells me he wasn't using his soul all that much even before it was taken."

They both fell silent for a while, staring out across the ocean. The pain of his body had started to subside, which meant he was healing; one angelic aspect that he'd never made any effort to suppress.

"This is nice," he said finally, reaching to take her hand.

"It is," she said, "but you know it's not real, right?"

Remy sighed, not wanting to see the truth in her gaze.

"I know. But I really don't care. I'll see you any way I can."

He felt her smile at him, and his heart did the same kind of acrobatics it had done when they'd first met.

"You're sweet," she said, leaning over to kiss him. "But you really should get going."

"You're probably right."

They kissed briefly, and then Remy stood up. He was no longer wearing his shorts; he was in his work clothes.

"Looks like I'm waking up," he said, giving himself the once-over.

"Looks like you're right," Madeline said, leaning back in her chair as if to relax.

"See you later?" Remy asked.

"You bet," she said with a smile, and closed her eyes.

Remy opened his eyes and found that he was laid out on an old, beat-up leather couch in the corner of a dark, filthy office.

He sat up with a grunt, flexing his fingers and moving his arms, just to be sure everything had healed while he and Madeline sat on the beach.

He could still smell the ocean.

Cautiously, he rose to his feet and looked around the gloom of the office. On the wall, in a dusty, crooked frame, was a certificate for a job well-done by Rudy Haberlin, from the home office of the Boys and Girls Clubs of America. He found the closed door and crossed the room toward it, surprised to find it unlocked.

He stepped out into a small corridor that took him to the lobby of the apparently abandoned Boys Club building, where he found a set of trash-strewn marble steps, leading to what looked like the front doors. He cautiously walked down, only to find that a thick chain and lock had been fastened between the doors, making his escape a little less probable. He thought about calling on the power of the Seraphim again, but decided against it. Maybe as a last resort; there had to be other ways out of the building, and besides, he was curious as to why he had been brought here.

He climbed the stairs back into the lobby and had a look around. Multiple doorways led farther into the darkened recesses of the building, and he was about to pick one at random, when he heard the unmistakable sounds of cheering from somewhere in the distance.

Navigating the darkness, he moved toward a particular doorway, finding another set of stairs descending farther into the belly of the Boys Club. That was where the sounds seemed to be coming from, so that was where he decided to go.

Holding on to the cold, metal railing, Remy descended, listening as the cries grew louder, and some truly unusual scents wafted through the air—expensive perfume, aftershave, liquor, sweat, blood, and the unearthly.

The emergency lights were functioning on this lower level, providing just enough light, as Remy followed the sounds and scents to a set of large swinging doors at the end of the corridor.

Carefully, he pushed open one of the doors a crack and found himself looking into an old swimming pool area. It was crowded, at least two hundred or so normal and paranormal beings circling the pool. Portable bleachers had been set up on either side, where it appeared that the more wealthy and influential were sitting.

Remy willed himself unseen and slipped into the room, maneuvering through the raucous crowd, trying to get closer for a look in the pool.

A demon in an expensive suit got a phone call and so moved aside, allowing Remy the opportunity to take his place for a look at what was holding the attention of so many.

The dry, Olympic-sized pool had been turned into a makeshift gladiatorial pit, and inside, locked in ferocious combat, were two beings, both showing the bloody signs of violence they had heaped upon each other. One appeared to be pretty much human, wearing only a pair of loose-fitting sweatpants. He was a big man, but older. The hair on his chest was white, resembling tufts of down from a torn pillow, and he wore his equally snow-white locks long and flowing past his powerful shoulder blades.

But the other fighter was anything but human. Remy wasn't sure exactly what it was, guessing maybe some sort of troll descendant.

The troll raked a clawed hand down the front of the human's chest, staining the downy whiteness a crimson red. The old man stumbled back away from the beast. He squatted down, his hands feeling around on the ground before falling on a wooden bat.

The troll bellowed, looking down and bending just long enough to recover its own club.

The old man charged, holding his bat high. The troll raised its own bludgeon to block the savage blow, but the old-timer had other plans. At the last moment, he bent low, bringing the bat down upon the troll's bare foot.

The sound of breaking bones, followed by the troll's bellow of pain, echoed in the chamber.

The crowd went wild. The man advanced on his opponent as it tried to back away. The troll limped, visibly impaired by the injury, but managed to bring its club back up. The white-haired man ducked beneath the swing that would have likely taken his head off if it'd had the chance to connect, and rose up to slam his own bat into the troll's left side. Remy winced at the savagery of the blow as the troll bent forward in agony.

The old man was relentless, raining blow after savage blow upon his opponent.

Smelling blood, the crowd went wild. And across the room, near the ladder that would bring the victor up from within the pool, Remy caught sight of the man and woman who had driven their truck through the window of the Nightingale Motel and had brought him here. They were cheering madly, caught up in the frenzied excitement of the furious battle below.

The troll's cry of pain drew Remy's eyes back to the conflict.

The old man circled the beast that had fallen to its knees. The troll tried to keep its opponent at bay, but it proved impossible. Lashing out with his bat, the old man struck at the troll's hand, causing it to drop its weapon, which went clattering to the pool floor. The man tossed his own weapon aside, and threw himself upon the back of the beast.

The creature tried to rise, but fell back, while the old man clung on, putting the troll in a headlock.

The crowd had begun to chant, sensing that the match was about to end. It took a moment for Remy to discern exactly what the crowd was repeating, over and over again, but once he did, it all made a twisted kind of sense; the long hair, the nearly super-human strength.

Remy saw the man lower his head, speaking into the troll's bleeding ear, before executing his final move.

The troll's eyes slowly closed, as the old man let loose with a bellow of rage, savagely twisting his adversary's neck, breaking it, and letting the limp body fall broken to the floor of the pool, where it twitched obscenely before going still.

The winner raised his hands and face to the crowd, and the place went wild with cries, howls, and whistles. Glancing across the room, Remy saw the man who had brought him there collecting large amounts of money. He was laughing, frantically counting as he was pelted with bills.

Somebody had made a small fortune on this bout.

The crowd was breaking up now; some heading toward the doors, others slipping into patches of shadow to disappear. Some had even conjured crackling passages of magickal energy that swallowed them whole before collapsing with sounds reminiscent of a slamming car door.

Remy remained where he was, watching as the woman descended into the pool to help the old man find his footing on the ladder. It was almost as if the man were blind.

They reached the top of the ladder, and the girl handed him a towel and a bottle of water.

"Thank you, little girl," he said, his voice low and rough.

"Did good tonight, Daddy," she said with a laugh, leaning in to kiss the side of his sweaty head.

Daddy?

"Excellent haul, Pops," the young man said, waving an enormous stack of bills beneath the man's nose.

"Is that what victory smells like?" he asked, and they all started to laugh.

A strange sound from the pool below distracted Remy, and he looked down. Things, about Marlowe's size, were ripping at the troll's body with razor-sharp teeth and a hunger that seemed insatiable.

Nose curling up in disgust, he could not help but watch the monster's body disappear, bones, blood, and all. In a matter of seconds, it was as if it had never been there at all.

The voracious beasts skittered away into the shadows of the pool, and Remy returned his gaze to the only three left in the area with him.

"Would someone care to explain what's going on?" Remy asked.

The old man jumped, his large head looking around.

"Who's that?" he asked his daughter, who was cleaning the claw marks on his chest with peroxide.

"It's the private eye," the woman said.

"You know, the Seraphim," the man added sarcastically.

The woman returned to dabbing the wounds with a cotton ball, when the old man gently moved her hands away. Slowly, carefully, he made his way toward Remy, and the milky film that covered his eyes told Remy he had been right. The old man was indeed blind.

"You're Remy Chandler, right?" the powerful old man said, extending a large hand in greeting.

Remy moved closer, placing his hand in the old man's calloused paw.

"I am," he said. "And you are Samson."

The old man's lips parted to reveal a wide yellow smile as he pumped Remy's hand enthusiastically.

"Yes, I am," he said with a laugh. "The one and only."

CHAPTER ELEVEN

Deryn began to awaken, thinking everything was all right.

She was back in Florida with her beautiful daughter, Zoe, and Carl . . . Carl was just out of the picture.

Maybe he was dead.

That thought brought her closer to consciousness, swimming up from the deep darkness where she had gone when . . .

She remembered the attack and awoke in a panic.

The room was set in a semigloom, rays of the sun creeping in from behind a sheet that had been placed over the window.

Deryn immediately sat up on the mattress, searching for her daughter. She hoped that at least one part of her dream was true, but it wasn't.

She felt groggy, and as she bent her arm, she experienced a bit of pain and remembered that the men who took her had given her a shot of something. Deryn strained her eyes as she studied the crook of her right arm, rubbing the thumb of her left hand across the sensitive area where she'd been stuck.

Crawling off the mattress that had been placed in the center of the room, she stood unsteadily. The room was large, but empty. It had beautiful hardwood floors and high, vaulted ceilings. It was what she imagined the rooms in one of those fancy Hollywood mansions would be like.

She held her hands out in front of her and crossed the room toward the white door that seemed to glow, suspended in the gloom. Her heart raced, and her thoughts were electric as she tried to figure out who would have done this to her—and why.

Try as she might, she couldn't think of a single reason . . . other than maybe something Carl had done to really piss off someone.

He could most certainly do that.

Her heart was hammering so hard in her chest that it hurt as she gripped the crystal doorknob. She was certain it wouldn't turn. But miraculously, it did.

Cautiously, she opened the door and stepped out into a long, carpeted hallway. A set of stairs was at the end of the corridor to her right, and she quietly moved toward them, past other closed doors, wondering whether Remy Chandler might be behind one of them, but afraid to find out. She stopped at the top of the stairway, listening, eyes darting about as she searched for signs of her attackers.

Seeing nothing but an elaborate entryway below her, Deryn carefully took hold of the dark wooden banister and slowly descended. Her heart began beating painfully fast again as she stepped from the final stair onto the black-and-white marble floor, and saw the front door before her. She lunged toward it, reaching for the knob and silently praying for the same kind of luck she'd had upstairs.

"Deryn?" a friendly voice called from somewhere behind her.

She froze, her hand gripping the cool metal of the brass handle. She almost answered but managed to stop herself.

"Deryn York, is that you out there?" the woman called out again. "Please, come join me in here."

Deryn had no idea why, but she did as the woman asked, letting go of the door and abandoning her chance for escape. She moved toward the left of the stairs, and down a short hallway to a small room—a sitting room—on the right. Slowly she entered to find an attractive, dark-haired woman sitting in the center of a high-backed love seat and pouring from a silver tea set.

"There you are," she said with a wide smile. "Would you care for some tea?"

A low moan followed the woman's question, and Deryn noticed a man slumped in a floral wingback chair at the other end of the love seat. He was dressed in a navy blue jogging suit, his complexion deathly pale. He seemed to be staring off into space, emitting groans from time to time.

"Oh, pay no attention to him," the woman said, waving with a bejeweled hand. "Come, sit beside me, and we'll talk about your daughter."

"My daughter?" Deryn asked, not sure she had heard correctly. "Did you say my daughter?"

"Yes, I most certainly did," the woman said. "Come—sit—before I lose my patience."

Deryn entered the room, her footfalls muffled by the elaborate oriental rug that covered the floor.

"What do you know about my daughter?" she demanded. "Who are you? Why was I . . . ?"

The woman interrupted her, laughing melodically. "There will be plenty of time for questions," she said, pouring tea into a china cup, which she placed on the table in front of the love seat. "We'll have a bit of refreshment first, and then we'll get down to business."

The woman smiled again, sipping from her own cup.

Silently Deryn sat on the other end of the love seat, staring . . . waiting.

"Do drink your tea," the woman instructed.

The man in the sweat suit shifted suddenly in his chair, bending forward to bury his head in his hands, softly screaming.

The woman ignored him, turning slightly to stare at Deryn with a powerful intensity.

And suddenly Deryn wanted her tea. She picked up her cup and took a sip, making a face as she set it back down on the saucer.

"Sugar?" the woman asked, setting down her own cup and picking up the sugar bowl.

"Who are you?" Deryn demanded.

The woman placed the sugar bowl close to Deryn's hand.

"My name is Delilah," she replied. "And your daughter has something that I want."

The man had begun to thrash, falling from the chair to the floor, his spastic movement nearly kicking over the coffee table.

"Oh, come now, Mr. Poole," Delilah scolded. "Have a little bit of control."

Deryn watched the man, feeling herself grow more and more afraid. "What's wrong with him?" she asked.

"Mr. Poole has a rather odd talent . . . an affliction really," Delilah explained. "He can read the psychic impressions left upon things, telling where they've been and, with the right incentive, where they are."

She looked at the man who was still lying on his stomach at the foot of the chair. "Isn't that right, Mr. Poole?"

Poole remained silent, twitching as he lay there.

"You said," Deryn began, addressing Delilah, "you said my daughter has something you want?"

Delilah nodded, and she picked up the silver teapot and refilled her own cup. "I wasn't sure at first, but after my trip to Florida, I'm certain it's she."

"Your trip to Florida?" Deryn asked. "Where . . ."

"Never mind about that, Deryn," Delilah said forcefully. "We have to find your little girl and get her back into your arms, don't we?"

Just the thought of holding Zoe made Deryn smile.

"I—I would really love that, but . . ."

Delilah held up one hand, bringing the teacup to her lips with the other. "No buts then," she said, taking a sip and setting her cup down once more. "That is what we will do. And when we find her, you will have your daughter back, and I will have what I want."

Delilah smiled so wide that Deryn imagined it must have hurt.

"What could she . . . What does Zoe have that you . . . ," Deryn started to ask, curious how her six-year-old daughter could have something that this fine woman so desperately needed.

"That is of no concern to you," Delilah said. "I doubt she even knows she has it, and when we find her, I will take it, and she will be none the wiser."

Deryn thought of Remy Chandler again. He was helping her, but at this stage, she didn't even know if he was still alive.

But this woman—this Delilah—seemed to know how to find her little girl. "How?" Deryn asked desperately. "How are we going to find my baby?"

Delilah was smiling again, but her smile quickly disappeared when she looked at Poole still lying upon the floor. "Get up now, Mr. Poole," she commanded.

Deryn felt a cold chill run up and down the length of her spine as Poole climbed to his knees with a grunt, staring with pleading eyes at the beautiful woman.

"We're going to find Ms. York's little girl," Delilah told him.

And he started to sob. "I . . . I need . . . I need to rest before . . ."

"There will be plenty of time for rest once the child is back in the custody of her mother," Delilah scolded, turning her gaze toward Deryn.

"Yes, please, Mr. Poole," Deryn said. "Please find my little girl."

Poole met her eyes, his face damp with tears. "She doesn't care about your child," he said, his eyes glistening with emotion. "All she cares about is . . ."

Delilah was a blur as she jumped up, yanked the man into the air by the front of his sweat suit, and slammed him back into the chair.

"Don't make me regret using your services, Mr. Poole," she snarled, still holding him by the twisted fabric of his nylon top.

"Kill me!" the man screamed. "Kill me now, you fucking bitch!"

"I'll do worse than that," she said, giving him a violent shake before letting him go.

Deryn sat silently, not sure exactly what was happening, but caring only about finding her little girl . . . finding her Zoe.

Delilah turned to her, that smile again stretching her features.

"Sorry about that," she said with a polite chuckle. "Mr. Poole and I have been working quite closely for the last few days, and we've started to wear on each other's nerves."

She held out her hand, and Deryn noticed how long and delicate her fingers were, and how sharp the scarlet nails seemed to be.

"Come here, Deryn," Delilah commanded.

Immediately, Deryn stood, walking around the coffee table, to stand before Delilah.

"Your hand, Mr. Poole," Delilah ordered, and the man offered his trembling appendage. "Take it, Deryn York."

Deryn reached out, but skittishly pulled her hand back. "What is he going to do?" she asked.

"He will read the psychic impressions left upon you by your lovely daughter," Delilah explained. "A mother's love for her child is a very powerful thing, and, hopefully, he will be able to follow those impressions through the ether to locate her present whereabouts."

Deryn hesitated, then grasped the man's cold, clammy hand. "Will it hurt?"

Mr. Poole began to laugh, and laugh, and laugh.

"If you think I've got a table for you assholes, you've got another think coming," the Asian man waiting inside the entrance to the China Lion said, slapping the menus in his hand against the side of his leg.

Samson let out an enormous laugh, pushing past his daughter and son to embrace the little man.

"Kenny, how the fuck are you, my little yellow brother?"

Kenny hugged back. "Haven't seen you in a while—I thought the food finally killed you."

"Not a fucking chance," Samson said, releasing the man.

"Table for four?" Kenny asked, holding up four fingers.

"Four it is," the big man agreed.

Remy still found it hard to believe the man was blind, but he guessed a life as long as Samson's had allowed him time to adapt, and from watching Samson move and interact with his surroundings, he certainly had.

He felt the hand of Marko, Samson's son, upon his back, as they all followed Samson and Kenny to the back of the Market Street restaurant.

"Hope I didn't hurt you too bad when I decked you," Marko said, walking beside him.

Remy heard Carla, the blind man's daughter, chuckle. For the briefest moment, in response to their lack of respect, he imagined reaching out with a hand bathed in the fires of Heaven and burning away the man's face, before moving on to the girl.

The Seraphim seemed to laugh from somewhere deep in the darkness of his being, but Remy ignored it.

"I can take it," he said instead, forcing a smile, while bringing a hand up to move his jaw from side to side.

Marko laughed, slapping Remy on the back as they entered a private dining room. Kenny pulled out a chair for Samson, guiding him into it and handing him a menu. The restaurant owner then pulled out the other seats, Remy taking the one to the left of Samson, and dispersed the rest of his menus.

"Any specials tonight, Ken?" Samson asked.

"Yeah, you get no food poisoning," the little man said as he briskly walked from the room.

Samson liked that one, laughing until he started to choke and cough.

Marko and Carla were looking at their menus. Remy had had no intention of eating, but the place did smell pretty good.

A cute waitress with a less-than-stellar grasp of the English language filled their water glasses and took their drink orders. Samson and his kids ordered Tsingtao beer, and Remy chose a Seven and Seven.

As they waited for their drinks, Remy decided he'd been patient long enough. Back at the Boys Club, he'd tried to get Samson to fill him in, but the big man had refused, saying he had to eat before he dropped dead.

Their drinks arrived, and they put their dinner orders in. Soon after that, three servings of Chinese dumplings arrived, which were promptly pounced upon by the table's residents.

"So, do you think you might be able to tell me what's going on now?" Remy asked finally, taking a sip of his drink. It tasted strongly of Seagram's, just the way Mulvehill and he liked a Seven and Seven. Remy was sure that if the China Lion were more in the neighborhood, Steven would be a regular, but Lynn was a little too far even for excellent Seven and Sevens.

Samson stabbed a dumpling with his fork, dipped it in the special soy sauce, and brought it to his mouth. The dark sauce dribbled from the corners of his mouth, down into his white beard.

"We thought you might know some stuff that would be helpful to us," the big man said, noisily chewing on the dumpling.

"So I'm guessing your kids' driving through the motel wall wasn't an accident?"

"I told them to follow you." Samson shrugged.

"And what's this information I might have?" Remy asked. There was one dumpling left, and he stabbed it with his fork.

"Methuselah thought you might have something," Samson said. He wiped the sauce from his beard, then picked up his bottle of beer.

"Methuselah?" Remy asked.

"You were at his place the other night, asking about the mark." Samson set his beer down and rubbed the back of one of his large hands.

"Yeah, I was," Remy said, breaking the dumpling in half with the side of his fork and popping the piece into his mouth. He chewed for a bit before continuing. "I was curious if anyone had ever seen something like it."

Marko and Carla chuckled as they sipped their Chinese beers.

"All right, so I'm guessing you guys know something I don't," Remy said. "How about we all be big kids and share."

Their dinners arrived. Carla got the Szechuan chicken, and Marko had ordered some sort of spicy shrimp dish served inside a half of a pineapple. Samson's dinner had something to do with duck and Paradise, and Remy relied on his old standby, General Tsao.

They dug into their meals, Remy still waiting for his answers.

"It's her mark," Samson finally said, feeding the crunchy fried skin of the duck into his mouth.

"Excuse me?" Remy asked, his fork holding some of General Tsao's chicken midway to his mouth.

"The kiss marks," Samson stated in explanation. "They're her mark . . . Delilah's."

Remy dropped his fork. With the inclusion of Samson in the puzzle, he should have known.

"Really," he said, taking another sip of his drink. "She's still around too, is she?"

"Oh, she's around all right," Samson said with a nod, reaching into his mouth to pick a piece of duck from his teeth. "I've been trying to kill that bitch for years."

He grabbed his beer and tipped it back, discovering with disgust that it was empty. "Hey, Kenny!" he bellowed toward the doorway. "Another round, you yellow bastard!"

"You can all go fuck yourselves," the owner replied.

Samson got very serious, his large, sausage-sized fingers intertwining at his chin. "I was born to be the champion of the Israelites," he said quietly. "To deliver my people from the tyranny of the Philistines. All I had to do was abstain from alcohol and not cut my hair."

The waitress returned with their drinks.

"Guess that was supposed to prove I was totally dedicated to God," the big man said as he brought the fresh beer to his lips. He drank nearly half of it before taking the bottle from his mouth again.

"Making up for lost time," he said, and then belched.

The kids thought this was a riot.

"I killed a lot of Philistines in my time," he said, flexing and unflexing his gigantic hands. "And had a lot of women, but nothing compared to her."

"Here we go," Marko said, rolling his eyes. "I'm going out for a smoke." Carla said she would join him, and they both left the table.

"Fucking kids," Samson growled. "No sense of history." He took another pull from his beer.

"So I'm guessing the *her* that no other woman compared to is Delilah."

"And you'd be correct," the big man agreed. "I fell in love with her on first sight. She was from a little village in the valley of Sorek. I was passing through there on the run from some Philistine jerkwads trying to make a name for themselves by taking me down."

He laughed, lifting his beer. "Yeah, good fucking luck with that.

"I hadn't planned on hanging around, but she had this certain quality. Once I was with her, I couldn't imagine being without her."

Samson grew quiet. Remy could tell that the old man's memory was still good enough to remember all the details, both the pleasant and the unpleasant.

"I shared everything with her," he said, still ashamed at how he'd been taken. "Told her about God's mission for me, and how I could be stopped only one way."

"The hair?" Remy said.

Samson nodded.

"So, could you please explain to me what the fuck is up with that?" Marko asked as he and Carla returned to the table, stinking of cigarette smoke. "You cut your hair and lose your strength? I don't get it."

"It's a God thing," Remy said. "I swear He comes up with the stuff off the top of His head."

"Exactly," Samson said. "Those were His rules, and I was supposed to stick to them."

"But Delilah betrayed you," Remy said sympathetically.

The old man clutched his beer bottle in a tightening grip. "Oh yeah, she did that all right. It just goes to show how you never really know a person," he said.

He finished his second beer before coming up for air.

"The Philistines had pulled her aside and made her an offer she couldn't refuse. Eleven hundred silver coins for the secret of my strength."

He shook his shaggy head, his white hair, in a ponytail now, swinging back and forth. He felt for his fork and picked it up, then began to work on one of his duck legs.

"She cut my hair while I was asleep, after a good schtuping—if you know what I mean." He made a fist and brought it back and forth. Remy knew what he meant.

"With the hair gone, my deal with God was canceled."

"God's a dick," Carla said, tipping back her beer.

"He is pretty anal about His rules," Remy said in a weak attempt at defending the All-Father.

"The rest you probably know," Samson said, feeding strips of duck meat into his mouth. "The Philistines captured me, blinded me, and used me as a slave to grind their grain."

Samson tore what remained of the leg from the duck carcass and brought it to his mouth.

"I just bided my time, praying to God every moment I had, swearing to serve Him for as long as He wanted me. He must've seen that I still had some good years left, and He gave me a little gift. He let my hair grow back overnight."

"Dad fucked up those Philistines good," Marko said, doing the fist bump with his sister.

"I did at that," the old man said wistfully. "Brought their whole friggin' temple down around their pointy ears."

The kids raised their beer bottles in salute to their father.

Remy finished his second drink, tipping the glass back so that some of the ice would fall into his mouth. "And what about Delilah?" he asked, crunching on the ice. "I'm pretty sure her story doesn't end there."

The large man shook his head again. He dropped the duck leg bone down onto his plate, wiping his greasy hands on his napkin.

"Not by a long shot," Samson said. "She took off after I was captured, and nobody really knew what happened to her. Probably started a new identity elsewhere, but it didn't change who she really was . . . and whom she betrayed."

Samson turned his blind eyes toward Remy.

"She didn't just betray me; she betrayed God." He pointed toward the ceiling. "And you know He hates to be fucked with."

The cute waitress came into the room to clear the table. There wasn't all that much remaining of the meals, but Marko asked for the leftovers.

"God cursed her," Samson said in a voice softer than usual. "Cursed her to live eternally, always knowing that what she had . . . always knowing that whatever she loved would die."

"And the mark?" Remy asked.

"Now, that's the interesting part," Samson said. "It seems that after God cursed her, she went through a bit of a change. Delilah became less human and more demonic with each passing century. She changed physically. She had the ability to command the weak-willed, and to feed off the souls of her victims. She became a succubus."

"She leaves her mark when she feeds on their souls," Remy said, finally understanding.

"The ultimate hickey," Marko said.

"So you're still looking for her?" Remy asked.

The waitress came back into the room with the bagged leftovers, asking if anybody wanted coffee or dessert. Marko and

Carla ordered the fried ice cream, while Samson ordered another beer and Remy asked for a cup of tea.

"I swore to God that I would serve Him for as long as He wanted," Samson said. "And my job is to find that soul-sucking bitch and put her out of His misery."

"All this time though, and you still haven't found her?"

"The bitch goes dormant," the strongman explained. "As if she's ceased to exist. A hundred years have been known to go by until she starts to use her twisted gifts again. I can feel it in my bones; makes them ache something awful. And I've been feeling pretty awful of late."

The waitress brought the desserts and drinks, and asked if they'd like anything else.

They all said no and thanked her. She told them she'd be back shortly with the check.

"She's been active all right," Remy said as he dunked the tea bag in his mug of hot water.

"And now you know why we picked you up," Samson said, pointing at Remy with his beer bottle. "So, that case you're working on, give me some details."

"It's a missing person's case," Remy said as he brought the mug of tea to his mouth. He took a sip of the hot liquid. "A six-year-old child. And it seems as though Delilah might be looking for her as well."

"She's been known to steal a few in her travels," Samson explained. "Raises them as her own; they grow up to serve her and all that. Of course, she feeds on their souls to make them more obedient."

Remy shook his head as he held on to his mug, warming his hands. "Seems a little more complicated than that. I think the child is gifted."

"What, she can spell well or do math problems off the top of her head?"

"No, the I-think-she-can-see-the-future kind of gifted."

"That could be useful," Carla said, licking her spoon clean of ice cream.

"But what would she need that for?" Samson asked. "There are seers all over the planet. What makes this kid so fucking special that it's brought her out of hiding?"

"I guess that's the million-dollar question," Remy said, sipping his tea. "I'm not sure if this means anything or not, but both Mom and Dad were once involved with a cult called the Church of Dagon."

"Dagon?" Samson asked, blind eyes squinting. "The Philistines worshipped a god named Dagon. Matter of fact, it was a Dagon temple I brought down on top of their worthless heads."

"The parents were supposed to provide a host body for Dagon in the form of their unborn child, but the ATF saw things a bit differently and broke up the party before the old god could take up residence."

The waitress brought the check on a small plastic tray and left it by Samson's right hand.

Remy reached for it, but Samson swatted his hand away.

"I got this," he said. "Marko, take care of this and I'll pay you back."

Marko laughed. "Yeah, right," he said as he took the check from his father.

"Disrespectful punk," Samson growled.

"So do you think there's some kind of connection between this church business and Delilah?" Remy asked.

"If there is, I can't see it, pardon the pun," the blind man said with a chuckle. "But it's good info, just in case."

"Delilah's goon squad took my client," Remy said. "I need to find her yesterday."

Samson nodded in agreement. "We'll keep our ears open. If we hear anything, you'll be the first person we call."

"Thanks," Remy said. "And thanks for dinner."

"No problem," the big man said. "Just remember to keep us in the loop if you should come across any promising leads."

"Will do," Remy told him.

Carla and Marko got up to pay the check and have another cigarette, leaving Samson and Remy to themselves again. The room was silent, each lost in his own thoughts.

"Married?" Remy asked, breaking the quiet.

"Who, me?" Samson said.

"Yeah, I thought with the kids, maybe . . ."

The big man chuckled. "After what I went through? I'd never trust another one of them. I'll fuck 'em, but I won't marry 'em."

He got a good laugh out of that, but Remy could sense a certain sadness in the man's words.

"Do you still love her?" Remy asked him.

Samson went stiff, his last beer almost to his mouth. "I should smash your fucking angel face in," he said with an animalistic growl.

"Answer the question . . . truthfully."

Samson downed the remainder of his beer, wiping at his mouth with the back of his hand.

"Yeah, I love her." He scowled. "I love her enough to want to strangle the life from her body with my bare hands. If that's not love, I don't know what the fuck is."

Marko and Carla dropped Remy back at the Nightingale Motor Lodge to pick up his car. They'd driven by the side of the building for a look, only to find the area cordoned off with wooden horses, the hole in the wall covered with sheets of opaque plastic that seemed to breathe in and out like some kind of gigantic, artificial lung.

Samson's kids got quite a kick out of the damage they'd caused.

They left Remy at his car, reminding him to give them a call if he should hear anything about where Delilah might be holed up.

The ride home was uneventful; the radio tuned to some talk show that he wasn't really listening to. His brain was caught in a loop, turning what few facts he had round and round inside his head.

Parking was particularly bad, so he was forced to park on Cambridge Street, and walk all the way up the hill, to his house on Pinckney Street.

Remy let himself into the brownstone to the sound of the most ferocious dog in the world. Marlowe barked like crazy, bounding from the living room to greet him at the door.

From the ruckus he was making, Remy knew Ashley was still there, and Marlowe was protecting her.

"Hey, Ash," Remy said as he came in, closing the door behind him. "Sorry I'm so late."

He found Ashley sitting on the floor in front of the coffee table, her schoolbooks spread out all around her.

"Hey, Remy," she said sleepily.

"Were you working or dozing?" Remy asked, standing in the doorway.

"A little of both really," she said. The television was on, and she grabbed the remote to shut it off.

He went into the kitchen, Marlowe at his heels. "Did Ashley let you out?" he asked.

"*No*," the dog told him.

Remy opened the door and let Marlowe out into the backyard.

"I just let him out," Ashley bellowed from the living room.

"He told me you didn't," Remy said.

"Well, he's a big fat liar then," she said.

"How dare you call my faithful canine companion a liar," Remy said, opening the screen door to let the dog back inside. "I bet she hasn't given you any snack either," he addressed the Labrador, knowing full well she probably had.

"*No snack*," Marlowe said, sitting down at Remy's feet, his tail sweeping the floor.

Remy got a few dog cookies from a monkey cookie jar on the counter.

"He's had a bunch of treats too," Ashley called out again.

"I know she lies," Remy whispered loud enough for Ashley to hear as he gave Marlowe two cookies, which he promptly inhaled.

"*Lies*," Marlowe agreed, hoping Remy would give him some more.

"That's enough for now, buddy," Remy said, reaching out to pat the dog's square head.

"All right, I'm getting out of here," Ashley said sleepily, standing in the doorway, her overstuffed book bag slung over her shoulder.

"Thanks for coming by," Remy told her. He reached into his pocket and pulled out some folded bills. Removing two twenties, he gave them to her. "Here ya go."

"What's that for?" she asked with a scowl, not taking what was offered.

"Your pay," he said. "Take it."

"No thanks," she said, walking to the door. "This wasn't an official gig," she told him.

"I'll catch you later then," he said.

"You do that," she agreed, giving him a smile that he was sure melted teenage boys' hearts all over Boston.

She was opening the door when she stopped.

"Hey," she said.

"Hey what?" Remy answered, about to make a pot of coffee.

"Who's the artist?" she asked, and gestured toward the living room.

He remembered he'd been going over Zoe's drawings last night and had left them out.

"A little girl who's gone missing," Remy said. "She's pretty good, eh?"

"Pretty freaky," Ashley stated. "I can't believe some of the stuff she drew."

"Anything particularly freaky?" he asked.

"The one of that hand thing," she said. Ashley dropped her bag at the door and went back to the living room. Remy and Marlowe followed her.

She had picked up the pieces of paper and was going through them. "When I first saw the drawing, I couldn't believe it, y'know? Why would a little kid be drawing something like that?"

Finding the drawing, she handed it to Remy. The picture was of what looked like a hand, with a stick, or nail, going through the center, blood dripping down the wrist from the entry point.

"Do you know what it is?"

"What, you don't?" she asked. "Don't tell me there's something I know that you don't?"

"Keep this up and I'll never call you again at a moment's notice to take care of my dog," he said in mock seriousness.

"I'm sorry, Mr. Chandler, sir; I'll be good."

They laughed, then turned their attention back to the drawing.

"Seriously, what is it?" Remy asked.

"It's a statue out in front of the old Boston archbishop's mansion in Brighton," she explained. "When Mom was working for

Catholic Charities, she used to take me there for special meetings and luncheons and stuff, and I used to see this creepy statue right out in front of the building. I think it's supposed to be Jesus' hand or something like that."

Remy continued to stare, ideas starting to formulate.

"I think the church is supposed to be selling the building to Boston College," she continued.

"I think you're right," Remy said.

"All right, I'm leaving," she said, walking to the door again.

Remy said nothing and did not move.

"Don't worry about me," she said sarcastically, opening the door and hauling herself and the heavy book bag out into the hall. "I can get the door and this two-ton book bag perfectly fine all by myself."

"Take it easy," he said, responding to the teenager on the most rudimentary level.

The detective's thoughts were elsewhere.

"Why would she have drawn this, Marlowe?" he asked.

The dog had climbed up onto the couch and was watching him.

"Why this?" he asked. "She must've seen it," he said. "It must mean something if she drew it."

The Labrador lowered his face between his paws and sighed. He wasn't at all interested in anything Remy had to say, not unless it had something to do with food, or a nighttime walk.

He'd left his cell on the kitchen table and went for it. From a wrinkled piece of napkin scrawled on at the China Lion, Remy read and punched in the number Samson had given him. It rang three times before being answered.

"Yeah," said a distinctly female voice.

"Carla?" Remy asked.

"No, this is Carol."

"Is Samson there?" Remy asked, concerned that he might have the wrong number.

"Yeah, wait a second," Carol said. A hand was placed over the phone, and he heard the girl call for her dad.

Another kid? Remy mused as he waited.

He paced around the kitchen, listening to the vague sounds from the other end. He could hear scuffling and the distant sound of music, something old, like big band music.

"Yeah?" Samson boomed.

Remy held the phone slightly away from his ear.

"It's Remy."

"Miss me already?" the old man asked, and laughed a rumbling laugh.

"Sure, that's it," Remy said. "I think I might have something."

The voice on the other end became suddenly serious.

"Let's hear it."

"Think I might have a location . . . the old archbishop's mansion in Brighton."

"And what makes you think this?" Samson asked curiously.

Remy had again walked into the living room, and was staring down at the drawing of an impaled and bleeding hand.

"Let's just say my source is pretty good."

The old man was silent for a bit, and Remy was about to ask if he was still there, when he spoke.

"We should probably move on this pretty quick," he said. "Delilah is not the nicest of people . . . if you could even call her *people* anymore. The longer your client is with her, the smaller her chances are of . . ."

"Why don't we meet in about an hour?" Remy said. "There's something I need to do before we do this."

"An hour it is," Samson said. "Just want you to know if this is what we think it might be, it isn't going to be a walk in the park. There are a lot of people willing to die for that bitch."

The ancient warrior's words slowly sank in.

"I understand," Remy told him. "I'll see you in an hour."

There was nothing more to say, and the phone went quiet in his hand.

CHAPTER TWELVE

Marlowe was awake.

Remy had hoped to sneak out, but he should have known that was asking a little too much.

"I have to go out for a while," he told the animal, who was sitting at attention on the couch where mere moments before he had been sound asleep.

"*Where?*" the Labrador asked, his head cocked to one side.

"To work," Remy said.

"*Go with?*" Marlowe asked, getting down from the couch and stretching.

"Not this time, pal."

The dog walked over and stared up at him. His tail began to wag.

"*Go with?*" he asked again.

Remy didn't have time for this. "You heard what I said. Stop being a brat."

"*No brat,*" Marlowe grumbled, insulted.

"Yes, you're being a brat," Remy told him.

The dog lowered his tail and slumped back toward the couch, lying down beside it, his face buried between his two front paws. He was playing the part of the saddest dog in the world, and Remy truly believed an Oscar might actually be in Marlowe's future.

"What's wrong?" Remy asked.

"*Sad.*" The Labrador refused to look at him.

"I'm very sorry you're sad, but I need to go." Remy went to the front door, feeling Marlowe's eyes on his back. And he couldn't stand it.

"I think I know what might make you less sad," he said, turning at the door and seeing the dog raise his head inquisitively.

Remy gestured for Marlowe to follow him to the kitchen and knelt down beside one of the lower cabinets. The dog had already figured out what was up, and he stood beside Remy, panting madly while his tail wagged furiously.

Remy reached into a bag inside the cabinet and pulled out one of Marlowe's favorite treats—a pig's ear. Madeline had always thought the greasy, rawhide delicacies were disgusting, but Marlowe loved them more than almost anything, and if something was to distract him from Remy's leaving, it would be this.

Marlowe was practically vibrating with excitement as Remy held out the pig's ear. "Will this make you happy?"

"*Yes,*" he barked, snatching the treat and running off to the living room floor.

"I'll be back as soon as I can," Remy called out, the sound of powerful jaws crunching on smoked cartilage escorting him out the door.

He walked back down the hill to Cambridge Street, grabbed his car, and drove up Charles Street on his way to Newbury. He had to pay a visit to Francis' place again.

There were certain things—certain dangerous things—that might be needed tonight, and he could think of only one place where they would be readily available to him.

He found a spot on the upper end of Commonwealth and jogged around the corner to the brownstone. Letting himself inside, he was again aware of the sad silence of the place and thought of his friend.

When Francis wasn't guarding one of the passages to the Hell prison of Tartarus, he was earning a living as one of this world's most deadly assassins. Working within the confines of his own strange moral code, he would kill for the highest bidder in order to afford one of the only things that made the exiled former Guardian angel truly happy.

Weapons.

He had a particular fondness for medieval weaponry, but anything he could use to end the life of some loathsome undesirable, for a ridiculous amount of money, was cool by him.

Remy unlocked the door to Francis' apartment and descended, going directly to the wardrobe where he'd found the key the other night.

He didn't want anything too obvious, so the swords and battle-axes probably weren't going to do the trick. But then he found it, in a velvet-lined drawer—a military Colt 45 Automatic. He hefted the heavy black weapon; it would serve him just fine. He found a shoulder holster and helped himself to that as well.

Remy then searched for some proper ammunition. Normal bullets were usually enough, but tonight, he would need something with a little more bite, especially if he intended to fight a soulless legion and Delilah herself.

And who knew how much more durable she'd become since being cursed by God.

Sometimes Remy had to wonder about the Lord's judgment on these things; it often seemed that He was just making things worse.

He found the supply of special bullets in a lower drawer, in a case that resembled a small treasure chest. They were pure silver, with intricate sigils scratched into their tips.

From what Francis had told him, these things were better than hollow points. Not only did they have amazing stopping power against the natural and supernatural, but the magick within the projectile that was released when the bullet entered cursed flesh was devastating.

He loaded the silver bullets into multiple clips, slid one into the butt of the Colt, and put the others in his jacket pocket.

Closing up the wardrobe, Remy climbed the stairs back up to the lobby and locked Francis' door behind him. He then left the building, locking that as well, and headed back to his car.

He wasn't sure exactly why he did it, but he found himself driving around the block to head back up Newbury Street, past the restaurant Piazza, in hopes that he might catch a glimpse of Linda Somerset.

Now, why am I doing this? Remy asked himself, checking out the tables, as well as the waitstaff moving amongst the patio tables, and found himself growing annoyed at his surprising actions.

And disappointed that he did not catch a glimpse of her.

A kid named Elijah had brought them to Pastor Zachariah's home.

Carl was awash with emotion as he held Zoe's hand, following the young man across the compound; afraid he would not be welcomed back into the flock, and ashamed for what he had done so long ago.

Supposedly the leader of the Church of the Holy Abundance, though quite ill, wanted to see him at once.

Carl's mind was racing, going over how he would beg for the holy man's forgiveness. He looked down at his little girl walking by his side.

She would have belonged to them—to the Church of Dagon; she would have been born something so very special.

Instead of like this.

Carl owed his little girl an apology as well.

Elijah led them up a stone path to a simple, single-story home. He removed a key from his pocket and unlocked the front door, then turned and gestured toward them.

"Come in," he said. "The pastor is waiting."

Carl led Zoe through the door and into a small foyer.

"Why don't you two have a seat," Elijah said, escorting them into the living room. "I'll tell the pastor you're here."

The handsome young man disappeared down a darkened hallway, leaving Carl alone with his daughter. He noticed that her hands had started to twitch, and she was making small moaning noises as she began to rock from side to side.

"Hey," Carl said, kneeling down in front of her. "I'll get you some paper and crayons in a little while," he told her, holding her shoulders while trying to look directly into her eyes. "But first we're going to meet a very great man. Somebody who was supposed to be a part of our lives, but your dad lost sight of the big picture and did some very stupid and selfish things."

He squeezed Zoe's shoulders. "But that's going to change now," he told her

Zoe moaned a little louder, her tiny, eager hands opening and closing.

"The pastor will see you now," Elijah said suddenly from behind Carl.

Carl gasped. *This is it.*

Elijah gestured for them to go down the corridor first, and Carl obliged, dragging the moaning little girl along behind him.

"Is she all right?" the young man asked as he followed.

"She's fine," Carl told him. "Just excited to meet a great man."

"It's the last door," Elijah said. "Go on in. He's expecting you."

Carl pulled his daughter along, stopping at the door long enough to take two deep breaths.

"Are you ready?" he asked his daughter.

She moaned, pulling back a bit as he grabbed hold of the knob, turned it, and pushed open the door.

Eager to be forgiven.

"Pastor Zachariah?" Carl asked, stepping into the darkness.

It was cold in the room, uncomfortably so, the hum of the air conditioner drowning out any other sound. Carl could make out lights from the machines that helped to keep the great man alive, and moved toward them, still holding on to his daughter's hand.

He noticed that the floor was covered, and thought briefly that it was odd, but that did not stop him. His eyes had begun to adjust to the lack of light in the room, and he could make out the shape of the hospital bed, which gradually appeared out of the black like a ship emerging from a fog bank.

"Pastor, I . . ."

"So, the Judas returns," Zachariah's old voice croaked.

Carl stopped in his tracks.

"I—I've returned to beg for your forgiveness," he said, surprised to hear the level of emotion in his voice. "Everything has been wrong in my life for so long that I was blind to the true cause . . . until now."

There was a strange gurgling sound from the bed, and Carl was curious whether the pastor was choking, but then he spoke. "You have no idea the level of damage you caused that day."

"I do," Carl proclaimed. "I do, and I beg you to forgive me. Please, I want to come back."

The bed creaked, and Carl could hear the sound of wet breathing over the hum of the air conditioner.

"What you did goes beyond the forgivable," Zachariah wheezed.

Carl felt his hopes begin to deflate, and he hung his head in sorrow. Without the forgiveness of the church, he would have nothing.

Nothing except his child.

He released her hand and pulled her in front of him. Zoe stumbled, her sneakered foot catching on the plastic covering the floor.

"Look, this is the child," he said desperately. "The one my wife and I promised you."

The bed creaked, and Carl imagined somebody leaning over the side for a better look.

"The child," Pastor Zachariah murmured. "The original host conceived for the glory of Dagon."

"Yes," Carl said. "My selfish actions have caused even her to suffer," he confessed.

Zoe moaned, flapping her hands in front of her face as she rocked back and forth.

"She is afflicted," the pastor observed.

Carl nodded in the darkness, feeling warm tears begin to spill from his eyes. "Yes, and it's all my fault. . . . I was punished. . . . My child was punished. . . ."

Emotion rolled from him unimpeded, and he found himself dropping to his knees, the plastic noisily crackling beneath them.

"And why have you brought this child before me?" the pastor asked from the darkness.

Carl, who had been bent over at the waist, straightened, his squinting eyes searching for a glimpse of the pastor.

"To show you," he said. "To show you how I've been made to suffer for my sins."

Zachariah laughed harshly.

"You do not know the true meaning of suffering," the pastor said.

"But I do," Carl begged. "I really do."

The pastor laughed again, an unnatural sound that made Carl think of somebody choking out their last breath. "I will show you suffering," he said.

Carl didn't like the sound of that, and instinctively reached for one of his daughter's flailing hands.

The blow landed savagely upon the back of his head, and he pitched forward to the plastic-covered floor.

"No," he managed to get out, but he sounded as though seriously drunk. He tried to get up, but a powerful arm closed around his throat from behind, cutting off most of his oxygen.

"Zoe," he gasped.

His attacker turned him toward the child. She was standing less than a foot from him, flapping her arms and moaning. She had begun to spin slowly in a circle, moving steadily away from him and farther into the darkened room.

Carl reached for her, but Elijah only increased his steely grip upon his throat.

"No," he choked desperately, "don't hurt . . ."

"We're going to make you watch," the handsome young man hissed into his ear. "That will be your penance."

"And when it's over, you will be forgiven."

The thing that had been worshipped as Dagon dropped over the side of the hospital bed, the tubes and connections to the various machines that helped to keep his rotting host alive ringing and beeping with a furious insistence.

Dagon landed upon the plastic-sheeted floor, honing in on the child. He could smell her fear, her youth, her purity. And like the great Leviathan smelling the blood of it victims awash upon the sea, he moved toward his prey.

The ancient deity's stomach gurgled impatiently, but he did not want this sacrifice to be over too quickly.

The traitor had to pay for his sins.

For what he had cost the god Dagon.

He would take this offering slowly, keeping the child alive for as long as possible so her father could see, and remember this for every remaining moment of his miserable life.

Dagon was a merciful god, but for what this human had wrought, he would be made to suffer.

He saw the child before him, spinning in the darkness, arms flapping as if to escape in flight. Her strange dance made him chuckle, and he salivated in hungry anticipation.

Elijah held the Judas at bay, forcing him to watch. Dagon saw Saylor's eyes bulge as the god emerged from the darkness, crawling across the floor like some loathsome insect; the years had not been kind to this human shell.

To house the power of a god was to do insurmountable damage to frail, human flesh.

Damage that only the ritual of sacrifice could temporarily reverse.

How many had he consumed over the years? How many ravaged bodies lay beneath the fertile soil of the compound garden?

Saylor struggled against Elijah's grip as Dagon reached a spidery hand toward his twirling prey.

The child didn't seem to realize what was to happen, and that disappointed the god Dagon, for a certain amount of terror always brought a special taste to the sacrament. He grabbed hold of the moaning child's arm, the jagged claws at the ends of his long fingers sinking into the tender flesh.

She stopped in midspin, and, finally looking upon his rotting visage, she began to scream. For a moment, Dagon thought the meat he was about to feast upon might be very tasty indeed.

But that was before searing white light, instead of blood, erupted from the five puncture wounds in the child's arm.

And Dagon was painfully reminded of what it was like to be in the presence of godlike power again as he was repelled across the room.

*   *   *

The former archbishop of Boston had lived in the three-story, Italian Renaissance–style mansion for most of his tenure, before leaving for a special appointment in Rome, after the ninety-million-dollar settlement for victims of the clerical sexual abuse scandal rocked the Commonwealth.

The Archdiocese had planned on selling the mansion and its forty-three adjoining acres. Boston College was rumored to have been interested in purchasing the property, but for now, it remained supposedly empty.

Remy found Samson and what appeared to be a small army, hidden in the shadows of the woods near the building.

"What the hell is this?" he asked in a hushed whisper as he approached.

Multiple guns were suddenly aimed in his direction by multiple young men and women. All bore similar appearances to Samson's children, Carla and Marko, who stepped forward to greet him, and to prevent him from being shot by the obviously enthusiastic gathering.

"He's cool," Marko said, and the guns were lowered as the small army went back to whatever it was they had been doing.

"Let me guess," Remy said, joining them. "Brothers and sisters."

"Half brothers and sisters," Carla corrected.

"It's good that he has a hobby," Remy said as the pair chuckled. "Where is he, by the way?"

Marko hefted a sawed-off shotgun over his shoulder and pointed it in the direction of the mansion in the distance.

Remy walked past the multiple members of the strongman's brood, marveling at their number. There had to be at least thirty of them, all carrying heavy artillery, and Remy had to wonder whether this had been Samson's intention all along, to procreate enough to have an army at his disposal.

The big man was leaning against a tree, smoking a cigarette.

"Nice gathering we have here," Remy said.

"About time you showed up," Samson answered, his blind eyes staring off into the shadows. "Made a few calls just in case. The kids are always happy to help their old man out."

Remy looked around again, watching as Samson's spawn prepared for what was to come.

"Is this all of them?" Remy asked.

The big man chuckled. "Around here, yeah."

One of Samson's kids, this one looking a bit younger than the others, ran over to his father from the direction of the mansion.

He was slightly out of breath, bending down, hands upon his knees, as he breathed in and out.

"What've you got, Stretch?" Samson asked.

Stretch straightened, enough to take the cigarette from his father's fingers for a puff.

"No guards posted. They have the windows covered with sheets, but they're definitely in there."

Stretch put the cigarette back in his father's fingers, and walked off to join the others.

Samson finished the smoke, flicking the remains away from him.

"That's it then," he said. "Are you ready?"

"Ready for what?" Remy asked. "Maybe you should fill me in on the plan."

Samson smiled. "Sorry about that, champ," he said. The big man put a tree limb–sized arm around Remy's shoulder and pulled him close. "Here's how it's going to go. We're going up to the house, getting inside, and finding your client."

"You're doing this all for me?" Remy asked, knowing full well this wasn't the case.

"Pretty much," Samson said. "And we'll probably take out Delilah while we're at it. Might as well if we get the chance."

"You do realize that's not much of a plan," Remy told him.

The big man removed his arm from around Remy's shoulder.

"Yeah, but it's not too bad for the spur of the moment," he said.

Samson snapped his fingers, and his children began to gather around him.

"So we all know the drill," he said to them. "We're going up to the mansion, getting inside, killing the traitorous bitch, and finding Remy's client." He hooked a thumb toward him. "What's her name again?" Samson asked.

"Deryn York," Remy said. "She's blond, in her mid-thirties, about five foot six."

The Samson spawn stared with frightfully blank expressions, and he hoped they were listening. He didn't relish the idea of having his client mistaken for one of Delilah's soulless followers, and taken out by one of the strongman's overzealous children.

"Any questions?" Samson asked, his sightless eyes roving over the crowd of his children.

One of Samson's boys tentatively raised his hand.

"Fred has his hand raised," Stretch informed his father.

"Figures," Samson grumbled. "What is it, Fred?"

"Are we sure she's up there?" he asked nervously. "The traitorous bitch, I mean?"

Samson slowly turned in the direction of the mansion, his blind eyes staring.

"Oh yeah," he said, the response uttered with more growl than voice. "I can feel her like a fucking rash."

He'd begun to scratch, and Remy noticed red, raised welts on the back of the big man's hand. It appeared as if Samson really was having some kind of physical reaction.

"All right then," Samson said, just loud enough so they could all hear. "Let's get this done, and remember . . . she's mine."

They moved en masse, quietly, sticking to the shadows, coming to a stop whenever a car would occasionally pass in the semi-isolated location. Remy's biggest fear was the campus security from BC across the way, but so far, so good.

They came up through the wooded area to the back of the house, Samson's children moving like trained special forces agents as they scoped out the lay of the land and made their way to the back of the house. Standing on either side of the door, automatic rifles at the ready, they waited for their father to reach their location.

Remy followed close behind, eyes searching every hidden corner and pocket of shadow for signs that they had been discovered. Seeing nothing, he followed the large man to the back door.

"Open it," Samson said.

Another of his kids removed herself from the pack and approached the door, lock picks emerging from a thin packet that she'd pulled from her back pocket.

"Showtime," she said, kneeling in front of the old lock. "This should take no time at . . ."

The doorknob began to move, turned from the inside.

Everybody froze. Remy watched as Samson's head cocked to one side, hearing the doorknob jiggle. He held up one large hand, signaling to his brood that they should stay right where they were.

A white-haired man, whom Remy immediately recognized, stepped outside, cigarette dangling from the corner of his mouth.

This was the man who almost put a bullet into Remy's skull back at the Nightingale Motor Lodge, a man perfectly comfortable without a soul. His lighter had just made it up to the tip of his smoke when he noticed the twin gun muzzles pointed at either side of his head, and the large form of Samson standing directly across from him.

The big man raised a sausage-sized finger to his lips, warning him to be quiet.

There was no fear in the man's expression; in fact, he smiled crookedly, still holding the cigarette in the corner of his mouth. He allowed the lighter to reach the smoke, igniting the tip.

"Samson and company," the man said, puffing smoke from the other side of his mouth. "Go right in," he said, the door open at his back. "You're expected."

One of Samson's other kids ran toward the door, pistol in hand, checking it out. "Looks clear," he called out.

Remy had moved to stand beside the big man, his eyes glued to the soulless man casually puffing on his cigarette.

"What do you think?" Remy asked.

"I think we're going in," Samson said. "But he's going first."

He pointed in the direction of the man as his son and daughter urged their captive back into the house at gunpoint.

The man let the cigarette fall from his mouth, grinding it out with the heel of his shoe.

"She doesn't allow us to smoke inside," he said, before walking back in, two automatic rifles pointed at his back. "Come on in. I'll take you to her."

More of Samson's kids, their firearms at the ready, swarmed in through the back door, making way for them to follow.

"Are you sure this is wise?" Remy asked, allowing Samson to hold on to his arm at they walked through the doorway into the house.

"When have I ever done anything wise?" he asked. "I'm just rolling with the punches as I've done for the last few thousand years."

The air-conditioning must have been turned to its maximum setting, making for a sharp transition going from the damp, warm mugginess of outside, to an almost deep-freeze chill inside.

Marko waited for them in the doorway leading from the kitchen.

"Anything?" Remy asked.

"There're voices coming from the front of the house, but no signs of aggression yet," Samson's son said.

"Go on ahead with the others," his father ordered. "We're right behind you."

Remy could feel the Seraphim coming awake, the potential for violence the perfect thing to stir it from its dormancy. But Remy held the power of Heaven in check, desperate not to call upon it unless an absolute necessity.

They passed through a heavy, swinging door into a hallway of dark mahogany. Remy could see Samson's sons and daughters up ahead, scanning every nook and cranny for potential danger, but none was to be found.

The white-haired, soulless man was still being led by the pair with the rifles, leading the train of young soldiers deeper into the house. The closer they got to the front of the elaborate dwelling, the louder the voices became. They were moving toward the sounds, the soulless man doing as he promised and delivering them to his mistress.

Remy escorted Samson down the center of the corridor, Samson's children on either side of them.

Up ahead, their prisoner was about to pass from the hallway into what could best be described as a den. The voices were louder now, and distinctly female. Remy felt Samson's grip upon his arm painfully tighten at the sound of one voice in particular; low and throaty, distinctly sexual, and charging the air with every uttered word.

"It's her," the large man hissed.

Samson started to move ahead of him, blindly bouncing off the hallway wall, as he moved in the direction of those speaking.

The powerful man's soldiers followed his lead, guns drawn and ready for firefight, as they filled the doorway to the parlor.

Remy pushed through the crowd to where Samson now swayed upon his feet.

"Delilah," he snarled, hate dripping like poison from the utterance of her name.

Remy was shocked to see Deryn York sitting upon a flowered love seat, sipping from a fine china cup, and, beside her, a dark-haired, dark-skinned woman of infinite beauty.

"Hello, Samson," the beautiful woman said, setting her cup and saucer down upon the coffee table before her. "It's been quite some time."

Remy could feel the magick in the woman's words, in her speech, keeping them all at bay, preventing tempers from igniting.

Deryn looked terrified, the base of her cup trembling against its saucer.

"Are you all right, Deryn?" Remy asked her.

She nodded, eyes wide as she stared at all the men and women in the doorway with their guns.

"I . . . I'm fine. . . . Really . . . I'm fine," she said.

"See," Delilah said, throwing up her hands. "She's perfectly fine."

The beautiful woman smiled, showing off perfect teeth as white as pearls. "So why don't we all calm down and turn our attention to a situation that requires our concern."

Delilah reached for her cup and saucer, reclining upon the couch as she brought the cup to her mouth.

"Deryn's daughter, for example," she said, sipping nonchalantly, dark eyes staring intensely over the rim of the fine china.

Samson began to scream, throwing back his arms and shoulders as if snapping some form of invisible restraints. "Succubus!"

He lunged toward the sound of Delilah's voice. "You've worked your last spell upon me, and upon this world."

There was murder in the man's intent, and rightfully so, but this woman—this Delilah—knew something about the child that Remy had been hired to find, and if Samson were to kill her, that information might be lost.

Remy moved at the speed of thought, getting between the strongman, the coffee table, and the woman who sat behind it.

"Samson, wait," Remy said, allowing the Seraphim to emerge. The fire of Heaven burned in his veins as he placed his hand upon the man's chest.

Samson's blind eyes dropped to where his hand had fallen.

"What the fuck do you think you're doing?" he snarled, flecks of spit shooting from his mouth. "Take your stinking hand off me and get the fuck out of the way."

"She knows something about the child," Remy said, his voice booming with the authority of one of His messengers. "Kill her, and we might never find her . . . never know what's truly going on here."

At that moment, Remy was prepared for just about anything. He could feel Samson's heart beating crazily, sense the rage churning at his core.

"Please, Samson," Remy said. "For the sake of the child."

Samson looked about to explode, his fists clenched at his sides like two wrecking balls, and Remy was prepared, prepared to unleash the full power of the Seraphim in order to keep the strongman at bay.

But it wouldn't be necessary, for Samson wrestled with his fury, managing to suppress his nearly uncontrollable anger.

"I'm good," he said, breathless with the strain as he stepped back.

Remy lowered his arm, feeling the Seraphim's disappointment that things had not come to violence.

"But this isn't over," Samson growled, directing what remained of his anger at the woman lounging upon the couch.

"Of course it isn't," Delilah said, one long, perfect leg crossed over the other. "We have an innocent child to save, and a piece of creation to retrieve."

Piece of creation?

Remy turned toward the women. "What was that?" he asked. The Seraphim continued to stir.

"It's why I'm looking for the child," Delilah said. "She has what I've been searching for . . . what I need."

Deryn was nodding furiously.

"It's why she's so different," the child's mother tried to explain. "This thing . . . this piece of . . ."

"Creation," Delilah finished. "A shard of God's power used to shape the world and everything in it. 'In the beginning God created the heaven and the earth. The earth was without form, and void: and darkness was on the face of the deep. Then God said, "Let there be light," and there was light.'"

She paused for dramatic effect, making sure it was sinking in.

It was sinking in all right.

"This seed of His holy power has existed on the earth since its formation, found by some of the earliest members of humanity, and protected."

"So how did it wind up with a six-year-old kid?" Samson asked, before Remy could.

Delilah raised a bloodred thumbnail to her mouth. "I've probably been a tad overzealous in my pursuit of it, and it sought a safe haven."

"Inside a little girl?" Samson questioned. "That doesn't make a whole lot of . . ."

But it does, Remy thought. "The piece of creation needed a safe place," he said aloud, "a place where it could hide and be protected."

"Yes," Delilah agreed, nodding her head.

Remy looked to Deryn. "When you and your husband were with the Church of Dagon . . . you were supposed to give birth to a child who would house the power of a god. The unborn Zoe had been prepared . . . but the ritual was interrupted, and the god never took up residence."

Delilah nodded again.

"Dagon's loss was the fragment of creation's gain. The child—this special child—was the perfect place for the power to hide from me," Delilah continued, tickled by this newest revelation.

It was all starting to make a twisted kind of sense; all but one very important thing.

"Why would someone like you be interested in something as potentially powerful as this?" Remy asked Delilah, feeling the power of Heaven lunge threateningly within.

It didn't like this woman, not one bit.

"Good fucking question," Samson said, and his children grunted in agreement, clutching their weapons.

"Quite simple really," Delilah answered. "It's no secret that I've grown tired of this cursed existence, and I want it to end." She played with the crease on the leg of her slacks. "There, I've said it."

"You want to be released from your punishment?" Remy asked.

"I want to die," she said. "Are you happy now?"

"And you think the fragment . . ."

"I *know* the fragment can release me," she said. "It came to me in a dream . . . divinely influenced, I'm sure . . . and it said if I found the creation piece, I would be released from my torment, which is why I've been searching so enthusiastically."

She stood up from the couch, her movements smooth, predatory.

"I'm tired of living . . . tired of watching those I've learned to love wither and die from sickness and old age . . . tired of running from the likes of you and your bastard children," she said, staring defiantly at Samson and his brood. "I'll do anything to see it end."

Delilah placed her hands upon her shapely hips. "Will you help me do this, and save the life of the child in the process?" she asked.

"Zoe is in danger?" Remy questioned, his concern escalating.

"Oh yes," Delilah said. "It seems that a very ancient power is still very much in the picture."

It was Deryn's turn to stand now.

"He did come," the woman explained. "When the ritual was interrupted, it didn't stop him from coming. . . . He came, but instead of a new body, he was forced to go into an old one."

"The pastor of the former Church of Dagon, and the new Church of His Holy Abundance," Delilah said. "The old god temporarily lives within a shell of decaying flesh, and will be dead very soon. . . ."

"Unless?" Remy asked, not liking where this was going.

"Carl brought her there," Deryn said, her voice starting to quake with emotion. "He brought our little girl back to the one she'd been promised to."

"Dagon has the child," Remy stated.

"Dagon has the power of creation," Delilah added.

Remy knew what had to be done. The child needed to be saved, and the power of God removed from the ancient deity's possession.

"Do you know where she is?" he asked.

Delilah smiled a predator's smile, bringing the scarlet thumbnail back up to her perfect teeth as she nodded once.

"We'll have to go there," Remy said, looking at Samson and the others. "We'll have to go there and bring Zoe back home."

"And the fragment?" Delilah asked.

"I don't think it's a good idea for Dagon to possess it."

"I couldn't agree with you more," Delilah said.

She turned toward her white-haired servant amongst Samson's army.

"Mathias, tell the others we're leaving," she said.

"Yes, mistress." Mathias stepped away from his captors and disappeared into the mansion.

"And we're going where?" Remy questioned.

"I'm going to get my coat," she explained. "There's a private jet waiting for us at T.F. Green." The succubus continued on from the room.

"We can't afford to waste any more time."

CHAPTER THIRTEEN

The power that still crackled through his decaying human form made him feel more alive than he had in countless millennia.

This was but a taste . . . a taste of what it was really like. . . .

Elijah came to him, crossing the room in an utter panic, blocking his view of the child . . . the glorious child.

"Get out of the way!" the thing that was Pastor Zachariah shrieked as he attempted to crawl to his feet. But the pain was excruciating, and he crumbled to the floor.

"Pastor," Elijah whispered, kneeling down beside him, "you're hurt. . . . Let me . . ."

He *was* hurt. Dagon could feel the broken bones, his ruptured internal workings struggling to perform their functions to keep him alive. His skin was charred black in places; red and bubbled in others.

The power . . . the wonderful power had done this to him.

The power of God.

Dagon knew he would expire soon, the frail human armature that had become his prison, failing by the second. But he had to stay alive—long enough to claim this power as his own; to take what had belonged to another far more powerful than he, for with it, he could achieve the greatness that had eluded him.

He could sense the life radiating from Elijah, the young man's concern for his health and well-being touching, but irrelevant in the grand scheme of things.

Using what strength remained in his failing body, Dagon turned his attention to the youth, grabbing him by the back of his neck with a charred and blackened hand, and yanking him down toward his hungry mouth.

The boy didn't even scream. It was almost as if he knew what was going to happen to him—that the sacrifice of his life would allow the old god to go on long enough to reclaim what had been lost so very long ago.

Dagon's teeth sank deep into Elijah's throat, and his face was suddenly awash in the spray of blood.

And life.

The deity felt himself growing stronger, and he knew it wouldn't last.

But it was enough.

He continued to gorge himself on Elijah's body, flesh and blood entering his hungry mouth and providing the fuel to keep his own ravaged body alive.

The child continued to stand where he touched her, stiff as a store mannequin, as the power of creation continued to leak from the punctures he'd put in her flesh and to swirl above her head.

Though fearing for his continued survival, he could not keep himself away, and began to crawl across the floor, dragging his shattered limbs behind him like a tail.

The child's eyes were suddenly upon him, her expression going from blank to complete revulsion.

"No! No! No! No!" she wailed, shaking her hands before her in total panic.

Flecks of divine power sprayed from her wounds, landing at her feet to form a barrier of pulsing radiance to keep him at bay.

Dagon recoiled from the brilliance, his single good eye nearly cooking in its damaged socket.

He needed the child . . . needed what thrived inside of her.

A ghostly moan close by captured Dagon's attention.

The child's father—the Judas—was still lying stunned upon the floor, but he had started to come around. Dagon saw that the child noticed this as well, a glint of expectation in her innocent eyes.

Daddy would save her.

Dagon scrabbled across the floor, reaching out and grabbing the father's ankle with charred claws, pulling him closer across the plastic-covered floor. The man struggled weakly, but he was no match for the desperate Dagon.

The dying deity crawled atop the man, hearing his screams of terror and urging him to carry on the histrionics.

The child noticed as well, peering over the growing barrier at her screaming father.

"That's it," Dagon gurgled through the fluids filling his throat. "Look here."

The child was staring now, panic on her face.

"Daddy," she said as she made a move to come closer, but the barrier stopped her with a crackling hum.

Who is the master here? Dagon wondered. The child had been bred as a receptacle for divinity, but had the power taken control, as he had the body of Pastor Zachariah?

"Drop the barrier," Dagon commanded.

The child stared, her eyes frozen in fear.

Dagon grabbed her father's head, smashing it down on the floor, stopping him from flailing.

"Drop it!" he ordered again.

And still the child remained safely behind the wall of burning power.

Dagon made sure she was watching as he gripped her father's

skull, pulling back on his head to expose the width of his throat. The ancient deity opened his mouth, showing the child he was prepared to bite.

"Daddy, no!" she shrieked, starting to whimper and cry.

"Then drop the barrier," Dagon said. He didn't have much time, the burst of strength he'd received from feeding upon his faithful disciple rapidly fading.

"Do it," he screamed, a spray of warm blood clouding the air from his outburst. His strength was failing, and it would not be long before he was no more.

Another ancient power gone from existence.

Forgotten.

He sensed the blood thrumming through the man's body under him and found himself gazing down at his throat; the carotid artery pulsing beneath the thin veneer of flesh.

Dagon didn't want to die and was desperate for as much life as he could have. He lowered his mouth, prepared to rip out the Judas' throat to sustain him for that much longer, when the child cried out.

"Don't hurt my daddy!" she screamed, stomping her foot upon the plastic-tarp-covered floor.

And as the foot landed upon the cover, the barrier was gone in a flash, the smell of burned ozone lingering in the air.

Dagon smiled, even as he was dying.

His suspicions were correct; the child did manage some amount of control over the power hidden inside her.

She had placed her hand over where his nails had punctured her flesh, and Dagon watched as she moved her frail hand away to reveal that the wounds were no longer there, a trace of red, irritated skin the only evidence that the injuries had been there at all.

Oh, to have such power, he thought as desperation filled him.

He would be dead in a matter of moments; all the suffering he had endured since crossing over to this forsaken world, for naught.

The child moved haltingly closer, tears streaming from her eyes as she looked upon her injured father. He was awakening; moaning aloud as his head thrashed from side to side.

"Daddy," she said as she reached out to him.

Dagon could smell it on her; the blessed stink of a power he had longed for.

The power of life. The power of creation.

Weak beyond words, he laid his head down upon the parent's chest, letting the rhythmic beating of the man's heart escort him down the path of oblivion.

"Don't want to die," he slurred, the blood leaking from his mouth staining the man's shirt beneath his face.

But it was too late for begging.

Or was it?

Finding a residual strength, he managed to open his remaining eye and saw that the girl child had come closer, standing over him as she reached down to her awakening father.

Dagon could feel the power calling to him as it thrummed within the child's body. His eye fixed upon her hand as it moved across his line of sight; the tiny blue vein in her wrist pulsing with the beat of her heart, her blood filled with the stuff of God.

He did not know where he found the strength; some last bit of life's flame about to go out, and to thus bring the darkness of oblivion. But Dagon used that fire, taking its rapidly denigrating power and using it to surge up toward the child's wrist, and then sinking his hungry teeth into her tender flesh.

Gouts of her blood filled his mouth as she thrashed, clawing at the skin of his face—at his remaining eye—as she tried to remove his hold upon her.

But Dagon held fast, greedily drinking her blood; the child's pathetic cries were drowned out by the roar of creation in his ears.

Remy thanked Ashley's mother and hung up his phone.

He had to make sure Marlowe would be fed, watered, and walked. He was sure he'd hear about it from Marlowe when he returned, but at least his friend would be looked after.

He saw Samson standing by himself, deep in thought, at the back of the property, smoking a cigarette.

Remy approached, clearing his throat. It wasn't wise to sneak up on a guy with superhuman strength. "You're ready for this?" he asked.

"I'm ready to go back in there and strangle the life from her," Samson roared, nervously puffing away.

"That's not a good idea."

He grunted and continued to smoke.

"We have to think about Zoe," Remy said, attempting to justify what they were about to do. "She's completely innocent in all of this."

"I understand that," Samson said. "But I don't trust Delilah. There's shit she's leaving out."

"Then we'll have to be on our toes," Remy added.

Samson grunted again, bringing the cigarette to his mouth and sucking on the end as if there were no tomorrow. Maybe he knew something Remy didn't.

"A piece of creation," the big man said, smoke billowing from his nose and mouth. "What the fuck is that supposed to mean?"

Remy thought for a moment, and the more he thought, the scarier it became. "It's a piece of Him," he said finally. "A piece of what makes Him God."

Samson laughed, but there was no humor in his expression. "Obviously it wasn't a part He needed too badly."

"From what I can figure out, the Creator sort of exploded when He created the heaven and the earth . . . pieces of His divinity shaping existence as we know it."

"The big bang," Samson said.

"Yeah, I guess," Remy acknowledged. "And I guess there were some unused slivers of God's big bang lying around just waiting to be found."

"Sparks from a fire," Samson grumbled, trying to visualize what it was all about.

The big man was quiet for a moment, thinking some more. "Do you think it's wise for her to have this?" he asked, turning his milky eyes toward Remy.

"No," Remy answered. "Which is why we need to keep an eye on her and make sure she uses it for exactly what she said it was for."

"To die?"

"You heard her," Remy said.

"I've heard her say a lot of things over the centuries," Samson said. "She even said she loved me more than life itself, and we saw how that turned out."

Remy heard the sounds of heavy tires on gravel and walked toward the side of the house to see multiple vans pulling up in front. These would be their rides to the airport. "The vans are here," he called over his shoulder.

One of Samson's offspring had appeared and was leading the large man back into the house.

"Gonna need some help with the not-letting-her-out-of-our-sight business," he said, pointing to his blind eyes.

"You've got it," Remy said, feeling the crawl of anticipation in his gut growing more prominent.

Deryn held the back door open for Samson and his son, asking the strongman if he had any cigarettes to spare.

She looked a little shell-shocked, but was holding up better than expected. It was one of the things Remy admired most about humanity—the ability to accept and adapt to the most insane situations.

Deryn saw him and smiled as she lit up her cigarette.

"Are you all right?" he asked her.

She nodded through a cloud of smoke as she shook out the match, letting it drop to the ground.

"I'm going to get my daughter back," she said. "I'll be fine."

"You really shouldn't be going," Remy told her. "Let me handle it from here. I'll bring Zoe back."

Deryn sucked on the end of her smoke.

"Can't do that," she said. "Delilah says I have a connection to her, and you need me to find her. I have to go."

"I'm sure there are other ways we could—"

"Delilah says I have to go," Deryn interrupted forcefully.

"I wouldn't believe everything Delilah has to say."

"But I can't afford not to believe her," the woman explained. "I'll do anything to get my daughter back."

"It might not be safe," Remy said, knowing the words were useless, but he had to try.

"Then I'll just need to be extra careful," she said as she finished her cigarette, not giving him the opportunity to attempt to convince her otherwise.

And soon he was standing there alone with his thoughts, that awful feeling of dread anticipation in his gut.

It was going to be there for a while.

Poole had never imagined the power of a mother's love.

He barely thought of his own mother and, in fact, seldom thought of her as a mother at all; an incubator was more like it. It was as if she'd forgotten he even existed as soon as he was ejected from her icy womb.

Poole's first memories were indifference, annoyance, and disgust. He had never known his father. As a child, Poole had been left in the care of neighbors in the working-class English village, while his mother, whom he came to know as Eunice, worked two jobs—one at a textiles factory and the other at the local pub, where she had been a waitress.

He guessed there was some form of attachment there, between him and her. She did provide him with food, and clothes and a roof over his head, but that pretty much had been it. As he'd grown older, they'd become more like roommates.

By the time he was thirteen, his gift had kicked in, and being the thoughtful, independent child he had been shaped into, he set out on his own, using the unique abilities he'd been born with to make his fortune in the world.

Sitting strapped into his seat aboard the private jet given to Delilah by one of her myriad and wealthy followers, Clifton Poole basked in the love of a mother for her child, the feelings left over from his bond with Deryn York, while wondering why his own mother had never loved him.

He glanced over to the seat beside him, reaching across to make sure the seat belt was fastened tightly across the child-shaped metal statue. He'd grown quite attached to the vessel, and he wondered if his own love could ever be as strong as Deryn York's.

The container secured, Poole let his fingers again run over its smooth surface, closing his eyes to the images that flooded his mind.

The power that Delilah had searched for had blocked his ability to locate it from every angle, but since the child's mother had added her own special magick, he was able to see exactly where the power had gone.

It was a marvelous feeling, traveling across thousands of miles without even leaving his seat, and he could not help himself from checking in on the child—and the power that resided within her—yet again.

The last time he'd checked, Zoe had been asleep in her father's lap, at some backwater location in West Virginia. Both he and the child's mother had eventually been able to find it on the map, and this had made his mistress very happy.

She'd even allowed him to have something to eat and to use the bathroom like a real person again. Life was good right now, and it was all because of a mother's love.

Poole felt the rush as he again traveled the path that the power had taken, zeroing in on the location of the child.

And finding that he was being watched.

The man gasped as yellow eyes studied him as if he were a bug crushed on a microscope slide. The power was in those eyes . . . those horrible eyes . . . and he tried to back away, to retreat to his body.

But the eyes held him firm.

Poole moaned and thrashed, hoping the others would come to his aid.

What is this? a voice that caused his bowels to loosen asked. He could feel that voice inside his head now, rummaging around, searching for his identity. It ripped at his brain, tearing away dripping chunks of gray matter, and when it had finished, it started to laugh.

It knew everything now.

It knew they were coming.

Poole squirmed in his seat, unable to open his eyes. He had to warn them . . . had to warn his mistress, but those eyes . . . those eyes would not let him go.

The voice spoke again, like thunder reverberating through his skull. It told him they were more than welcome to try to take what was now his.

They were welcome to try, but they would all die horribly in the process.

Poole tried to tell the presence inside his head that he would do this—that he would pass on the warning—but the voice said he would rather deliver a warning of his own.

An example of what they would be facing.

And suddenly there was an entire beast inside his mind—a beast with fangs and claws, and an insatiable hunger for flesh and blood, and the human soul.

The Boeing Business Jet flew along at thirty-two thousand feet as Remy sipped his soda water with lime. They'd been in the air a little more than an hour, and he figured they would be reaching their destination shortly.

He looked around the cabin, strangely intrigued that Delilah could simply pick up the phone and have something like this at her disposal in a matter of minutes. He wondered how far her influence actually went; how many individuals had experienced her lips, and were now beholden to her in every way.

The more he thought about this, the more he realized that Samson's job was totally justified. Delilah was just too damn powerful to be allowed to live.

But then again, she wanted to die, and if things went according to plan, that was exactly what would happen once Zoe was freed from Dagon and the Church of His Holy Abundance.

If things were on the up-and-up.

Remy glanced around to see Samson fast asleep. His kids were scattered around him, some also sleeping while others listened to iPods or played handheld video games.

Samson didn't trust the woman, and Remy could understand why. He really didn't trust her either, but in order to find the child, he had to go along with the idea that what she was saying was true.

But what if it isn't? that nagging voice at the back of his mind asked.

Remy unbuckled his seat belt and headed up closer to the front of the plane. He passed a sleepy Deryn York, and again wished she had listened to his warning. But then again, if it had been his child, would he have listened?

Two of Delilah's soulless thugs blocked his way.

"I need to speak to her," Remy said, attempting to keep his annoyance in check.

"The mistress does not wish to be disturbed," one of the two men blocking his way said. His voice was emotionless, like something spat out from a computer program.

Remy could feel his Seraphim nature recoil, disgusted that something so empty and vacant as this man would be allowed to walk about freely. He hated to think what fate would have befallen the man—all of the men in Delilah's service—if his true self were allowed to walk about freely.

"I'm not going to tell you again," Remy said. "I need to speak to Delilah."

The men stood their ground, and Remy felt his anger reach a critical point. He was just about to force his way through, when he heard a voice call out.

"Let him pass," Delilah called.

The men obediently stepped aside, allowing him to walk down the aisle to where Delilah was sitting. Mathias stood beside her chair like a faithful guard dog.

"I want to speak to you, alone," Remy said to her, but his eyes were locked on Mathias.

"What you say to her, you can say to me," the soulless man answered.

"Boys, boys," Delilah said, holding a flute of champagne. "There's no need for these displays of aggression. We're all on the same side.

"Very well." She sighed. "Mathias, please, let us be for a bit."

The man looked hurt.

"Be a dear and listen," she added, a touch of venom in her words.

Begrudgingly, Mathias agreed, leaving the section at the front of the plane to join the others in Delilah's thrall.

"Would you like some champagne?" she asked Remy as he took the seat across from her.

"No, thank you."

"So, what do you wish to talk to me about?" she asked, eyeing him over the top of her glass as she took another sip.

Remy paused, feeling the raw sensuality of a seductress, knowing that if he were truly human, he would have had no power against someone like her.

"I want to be certain we understand each other," he said finally, his voice soft, without a hint of emotion.

She smiled that extra-wide smile that made him feel uneasy.

"Of course we understand each other," she said, nibbling on the edge of her glass. "We're all in this together. By retrieving the child, we all get what we want: You help a child return to her loving parent, and I gain access to an ancient power that will finally release me from my curse."

She laughed before having some more of her drink.

"Even that muscle-bound buffoon and his army of urchins get what they want when I'm finally allowed to die," she said, gesturing with her nearly empty glass.

Delilah giggled as she removed the bottle from the ice pail and poured herself another glass. "A shining example of cooperation," she said, placing the almost-empty bottle back where she'd found it, and leaning back in her seat. "Does that make you feel better, Remy?" she asked.

Remy let the Seraphim show its face. He felt his eyes become like fire, and his flesh begin to radiate light and heat.

"I know what you are," he said, his voice losing any trace of humanity. "If you should betray me . . . or if any harm should come to the child, her mother, or my companions, I will show you what it truly means to suffer, and there will be nothing in Heaven or on Earth that will release you from this torture."

He drew back upon the Seraphim, putting it back where it belonged. "I hope we understand each other," Remy said, getting up.

Delilah looked about to say something, but she was interrupted by the most unholy of sounds: a scream that had traveled from the far end of the plane to the front.

Remy reacted at once, dashing down the aisle, pushing past the soulless, as well as past Samson's children, who had risen from their seats but had gone no farther to inspect.

Deryn's hand shot out, grabbing his arm as he passed.

"That's Poole," she said, staring down the aisle where the horrible sound had originated.

Remy had seen the man briefly. He had appeared quite crazy as he had boarded the plane, clutching some kind of metal statue in the shape of an infant child. He'd gone directly to the very last row of the private jet to sit alone.

"Stay here," Remy told Deryn, removing her hand from his arm.

He could see the top of Poole's head sticking up above the seat, his wispy hair moving in the breeze of the circulating air.

With great trepidation he came around the side of the seat, and was horrified at what he found.

Poole sat perfectly rigid, still strapped into his seat. He was covered in blood, his clothes torn to shreds, as was his flesh. His stomach had been ripped open, and his insides had spilled out onto the floor to pool at his feet. Remy leaned into the larger of the wounds, examining the broken rib cage, and how the direction of the shattered bones appeared to be pointing outward.

As if something had punched its way out from the inside.

*   *   *

Dagon burned with the fires of creation, and it was good.

The ancient deity could feel his decaying body rebuilding itself, discarding the human form that had been more like a prison, and replacing it with something so much better—something beautiful, divine.

With trembling fingers, Dagon reached up and pulled away the rotting flesh to reveal golden-scaled skin beneath. The old flesh had turned gelatinous, continuing to decay in his very grasp. The god threw handfuls of the foul waste onto the floor; tearing more and more of the humanity he had worn away to reveal what he was always supposed to be.

What he dreamed he'd be.

The child sat beside her still-unconscious father, rocking from side to side and muttering unintelligibly. Dagon could still sense the raw power churning inside her and was tempted to feed upon her some more, but decided against it.

The totality of the power that existed within this child could very well be too great even for one such as Dagon to contain. But he would keep her as his own, eventually taming the unbridled God-power that lived within her to bend to his desires.

The child had slipped from her fuguelike state again, and he could feel her fear-filled eyes upon him.

"Do not fear me, little one," Dagon proclaimed, spreading his arms to show her the beauty of his naked form. "I have come to make this world a better place."

The little girl gasped, crawling to cower against the prone form of her parent as Dagon's horns began to grow; curling long and beautiful from his bony forehead, a crown to his glory.

The glory that he was now becoming.

They would be coming for the power soon; Dagon had no idea who they were, but he understood why they would come.

"So be it," he growled, flexing the muscles of his powerful new form.

He had shown them an example of his might, reaching down through the child conduit, to the observer who attempted to spy upon him.

Dagon had horribly slain that one, but doubted it would do much to deter them. The power of creation was something to fight for.

And he was perfectly willing to let them.

Before slaying them all for such an affront to his godliness.

CHAPTER FOURTEEN

Remy watched as two of Delilah's followers disembarked the plane, each holding the end of a blanket that contained the bloodied remains of Clifton Poole.

"That's it," Delilah said, watching from the tarmac of a little-used runway at the small West Virginia airfield. "Carefully, now."

And just as she spoke, one of the men lost his footing, stumbling and dropping his end of the blanket.

Clifton Poole's body tumbled from its wrapping, landing at the bottom of the stairs in a broken pile.

Delilah rolled her eyes and sighed with exasperation. "Please pick that up," she said, pointing to the body. "We don't need to draw any further attention to ourselves."

The two who had been carrying Poole's corpse hustled to stuff it back inside the blanket and carry it to a waiting van.

The side of the van said it was from a flooring company, and Remy noticed the two drivers staring at Delilah, mesmerized. She approached the driver's side window of the van.

"Be a pair of dears and dispose of that for me, would you?" she asked, blowing them kisses as, with a screech of tires, they drove away.

Anything for their mistress, Remy thought with a scowl, *especially if she has a piece of their souls.*

Remy stood off by himself, noticing that Samson and his family were standing on one side of the tarmac, while Delilah's followers stood on the other. Remy wondered how this would work; if they were going to be fighting together, could one side actually depend upon the other?

He caught the approach of Deryn out of the corner of his eye and turned toward her. She was pale and sickly looking, and she was still wrapped in her own blanket from the flight, even though the air was quite humid.

"You okay?" he asked her.

She smiled as she nodded. "I keep seeing him all torn up like that," she said, and brought a hand to her mouth to stifle the tears. "And then I start to wonder how something like that is possible, and then . . . and then I realize that you're . . . that all of you aren't what you appear to be and . . ."

The woman was on the verge of complete shock, the glimpse of a strange and brutal world being more than her human mind could comprehend.

Remy stepped closer, using the voice of the Seraphim to calm her.

"Now, let's hold it together," he said to her.

She looked up into his eyes, and he willed her to calm down with his gaze.

"Remember that Zoe needs you. She's waiting for you, and you won't do her, or anybody else, any good if you come apart at the seams."

He could feel her begin to relax, the nervous energy that her body was emitting dwindling down to the faintest of crackles.

"This will all be over soon," Remy said, and he pulled her close for a hug. "Just a little more craziness and it'll all be done."

"A little more craziness?" she asked, and he felt a tremble go through her body as he held her.

*   *   *

"I'm not sure how much more I can take," Deryn said, letting herself be held by the private eye.

She didn't know what it was, but there was something about him; the way she felt whenever he was even close by. Remy Chandler made her feel safe, and she totally believed him that things were going to work out.

Deryn had been on the verge of panic since her daughter's disappearance, but after having met the man in Zoe's drawings, and having spoken to him about finding her daughter, she had believed then that things were going to be okay.

But that was all before she was taken from the motel.

Her panic threatened to rise again, but the closeness to Remy Chandler helped her to keep it all under control.

She knew things were not normal with the woman called Delilah, and with the people who seemed to worship her every word. To look at her, one saw a beautiful woman in her early thirties, apparently wealthy and very much used to getting what she wanted.

But there was something else, something occasionally caught from the corner of the eye, something that hinted to Deryn that this woman was not what she appeared to be.

That they all: Delilah, her servants, the blind man—Samson—and his children, and even Remy Chandler . . .

They were all not what they appeared to be.

But being held by the private investigator seemed to make everything all right.

Deryn always suspected that her daughter's odd talents, the ability to predict the future through her drawings, would take her to some interesting places; that the door to another world could possibly be opened to her.

But she never imagined the door opening so wide.

"How sweet," a woman's voice commented, and Deryn found herself stepping back from Chandler's arms.

And she immediately felt the effects of a world, far stranger than she ever imagined, begin to exert its influence upon her.

"The cars are here and we're ready to go," Delilah informed them.

Six black SUVs had silently appeared upon the runway, waiting for them.

"All right," Deryn said, starting toward where the trucks were parked.

Delilah's hand shot out as she passed, gripping her elbow in a hold so powerful that it made her wince.

Remy had started toward them at seeing this, when Delilah specifically addressed Deryn.

"We're ready to go," Delilah said again.

Deryn didn't understand.

"Where are we going, dear?" the woman, who maybe wasn't a woman at all, asked her.

"I'm not sure I . . ."

"Poole is dead, so we no longer have our Hound," Delilah informed her. "But I believe your connection to him was likely enough to have left some kind of residual impression to where we should be going next."

Deryn looked at Remy, her anxiety starting to escalate. She wanted to be in his arms again, to feel as though everything was safe.

"Think of your daughter," Delilah commanded. "Think about how badly you want to hold her again."

She found herself doing exactly as the odd woman commanded, and found her head filled with the staccato images of a place she had never been, but where she somehow knew her daughter to be.

When she opened her eyes, Remy was standing beside her, a look of concern on his face.

But she was fine; she knew where her daughter was.

"We need to go that way," Deryn said, pointing toward an open gate far in the distance.

The alarm wailed in the night, calling forth his followers from the safety of their beds.

Dagon stood before the dwelling of Pastor Zachariah, as the sirens howled, and waited for the faithful.

He held the child's tiny hand firmly in his own, feeling the continued presence of a power that could very well reshape the world, pulsing within her fragile, human form.

Dagon glanced down at her, sensing that it was no longer the child who controlled the little girl's body, but the power of creation that had emerged, peeking out through the child's eyes.

This power, now coursing through his own form as well, had lain becalmed for countless millennia, watched over by holy men, protected, until the woman—*the soul eater*—had begun her search, and it had found refuge in a child's body.

Dagon saw the woman inside his mind, the one who was going to try to take his prize from him.

She would fail.

With new eyes that could see in darkness as clear as day, Dagon watched his followers come to him. The expressions on their faces were humorous to behold. They had no idea what they were looking at . . . what they were in the presence of.

He raised his perfectly muscled arm and waved them closer.

"Come to me, my faithful," he said, his voice booming in the night like Gabriel's trumpet. "Come, and stand before your god."

They moved closer, but not too close. They were afraid, and he could understand their fear.

For he doubted that these mortals had ever stood before something so wonderful.

Their frightened murmurings filled the air like insect song as he began to address his acolytes.

"Be not afraid," he told them, "for I mean you no harm."

Their chatter grew more intense, and then an older woman in a flowered nightgown stepped from the crowd.

"What are you?" she asked, her voice raised in fear. "Where . . . where is Elijah? . . . Where is Pastor Zachariah?"

The crowd murmured, not yet convinced that they were in the proximity of greatness.

"I am your lord and god," he told them. "The one you have prayed to for so many years." He paused for a moment, smiling as he raised a perfect hand to the sky.

"I am Dagon."

The crowd buzzed, and he basked in their fear, surprise, and adulation.

"Where is the pastor?" the woman asked again.

"He no longer exists," Dagon explained. "He and I were one, but now only I am here."

The woman stepped back into the protection of the crowd.

"You look like the Devil," she said, and the gathering agreed.

Dagon laughed at the superstitious lot, his laugh a booming sound that cleaved the silent night like a thunderclap.

"Certainly you can't be serious," he said, his patience waning. "I have come for you—I have come to save you all."

"Everything I'd expect a devil to say," the woman cried.

Dagon was tempted to silence her, but knew that any act directed toward her would be seen as proof of her accusation.

No, he had to show them the truth.

He closed his eyes, feeling the power that coursed through his every muscle burn like the sun. They had to be shown the glory of what stood before them; the glory of what he was.

A messenger was needed to proclaim his coming.

The god growled as he reached out with his mind, taking hold of the one who would best serve his purpose, and calling him forth.

The little girl gasped, her own eyes closing as he exerted his strength. The power within her crackled about her head, joining with his own.

She looked up at him with large, vague eyes.

"I will show them," he told her.

The crowd was growing anxious, and he could sense their fear and confusion increasing. He hoped what he had to show them would belay their concerns.

The sound of a door opening behind him made Dagon smile.

He listened to the creak of the porch beneath the weight of a footfall as a figure emerged from the house.

Dagon stepped to the side, pulling the child along, and they both watched the figure sway on the top of the porch, preparing to descend.

"It's Elijah," the woman proclaimed, and the crowd murmured enthusiastically.

The young man looked out over the gathering. His clothing was stained nearly black with blood, but the crowd seemed not to notice. Nor did they see the jagged hole in his throat—until he began to awkwardly descend the porch steps.

"Look at him!" somebody yelled.

"Is that blood?" cried another.

The crowd began to back away, but Elijah continued to stand before them, watching, his head tilted loosely to one side.

It was suddenly eerily quiet in the compound.

Dagon closed his eyes, reaching out to his puppet, manipulating brain functions and vocal cords for this, his most special moment.

"I . . . ," Elijah began, his voice horribly rough and gravelly. "I was . . . I was dead." The young man raised his bloody hands for all to see, and then showed them the mortal wound torn in his neck.

Dagon could feel the fear slowly turning to awe, and he knew he had them.

He had them all.

"But now . . . ," Elijah croaked, "now I am alive." He spread his arms. "Praise him. . . . Praise Dagon."

Dagon smiled.

"Praise him!" somebody screamed.

"Praise Dagon!" bellowed another.

And soon they were all singing his praises, and he allowed his influence to slowly creep within each of them.

They were his, body, mind, and soul.

CHAPTER FIFTEEN

Remy sat in the back of the black SUV as it sped down the dark West Virginia road.

"We're close," Deryn said from the front seat, between Mathias, who was driving, and Delilah. "We're really, really close."

Delilah placed a comforting arm around the mother, pulling her close. "And soon you'll be holding your little girl in your arms again," she said, leaning her head against Deryn's. "And I will be holding mine."

Remy's ears perked up, and he was about to ask what she had meant by that, when the first of the attackers spilled from the woods down onto the road. They came from both sides, many of them wearing dark clothing, their screaming faces seeming to float in the stygian darkness as they jumped into the path of the speeding vehicle.

Mathias barely slowed as he plowed into the first of the fleshy obstacles.

Tires screeched, and the windshield turned to a frosted red, ice tinged with crimson, before the air bag erupted from the steering column. The sound of impact was horrible; the screams of those hit even worse.

Deryn was screaming too as the car spun and came to a neck-snapping stop.

"Deal with this," Delilah ordered her driver, before turning in her seat to look at Remy and at those beside him.

Without question, they all left the car.

Remy was torn as he heard the sounds of fighting from outside.

"Go, angel," she told him, her arms still around his crying client. "They need you out there. She'll be perfectly safe with me."

Remy hesitated until the first blast of gunfire.

"Go," Delilah hissed, her eyes glistening in the darkness of the car.

He pushed open the car door. It was chaos outside, Samson's children and Delilah's soulless warriors fighting together against a common foe.

A woman wearing a hooded sweatshirt and torn sweatpants came at him with a kitchen knife. She screamed something unintelligible, thrusting the blade toward him. Remy moved aside, grabbing hold of her arm and twisting it enough so that she dropped the blade.

"Fucking bastard!" she got out between screams of pain.

But that didn't stop her; she continued to fight, clawing at his face in her frenzy.

He hated to do it, but he punched her, and blood sprayed from her nose as she at last dropped to her knees and fell sideways to the ground.

"Nice one," he heard a voice say, and he glanced over to see Marko grinning, just before Remy delivered a roundhouse kick to an attacker wielding a baseball bat. "Did you imagine maybe it was your wife or girlfriend when you did that?"

The man's words were meant as a joke, but they, like the current situation, just pissed him off.

The Seraphim was eager to be free, as it always seemed to be these days, and Remy cut it some slack, letting it emerge enough to fill him with a warrior's fury.

And the hunger for battle.

The ground was littered with bodies; he did not take the time to identify each and every one, but he knew that some of Samson's children, as well as Delilah's minions, had fallen.

But so had their enemy.

He snatched up the baseball bat dropped by Marko's fallen enemy, hefting it in his hand, and waded into combat.

As he swung, blocked, and struck out with the weapon, his mind flashed back to an earlier time—a time when he fought on the side of the Almighty against those who had attempted to usurp His holy rule. Remy remembered the anger, and disgust, he'd felt for his enemy—those who had once been his brothers— and immersed himself in battle.

The Seraphim was elated, attempting more and more to exert its influence, trying with all its might to persuade Remy to let it be completely free.

It whined pathetically in Remy's ear, telling him that the battle in which he now fought would be over in a matter of seconds if only he would let go.

The temptation was great, as it always was, but Remy remained in control, letting his fragile human nature hold sway over the power of Heaven.

The Seraphim was not in the least bit happy with this as it moved about the road, smiting its enemies with savage precision, but it knew that it must take what it was offered. Always holding out hope that someday it would be free, and that not a trace of the false humanity that held back its full essence would exist to suppress its holy might.

It could dream, Remy thought as he smashed a man with his handgun across the face in a shower of teeth and blood.

At least he could give it that.

As the newest to face his angelic wrath dropped to the road in a twitching pile, Remy saw that others were running, abandoning the fight.

Still at the ready, he stopped, examining the situation.

Samson was in the process of picking up a squirming man and smashing him down onto the ground. Samson's spawn and Delilah's faithful watched as their enemies suddenly stopped their fighting, turning tail to disappear into the shadows of the woods around them.

"Looks like they had enough," one of Samson's daughters, a young lady in her mid-twenties with a lime green Mohawk, proclaimed as she pumped her fist in the air victoriously.

The Seraphim wanted more. It always wanted more; more fighting, more blood, more violence, but Remy forced it back, putting the genie in the bottle yet again.

"What do you think, Samson?" Remy asked, still holding his baseball bat, glinting oily black in the light of the half-moon.

"Not sure," the big man said, sniffing the air. "Could've just been a test."

"A test?"

"Yeah, to try us on for size . . . see how much of a threat we might be."

It sounded logical enough to him. "Obviously they saw enough."

"Yeah," Samson said, again looking around with his blind eyes, his nose twitching.

Remy heard the sound of a voice speaking rapidly, and he searched for the source. Over to the side, nearly hidden in some tall brush, he saw one of Delilah's men standing over one of their fallen enemies, a machete ready to descend.

Moving quickly, Remy grabbed hold of the man's wrist just as the blood-speckled blade began to fall. "No more," he said, his eyes burning into the man's.

Delilah's follower had the stink of one on the verge of losing everything. From what Remy could sense, he still had some of his soul, but it wouldn't be long until that too was gone.

The man snarled, attempting to pull his arm away, but Remy held fast.

"I'll break it at the wrist," Remy warned, causing the man to stop his struggles. "Go," Remy ordered, releasing his hold.

At first it appeared the man was going to defy him, but he then thought better of it—a wise choice.

Remy knelt beside the fallen man, who still lay upon the ground. Severely injured, he clutched his blood-soaked side where he had been stabbed.

The stink of approaching death was upon him, and Remy leaned in to hear what he was saying.

"He came . . . just like the pastor said he would," the man said. There was blood on his lips now, signifying some sort of internal injury. "He came to us . . . only to us to prove we are the faithful. We are the faithful, oh yes."

"Who came?" Remy asked, laying a calming hand upon the man's shoulder.

The man's eyes focused upon him, seeing him for the first time.

"Dagon," he said with a laugh. There were tears in his eyes, tears of joy. "Dagon came to us. . . ."

He began to cough, spatters of blood freckling his face, as streams ran down from the sides of his mouth.

"I'm looking for a little girl," Remy said urgently, sensing that death was near. "Was she there with you?"

The dying man seemed to momentarily focus, listening to Remy's question.

"Yes." His voice was no more than a whisper now. "Yes . . . the Judas and his child."

Remy felt his heart begin to beat faster.

"Are they all right?" he asked.

The follower of Dagon didn't answer, his eyes beginning to glaze over as he gazed into the beyond.

Remy could sense the Angel of Death's approach. Grabbing the man by the shoulders, he attempted to infuse just a little bit of his own life force into the man so that he would be able to answer.

But it was too late, and the man was gone, the last of his breath whistling from his lungs like air from a punctured tire.

"Anything?" Samson asked, approaching with his children.

"He said the father and child are there," Remy said, rising to his feet. "But that's all I know."

"Seems like enough," Samson said with a nod. "We'll continue on and take it from there."

Remy agreed, heading back to the SUVs stopped by the side of the desolate, backwoods road.

He watched as Samson's children took care of their fallen, carrying them gently to the trucks, placing them in the back. The same could not be said of Delilah's followers; their fallen were left in the road where they'd been killed, along with the bodies of the enemy.

Remy was tempted to do something, but time was now of the essence. Dagon's followers who had fled the battle would return to the compound, warning the ancient deity that they were coming. At the moment, there was no time to respect the dead.

Going to the SUV where he'd left Deryn and Delilah, he found the passenger-side front door open, and suddenly he experienced a very bad feeling.

"Deryn," Remy called out, hanging on to the door and finding the vehicle empty.

"Deryn!" he cried again, thinking maybe they had been forced from the car and were hiding nearby. "Deryn, are you out there?"

"They're gone, aren't they?" he heard Samson say.

"Yeah," Remy said, immediately fearing the worst.

The big man chuckled. "Are you surprised?" he asked. "Delilah really has her heart set on finding that little girl."

"And you think she took Deryn so she'd get there first?" Remy asked.

"Do you see her boy toy, Mathias, around anyplace?" he then asked.

Remy searched the crowd, and even the dead.

"No, looks like he's gone too."

"Then the answer to your question is yes," Samson said. He started toward the row of SUVs parked behind the first. "We probably want to get to that compound as quickly as we can before Delilah has the chance to get into what she's really up to."

It was Mathias who had found her at last.

Nothing but withered flesh and bones, she was curled in the fetal position in the lowest section of the archaeological dig.

She'd returned home, long before the Palestinian settlement of Sorek had been rediscovered, hoping to find—*to remember*—a time when she had been human. The city had been buried deep beneath the shifting sands, covered up by the passage of time, but she'd known it was there, homing in on the place as if following posted signs by the side of the road.

Delilah could sense it there beneath her. She could practically hear the sounds of the marketplace again, the children at play.

The cries of her lost humanity calling out.

A reminder that she must suffer for her sins.

Suffer she did, and as she suffered, she was transformed into something fearful, and so far from God that she couldn't imagine ever finding her way back.

But she tried, even after the deaths of loved ones—struck down, she believed, by an angry God—searching for a way she could show she was sorry.

This was why she had returned to the city of her birth, a city long since dead, but the place where it had all begun for her.

Like an animal of the earth, she had burrowed down into the sand, returning to a place where she had once felt safe.

And she found that trace of peace again beneath the desert sand, and she nested there in the home that had belonged to her family for generations.

That was where she lay, unfound, unnoticed, and unloved.

Until he found her.

Mathias.

She hadn't noticed how much grayer his hair had become over their time together.

Delilah looked at him—really looked at him—as they paused in the darkness on the outskirts of the church compound.

When did he become so old? she asked herself, barely aware of the passage of time since the death of her humanity. He had been so handsome when she'd first laid eyes upon him.

Delilah could still remember the feeling of his rough hands as they plunged down into the sand and drew her upward. For some reason he had been drawn to her, to the archaeological dig that had uncovered her home and village.

He'd said he could hear her crying inside his head, and before he went mad, he'd gone in search of her.

How horrible she must've looked after all that time beneath the ground, but that did not stop him. She recalled how he tenderly brushed the sand from her mummified lips, and slowly . . . longingly . . . placed his own lips to hers, feeding her for the first time in . . .

The former mercenary held up a hand, directing them to stop, as he scanned the area for threats.

"She's close by," Deryn said as softly as she was able to in her present condition, ringing her hands together as she almost ran in place.

It hadn't taken much to convince the woman to leave the safety of the SUV. Her daughter's presence was practically screaming for her to follow.

And Delilah was more than happy to oblige.

Mathias gestured for them to follow him. They carefully negotiated a heavily overgrown hill, moving through the bushes and bramble to come out at the back of a row of buildings. There were trash barrels outside the doors, and clotheslines strung between the buildings, and trees directly across; Delilah guessed these were the church's living quarters.

They waited, she and Mathias, looking toward Deryn to show them the way.

The woman held out a trembling hand, pointing down a ways to the back of a much larger, brick structure. They continued on to it cautiously. A single light burned above the door, and Mathias reached up to unscrew it, plunging the area into darkness.

"She's inside," Deryn said, barely able to contain her emotion.

"Then that's where we need to be," Delilah said, placing a comforting hand upon the woman's shoulder.

She could hardly manage her own excitement, sensing the power of the thing she'd desired for so many years . . . the key to her freedom.

"Mathias," she urged.

The man first tried the door and found it locked. From his back pocket, he produced a pocketknife and, kneeling down, went to work on the door.

It felt right that Mathias would be here with her; that he

would be the one who would help her achieve her goal. Of all she had feasted upon, he was the strongest.

Delilah had always been amused by the former soldier's ability to function without a soul. While others eventually withered and died, Mathias had kept going.

It was almost as if he were made especially for her.

She had not taken his soul all at once, instead choosing to feed upon it a little at a time, slowly returning to health.

To beauty.

It wasn't long after her return that she had had the dream telling her how she could free herself, but why just be free, when the power of God could be used to make things right?

Delilah hoped she remembered them all, the husbands and children who were once part of her life, but she was sure the stuff of creation would help her to remember if necessary.

Tingling with anticipation, she heard the creak of hinges as the door swung open to allow them admittance.

Mathias turned and looked at her as he slipped the tool back into his pocket. She could see he wanted her praise; anything to set him apart from the others she possessed.

But she said nothing, walking past him through the door and into the semidarkness of a corridor, lit only by the red glow of an emergency exit sign.

"Always leave them hungry" had been her motto for millennia, and she wasn't about to forget it now.

She could feel the object as she had in Vietnam, only this time it was stronger, calling out to her, teasing her. She was starting down the hall when someone moved past her at a run.

"She's down here," Deryn York said, pushing her aside. "Zoe," the mother called out. "Zoe, honey, it's Mommy."

She was running now, heels clicking upon the linoleum floor.

"Get her back here!" Mathias hissed.

"Deryn," Delilah said, attempting to use her ability to snag the woman's attention and bring her back.

But it had no effect.

She continued down the corridor, Delilah and Mathias close behind.

The corridor turned right into darkness, and Mathias reached out to halt the woman's progress, but she evaded his grasp, plunging into the shadows, desperately calling out her daughter's name.

Delilah held back, centuries of survival instincts suddenly coming alive and warning her that all was not as it seemed.

"Zoe?" Deryn called out. "Come out . . . please. . . . It's Mommy, honey. . . ."

The room was suddenly illuminated in a soft, pulsing glow.

"Mommy?" a tiny voice asked.

The child sat upon the floor, the light of creation that radiated from her tiny form pushing back the darkness that threatened to overwhelm her on both sides.

Delilah gasped at the vision; she was so close after all this time. She started to move toward the mother and child, when Mathias' hand stopped her.

Deryn pushed through the shadows toward her daughter, unaware that she was not alone in the darkness.

It emerged just as she reached the little girl, jumping out to block her.

Delilah knew that at one time it had been a man, but now . . .

"Hello, Deryn," the man said, the voice hollow, lacking humanity.

"Carl?" the woman questioned, but she did not back away, even as the man brought his hand up, emerging from the darkness that seemed to surround him like a shroud.

In a glinting arc, he thrust the blade into her belly.

"You shouldn't have come," the man said in that same, chilling monotone. "She doesn't belong to us anymore. She belongs to Dagon."

They'd driven a ways farther down the lonely, backwoods road, when Samson began to act up.

No longer having Deryn to guide them, they thought they might have some problems, but the big man picked up on Delilah's scent without any problem.

"Think we should pull over here," Samson said from the front seat of the SUV, moving his shaggy head around. "The bitch's stink is pretty strong right here."

From the backseat, Remy turned around to see that the other vehicles were pulling over as well, their army climbing from the trucks, weapons in hand.

He was still carrying the Colt 45, and unnecessarily checked the clip to make sure it was still loaded with its special bullets. Everything as expected, he slipped the gun back into the holster he wore beneath his arm.

"You want something bigger?" Marko asked him.

"No, this should be fine," Remy told him.

"Think I might have an extra shotgun, or Mac 10 if you—"

"No, this'll be fine," he told the man again.

"Suit yourself," Marko said, climbing from the car to retrieve his own weapons in the back of the vehicle, pushing aside some of the dead they carried to get at them.

Samson still sat in the passenger seat, his sightless eyes gazing out at the West Virginian night.

"Are you ready for this?" Remy asked, placing a hand upon the big man's shoulder.

"I've been ready for this for . . ." He thought for a moment but then gave up on the specifics. "Let's just say for a long fucking time."

Curiosity got the better of Remy, and he found the question slipping out before he could think better of it.

"And then what?" Remy asked him.

"What do you mean?"

"After this . . . Delilah will most likely be dead, and your purpose, your special task will be done. What then?"

Samson said nothing but fished in his shirt pocket to remove his crumpled pack of cigarettes. He remained silent as he fished one out, returned the pack to where he'd found it, and then lit up.

"I've lived a very long time, Remy," he said, tilting his head back to make sure Remy could hear him. "And even with the mission, I've done some pretty amazing things while I've been here." He puffed on his smoke. "Have done some pretty fucking stupid things too, but everybody does that despite what they say."

"I hear you," Remy agreed.

"Think I might call it a day," the strongman said.

"Really?" Remy asked, surprised by the answer.

"Yeah, it's been a good run, but the bitch . . . Delilah was my fuel," he explained. "My passion. With her gone, I just wouldn't be angry enough anymore to keep the furnaces stoked . . . to keep the machine going."

"Interesting," Remy said.

"Yeah, but remember, this is all based on the fact that she's going to bite it," Samson explained. "But I happen to know she's got more fucking lives than a cat with multiple personalities."

"There's that," Remy said as he remembered Delilah's explanation, her passionate plea as she explained that she wanted to die.

He remembered the odd statement she'd made in the car before the attack—that soon she'd be holding her own again.

"Did she ever have any children?" Remy asked.

"Who? Delilah?" Samson responded, a bit surprised.

"Yeah, I was just thinking about something she said earlier tonight that confused me."

"Yeah," Samson said. "She's been around as long as I have. . . . She had lots of kids . . . husbands. The whole package."

He paused. Remy could sense there was more.

"Didn't work out well for any of them though," the big man said, finishing up his cigarette.

"How so?"

"God would only allow her temporary happiness, before He took it all away."

"Sounds like Him," Remy grumbled.

"Yeah, but remember, she was cursed. So she'd think she was doing okay, let her guard down, and then the Big Guy would do something to show her how fucked she still was—disease, natural disasters, birth defects. Hell, even my kids and I found her living happily ever after a few times over the centuries."

"But she got away."

"Yeah, she did," Samson said.

"And her family?"

Samson didn't answer the question before he opened the SUV door.

"Think we should get this party started," the big man said, a somber chill now in his voice.

"A party," Remy said, climbing from the vehicle as well. "Yeah, right."

They were all standing around outside their vehicles, weapons drawn and ready for war.

Is that what this is? Remy thought, staring at them all, the soulless as well as the children of a near immortal. He guessed that was the case, but usually in war, there was at least a unified reason as to why the battle must be fought. In this case, there were multiple sides, each of them fighting for something different. Only the battlefield was the same.

Remy knew why he was fighting, and whom he was fighting for, and that was all that really mattered at this stage of the game.

Samson was giving a sort of pep talk to the troops. He could see the large man's children listening to every word, while Delilah's people just stared ahead blankly, murder in their gazes. They did what Delilah had instructed them to do, and that was pretty much it. But as long as they weren't fighting one another at the moment, things were working out all right.

It was hot and extremely humid in West Virginia, the nighttime life all singing one cacophonous song composed of buzzing, chirping, shrieking, and croaking.

That all went quiet as the warriors started into the woods.

Samson and his kids led the way, with Delilah's minions backing up the rear. One of Samson's youngest, somebody they called Little Shit, had run on ahead, moving from tree to tree, shadow to shadow, before being swallowed up by the woods.

It wasn't too long before he was back with his intel.

"Straight ahead, up the hill and down," the youngster explained in a whisper. "Looks like they plant their own crops and shit. We can make it right onto the compound property by cutting through the cornfields."

"Then that's what we'll do," Samson said, directing another of his kids to go back and tell the others what their plan was.

"Do you think the kid's all right?" Samson asked, sensing that Remy had come to stand beside him.

"Don't know," Remy said, fearing the worst. "Hope so."

"Me too," Samson answered before cracking the knuckles on both large hands. "I'd like to at least see something good come out of the mess that I think is about to go down."

Little Shit led them now, bringing them up the hill, halting them with an upheld fist, as he scanned the area down below.

"All right, it's clear," he said, gesturing for them to follow him.

They came down the incline into the crops, spreading out to walk between the rows. The corn still hung upon the tall stalks, large ears waiting to be harvested.

Moving between the rows, doing their best to remain as silent as possible, Remy hadn't noticed that the nighttime life had grown accustomed to their presence, and had resumed its songs.

Until it went silent again.

He felt it almost immediately, a shift in the atmosphere telling him that something unnatural was about to happen. Remy almost cried out a warning, but it was already too late.

The corn ignited with an eerie blue flame.

All the stalks exploded into a smokeless fire, burning down to the ground in a matter of seconds and leaving them all completely exposed.

And then it was as if the sun had suddenly risen in the sky as the entire area became bathed in an eerie yellow light.

"It's times like these when I'm glad I can't see," Samson said over to his left.

Remy shielded his eyes from the blazing light to see figures now standing up ahead.

"There you are," the lead figure said with a growling chuckle.

Remy had no doubt that he was in the presence of the ancient god Dagon. He wasn't sure what it was exactly, but it was either the golden, scaled skin, or the horns sprouting from his head that gave it away.

The warriors, now exposed, prepared to fight, the sounds of multiple weapons being readied to fire filling the night air. Remy looked around to see that the guns were all pointed straight ahead at their targets.

"Oh really," Dagon said, bemused.

"Is he naked?" Samson asked.

Distracted, Remy looked over to the big man. "What?"

"Is the guy doing all the talking naked?"

"Yeah," Remy said, "but I don't think now's the time to . . ."

"Can never take somebody who's naked seriously," Samson grumbled with a shake of his head, before issuing his command.

"Take 'em down!" Samson screamed, and his children, as well as Delilah's soulless soldiers, opened fire.

Startled by the sudden violence, Remy ducked down, staring ahead to see the extent of the damage. The air was filled with the billowing smoke of the weapons' discharge, but as it began to clear, he was met with the most disturbing of sights.

Those who had been attacking were down, their bodies bloodied by gunfire, but the god . . .

The god was untouched.

"How'd we do?" Samson asked.

"Not too bad, unless we were trying to take out Dagon."

"Ah shit," the strongman said, kicking the dirt. "Why can't anything be easy?"

Dagon first looked to the left, then to the right, studying the corpses of his acolytes.

His body seemed to glow all the brighter as he started to walk toward them. He walked about three feet before coming to a stop. The god then seemed to survey his surroundings, studying the dark earth now void of vegetation.

Some of Delilah's followers had started to shoot again, but the bullets had zero effect, and the ancient deity seemed not to notice.

"Give me the bad news," Samson requested.

"I really don't know," Remy said.

The god knelt upon one knee and brought one of his large hands forward, pushing his fingers down into the dirt.

"He's touching the dirt," Remy reported.

"What's he doing that for?" Samson asked.

Remy remained silent, continuing to watch as a flash of divine energy was emitted from the god's hand, the entire ground suddenly illuminated in a white-hot flash.

"Answer me, Remy. What's going on?" Samson demanded to know.

Remy wasn't sure how to answer, but the first of the screams to pierce the night was enough to tell them all that it wasn't good.

Remy looked toward the sound to see a group of Delilah's soldiers spinning around, searching for something, their guns at the ready. One of the men was suddenly gone, yanked down beneath the ground before he could cry out. It was repeated again, and again, one soldier after the next being pulled down beneath the ground by something unseen.

Dagon had risen to his full height, staring out across the empty field. The ground around him began to bubble and churn as if it were liquid.

And one after another, corpses in various stages of disrepair began to emerge, pulling themselves up out of the earth.

"I'm not going to ask you again, Chandler," Samson said. He began to lumber toward the sounds of the sickly moans as the dead crawled up from the dirt.

"It's times like these you should be glad you can't see," Remy said, pulling the Colt 45 from the holster beneath his arm and chambering a round into the weapon.

CHAPTER SIXTEEN

The first question that popped into Remy's head as he watched with abject fascination as the corpses shambled toward them was why there were so many bodies buried beneath a cornfield.

They were surrounded by the reanimated dead; even Dagon's followers, just cut down in the hail of bullets, were struggling to their feet to stand with their leader.

Samson sniffed the air as he turned in a circle.

"Dead guys, right?" he asked Remy.

"Lots of them."

"Wonder if they're fast or slow," the strongman asked, just before the corpses attacked.

The reanimated screamed their rage as they charged, a wave of rotted flesh and anger coming at them from all sides.

"Fast," Remy said, firing into the first of the moving corpses to reach him. He looked to be a slightly overweight teen, dressed in a ripped T-shirt and baggy jeans. His throat had been torn out, but it didn't appear he had been dead all that long.

The Colt fired an enhanced bullet into the dead kid's face, stopping him almost immediately in his tracks. Punching through the thick skull, the bullet lodged in the decaying brain, working its magick on the unnatural power that made the body mobile. But it was only the first.

The dead were like a swarm of ants, rushing at them even through a hail of gunfire.

"Form a circle!" Samson bellowed over the roars and moans of the reanimated. His kids obeyed to the best of their ability, shooting off their pistols and rifles in an attempt to reach their siblings and father.

Some made it; others . . .

Delilah's people were less inclined to listen, choosing instead to hold their ground.

Remy saw they weren't doing all that well; every corpse to fall was quickly replaced by three or four others. He did the best he could, firing his enhanced weaponry and taking down their attackers one at a time.

But it wasn't enough.

"Any tricks up your sleeves would be greatly appreciated," Samson said as the corpse of a legless woman scrambled between them, biting into the thigh of the big man with jagged yellow teeth.

Samson bellowed, reaching down to tear the woman from her hold. He broke the corpse, snapping and folding it as if getting ready to throw a cardboard box in the trash.

"Holy Hand Grenade, a one-time divine-intervention phone call," he said, tossing aside the pulverized body. "Anything, anything at all."

Remy glanced over to see Dagon standing there, his arms spread to the Heavens, a divine power crackling from his hands.

This was the power that Delilah had been seeking; the power of creation, the power of life over death.

This was the power that had to be shut off if they were going to survive this, but was that possible?

Remy knew this power; he had felt it exude from That which was his Creator. This was the power that had made the universe . . . the power that had made him . . . the power that had made them all.

It made him feel sick to see it being used in such a tawdry fashion. And he didn't want to even think about how this creature had acquired it.

More and more of Remy's comrades were falling, and as they fell and were torn apart by the vicious dead, they too rose to join the legions of the reanimated against their brethren. The dead were relentless in their attack.

Remy ejected an empty clip from his Colt, quickly snapping in the next in one fluid movement. He took down an old woman in a flowered nightgown, her white hair already speckled with blood and brains, even before two of the special bullets were unloaded into what remained of her face.

Their own number had dwindled by half, most of Delilah's followers having already been taken to join the ranks of their attackers.

Automatic gunfire blared like staccato blasts of thunder as those who had managed to hold their own continued their struggle. Samson, his clothes torn and bloody, continuously lashed out, powerful blows falling upon the dead with the force to pulverize.

And still they kept coming.

Remy knew what he had to do, and though it was excruciating to admit, little else would suffice.

Reaching down beneath his human façade, he found the power of Heaven waiting, and he extended his hand.

I have need of you, Remy called, urging the power to come forth. And as it surged upward, his body flushing with the power of God, he felt it recede as quickly as it had arrived.

Remy was shaken, his body filled with the agony of his true nature repressed. He looked toward the ancient god whose gaze had fallen directly upon him.

"I know what you are," the deity roared inside Remy's head. *"And you are not wanted here, warrior of Heaven."*

By now the dead were at him, so close, and so many, that his weapon could do little. The dead had him, dragging him down to the ground, the sickening stench of blood and decay flooding his nostrils enough to suffocate him . . .

As the dead made great efforts to make him one of their own.

Delilah held the metal bowl against herself, moving the electric mixer around through the golden cake batter until all lumps had disappeared.

Satisfied, she turned the mixer off, ejecting the beaters onto a waiting paper towel from which she picked up one of them, hungrily licking the batter from the blades.

Perfect, she thought, enjoying the taste of the cake batter she had made from scratch. She spooned the thick contents of the bowl into the cake pan. Completely content in her actions—indeed, in her life—Delilah hummed a song, the name of which she did not know.

Right then she experienced a moment of perfect bliss. She couldn't imagine life being any better.

Smoothing out the batter with a spatula, she opened the preheated oven and slid the cake inside to bake. Setting the timer, she prepared to clean up, and then get the dining room decorated for the party.

It was her youngest's birthday. David was going to be six years old. He would be starting school this year, and she experienced a pang of sadness, which quickly went away when she felt the stirring of life in her protruding belly.

Five months pregnant, she thought with a smile as she laid her hands upon the material of her flowered maternity dress. She and her husband had assumed they were done with babies.

This thought made her laugh as she strolled from the kitchen toward the dining room. She could hear the kids going wild outside with their father, and she strolled over to the sliding glass door to see what they were all up to.

It was warm outside, and the kids were enjoying the pool, as well as squirt guns and the hose.

There were children everywhere she looked, and for a moment, she fought to catch her breath.

How many children do I have?

The thought was totally bizarre, and she had no idea where it came from. She had as many children as she had, and that was that.

A water balloon struck the glass door, exploding in wetness, and she instinctively screamed aloud, jumping back.

Her husband, Sam, was looking at her through the door, a huge smile upon his rugged face. Looking at him standing there, wearing only his shorts, his muscular body exposed, she could understand completely why they had as many children as they did.

She slid the door open a crack to speak to him.

"It's a good thing for you I'm pregnant," she said, shaking her fist.

He pretended to cower in fear, just as six of her children, three boys and three girls, between the ages of eight and twelve, attacked him with their own water artillery.

She laughed uproariously as she watched them chase her husband around the yard, shrieking at the top of their lungs, as he narrowly evaded being hit by the water-filled balloons.

Perfect, she said to herself, again thinking of her life and how absolutely rewarding and wonderful it all was. She couldn't imagine it being any better.

Delilah sensed she wasn't alone in the dining room, and she turned from the view of her family to see a little girl, no older than six, sitting on the floor beside her dining room table. The child rocked from side to side, staring ahead at something Delilah was not privy to see.

"Who are you, darling?" she asked, cautiously moving closer, not wanting to scare the little girl. "Are you here to play with the kids?" she asked.

The girl must've been one of her kids' friends, but she didn't recognize her from the neighborhood. The child said nothing, continuing to rock back and forth and to stare intensely ahead.

"Hey, are you all right?" Delilah asked her. "Do you . . . do you want me to call your mommy?"

The girl suddenly sat up bolt straight, her eyes widening as if she were seeing something terrible.

"My mommy's hurt," she said, her voice rising to the level of a scream.

"Oh, honey," Delilah said, grabbing hold of the back of one of the dining room chairs as she lowered herself down to the child's level. It wasn't as easy as it used to be with her belly growing so . . .

Delilah looked down to see her stomach strangely flat.

That's odd, she thought, staring down at where the bulge of life used to be. *To look at it this way, it almost looks as though I'm not pregnant anymore.*

"She's hurt," the child was screaming now, climbing to her feet. "My daddy hurt my mommy!"

Delilah reached out to the child, wanting to take her into her arms and comfort her. She wanted to tell her everything was going to be all right.

Perfect.

But something told her that this wasn't the case, that things were far from perfect. There was a nearly deafening rumble from outside, and Delilah turned to glance toward the sliding glass door. If there was a storm coming, she wanted her family to come inside.

She wanted them there with her.

But it had grown dark as night out where the sun had once been shining on a—*dare she think it*—perfect day.

"Sam," she said, calling out her husband's name. "Kids!"

Standing at the glass door, she peered out into the darkness. No longer could she see her children playing, or her husband, or even her yard, for that matter.

There was only darkness.

Delilah turned from the glass door to speak to the mysterious child. Somehow she knew this little girl would know what had happened.

"Where are they?" Delilah asked, suddenly on the verge of hysteria. "Where is my family?"

"Gone," the little girl said with a stamp of her foot. "All gone."

And the world . . . Delilah's world . . . wasn't so perfect anymore.

Mathias twitched uncontrollably and moaned as he thrust, climaxing for the fourth time since he and the woman he loved had awakened aroused, hungry for love.

He slumped atop her supple form, jamming his panting face against her neck as she squirmed beneath him.

"Is that all you have?" Delilah asked in a panting whisper, her hand already on the way down between their legs to arouse him to prominence again.

He kissed her neck, his tongue sneaking out to lick at the saltiness of her sweating flesh.

"You're going to kill me," he said with a lascivious chuckle. She responded in kind, working her magic yet again on what he believed, up until a few moments ago, to be a tired and withered member.

Delilah rolled him onto his back as she squirmed out from beneath his weight.

"It appears you still have some life left in you," she said, working his growing stiffness with a voracious smile.

Mathias smiled in return, filled to bursting with his love and passion for this woman who had become his life.

Fully erect now, she climbed astride him, lowering herself down onto his swollen manhood.

"So we'd better take advantage," she said, beginning to move slowly up and down, riding him. "For who knows how much longer we actually have?"

He surrendered to her passions, closing his eyes and immersing himself in the unbelievable pleasure of her. She was everything to him, and he couldn't imagine a world in which she wasn't his—body and soul.

Entering a kind of fugue state, he lay there listening to the moans of her pleasure, adding his own sounds of bliss to their symphony of passion as they both grew closer to yet another climax.

But suddenly Delilah stopped her rhythmic pounding and was speaking to someone.

"Hello there," his love said.

His eyes snapped open as she disengaged herself from their lovemaking, crawling off him.

"What's wrong?" he asked, looking to see that his woman was staring across the room.

There was a little girl sitting upon the floor.

Mathias crawled to the foot of the bed to join his love, who now covered her glorious nakedness with a sheet. He wasn't sure why, but seeing this child filled him with a sense of overwhelming dread.

"Who could she be?" Delilah asked.

And Mathias just stared at the silent little girl, who rocked to her own inaudible rhythm; suddenly he knew exactly who she was.

She was the end of it all.

The water was glorious.

The sun was slowly fading, reflecting off the ocean and giving it a strange, coppery hue.

Almost like . . .

Deryn didn't even want to go there; thoughts like that didn't belong in her head. She had to stay positive, if not for herself, for Zoe.

The smiling child, water wings inflated upon her arms, and a life jacket securely fastened about her neck and waist, was slowly dog paddling toward her with the help of her husband.

Things are good now, she thought as she watched the two loves of her life approach.

It had been a trial, with Zoe being sick and all, but since Boston, things seemed to be moving in a positive direction.

Deryn held out her hands to the paddling child.

"Come on, big girl, you can do it."

She loved how Carl, her great protector from harm, doted on the little girl. It wasn't too long ago that she had been afraid they wouldn't make it as a couple; that his joblessness and Zoe's illness would just be too much for them.

But she had faith; faith in her child, and faith in angels.

The thought threw her. She'd never been a religious person, so didn't really understand where the sudden belief in winged servants of God even came from, but if it was this belief that helped to make their life better, then she guessed she was more religious than she'd thought.

The sun was pretty much gone now, a sleepy eye peering over the gulf horizon. There was no doubting what the water resembled now, and she swam around in a circle to greet her child and husband—to dispel the nasty thought.

But they were gone.

How is this possible? she wondered, treading water. *They were here just a moment ago.*

"Carl?" she called out, looking all around. "Zoe?"

The water seemed to have grown heavier, thicker, and a strong smell—*the stink of metal*—assailed her senses.

She knew the smell, and what it was trying to tell her.

"Oh God," she said, starting to swim toward shore. It splashed in her mouth as she paddled furiously; the taste of copper and iron.

On the shore ahead, she saw the figure of a child waiting for her. At first she wasn't sure, but she realized it was her daughter, but not the smiling, happy child who had been swimming out to her seconds ago.

This child was different.

"Zoe!" Deryn cried out as the water grew choppier and the clouds in the sky above churned with darkness. Nothing would stop her from reaching her child.

Nothing would keep her from holding on to the happiness she had attained.

The scarlet waters churned, and an undertow like nothing she had ever experienced in these waters pulled her down beneath the waves.

Down into a sea of blood.

"It's bad, isn't it?" Madeline said from her beach chair.

Remy sat across from her in his own chair, his body bloodied, scratched, and bitten. He didn't want to answer . . . didn't want to worry her.

The beach was as black as night, even though he knew it had

to be midafternoon. That was when they'd gone to the beach most often, midafternoon.

"Yeah, it's bad," he said.

"Then what are you doing here?" she asked him.

He shrugged, reopening a wound on his shoulder, allowing a crimson trail to run down his chest toward his taut stomach.

"Something's wrong," Remy said, dabbing at the blood with his fingertips. "Something's keeping the Seraphim locked up."

A warm wind came up suddenly off the water. It smelled of death.

"And you need it?" Madeline asked, holding on to the large brim of her hat.

Remy didn't answer.

"Why is it so hard for you to admit that sometimes you need to be what you actually are?"

He looked at the woman he loved, feeling a nearly overwhelming sadness with the intrusive memory that she was now gone from his life.

"Because I don't want to be that," he said.

She smiled at him then, shaking her head in that sometimes-you're-so-gosh-darn-cute way.

"And you won't be," she told him. "Not now . . . not after all you've been through. You could never be the way you were again. You've gone through . . . you've *lived* through so much."

"I guess," he said. "But it still doesn't change that something's preventing me from getting in touch with my other side."

"Dagon?" she guessed.

"Yeah," he said, gazing out over the dark surf. It resembled a sea of oil, it was so black. "It looks as though he somehow gained possession of that fragment of creation Delilah was looking for."

She shoved her delicate feet beneath the sand, burying them.

"So that's it then," she said. "You give up?"

"I'm trying, but I've got, like, sixty dead guys clawing and biting at me, and I can't. . . ."

"So case closed?"

"No," he said, refusing to let her push his buttons. "Not case closed."

"Then what are you doing here?" she asked him.

He could see the smirk on her face as she stared ahead at the pounding, black surf, knowing full well she was getting under his skin.

"I really don't know," he said. "And I guess I should probably get back there."

"You probably should," she said, pretending to ignore him as he got up from his chair.

His body was in pain, gashes, cuts, and bites bleeding profusely.

"I'll see you later?" he asked.

"You bet," she said, looking his way and giving him a wink.

He hated to leave her, but he had a god to kill.

And a little girl to save.

Zoe always knew she was special.

Even as a little, little baby, she had known she was unlike anybody else; unlike Mommy, unlike Daddy, unlike all the other kids she would see in Florida.

Because she had something special inside of her that nobody else in the whole wide world had.

At least that was how it had been.

Until the monster stole some of her specialness from her. That had hurt really bad, and she had decided to go deep inside herself, to find a place to hide until the monster had gone away.

Her specialness was in this place hiding too, and it was sad because it wasn't whole anymore.

Zoe was very upset that it was sad, and she asked it if she could do anything to make it happy again.

It did not answer her, which really wasn't so strange, but it decided to show her things . . . pictures inside her head that sometimes she would like to draw later.

Zoe saw all kinds of things; things that might happen, and things that had already happened. She saw the man with the black doggy again. Zoe liked this man and hoped someday she might get to play with his doggy. She saw her mommy and daddy, and she knew her daddy had been bad, taking her away so that Mommy could not find her. But her mommy was close by—she knew this; she could feel this. . . .

The monster made her want to hide deeper and deeper. At first he had been an old man, but after he had taken some of the specialness . . .

Scared now, she asked the specialness to stop showing her these things, but it ignored her, whispering that it had to show her, that she needed to see what was happening so she could make things right . . . so she could make the specialness whole again.

Zoe didn't understand what it meant, knowing full well the monster was not going to give it back.

She wanted her mommy. She wanted to feel one of her special hugs; she wanted to lie down with her on the couch and watch cartoons. Her mommy would make it so she wasn't afraid anymore.

But the specialness told her *no*.

Zoe was angry, telling the specialness it was being mean.

And the specialness said nothing, choosing instead to show her more pictures inside her head; only this time what was going to happen wasn't what she saw.

The monster had done something to her daddy while she was hiding, making him do things he didn't want to. Her daddy had brought her to a schoolroom like the ones where the big kids went, and where she would one day go when she got big.

Zoe knew these pictures had already happened while she was hiding inside her head. It was dark inside the big kids' classroom, and she and her daddy were hiding.

But from whom?

Someone came running around the corner, and suddenly Zoe knew who it was. She had felt her mommy coming, and she was here.

Mommy will protect me, she thought as she crawled out from inside her head, just in time to see her daddy do something very bad.

Daddy had a knife in his hand as he went to see Mommy.

Zoe thought that maybe they would be nice to each other now . . . that they would be happy to see each other . . . that they wouldn't fight.

She thought they were hugging, but as Daddy stepped back, she saw that Mommy was holding her belly, and that there was red . . . *blood* . . . on her stomach and her hands.

Daddy had done something to Mommy.

Zoe watched in horror as her mommy fell down on the floor with so much blood coming from her.

And that was when the specialness whispered in her ear like a buzzing bee.

You have to take it back, or your mommy will die.

Remy wasn't sure how long he'd blacked out, but at least he was still alive.

The stink of the dead was incredibly foul, their fetid mass pressing him down to the ground as they attempted to get at him.

He tried to summon his true self again, but found the power still blocked by something stronger.

He fought, striking out at the decaying flesh of his enemies. Swimming to the surface of this sea of reanimated corpses, he caught sight of Dagon, the ancient deity presiding over this bloodbath. The god still stood there, the power of creation radiating from his loathsome form, a beatific smile upon his monstrous face.

Their gaze connected again as Remy was about to be pulled down in a squirming undertow of rot and decay, but he found an untapped reserve of strength, fighting to remain above the clawing dead.

"Such spirit," Dagon announced as he reached down to grab him by the throat, yanking him up from the writhing sea of reanimated corpses.

Remy struggled in the deity's grasp, still hearing the sounds of fighting somewhere in the distance behind him; the sporadic blasts of gunfire, and dwindling battle cries. Some of them had managed to survive; some of them were still fighting.

"It seems such a waste to allow one as strong as you to die in such a way," Dagon said with a chuckle. "All that power churning around inside you."

Remy struggled in the deity's grasp, lashing out in any way he could, functioning now on purely the basest of instincts.

"Ferocious," Dagon said mockingly, holding Remy's thrashing form at a distance. "I'm curious though; did *He* send you to find me?"

"I don't . . . don't know who you . . . mean," Remy wheezed as the grip upon his throat grew tighter.

"Don't play stupid with me, Seraphim," Dagon roared, giving him a vicious shake. "Why else would a soldier of God be amongst this rabble? The All-Father wants His power back, and I have no intention of giving it to Him."

Darkness danced at the corners of his vision, threatening to plunge him into unconsciousness, but Remy held on long enough to ask the question. He had to know if all this—the fighting and the death—if it had all been for nothing.

"The child," he croaked, still dangling from the monstrous being's clutches, "does she still live?"

Dagon appeared taken aback by the question.

"The child?" he asked. "Your concern is for the child?" He started to laugh, a horrible sound that echoed through the night.

"She lives . . . for now," he said, drawing Remy closer. "But soon all that is special inside of her"—he patted his scaled breast—"all of it will reside within me."

The deity's smile grew enormous. "And then there won't be a thing that God, or His winged soldiers, will be able to do to stop me."

It was Remy's turn to laugh.

Dagon loosened his grip.

"Did I say something to amuse you, Seraphim?"

Remy's eyes had been closed, but he slowly opened them to look into Dagon's angry gaze.

"You amuse me. You're nothing but a nearly forgotten deity that's only received a reprieve from oblivion by stumbling onto something that's given him a taste of power, the likes of which he's never before tasted," Remy told him with a sneer. "God eats punks like you for breakfast."

Dagon laughed sharply.

"Speaking of breakfast," he said, drawing Remy closer to him, "I've never tasted angel before."

Dagon's mouth grew incredibly wide.

"Wonder if you'll taste as good as you smell."

And he prepared to take a bite.

*   *   *

Delilah opened her eyes to the sound of a child's screams, and the world had changed.

She looked around, realizing she was not in a place she recognized. Moments before she had been in her home, but now . . .

It took her a moment to get her bearings as she tried desperately to recall what had happened and whether she had turned off the oven.

And then she remembered the strange child in her dining room.

"Sam!" she cried out for her husband, her eyes scanning her surroundings for a sign of something—*anything*—that was familiar.

There was a man standing beside her, and as she looked at him, he began to sob. She recalled suddenly that his name was Mathias, and that he loved her more than anything because she made him that way.

The man was crying as she reached out.

Mathias grabbed her hand and brought it to his mouth, kissing it over and over again, drenching it with his plaintive tears.

"I want it back," he said through trembling lips. "Please let it come back to me. . . . Please . . ."

And little by little, bit by bit, Delilah remembered.

She remembered what the truth was.

A powerful rage filled her as she realized she had been manipulated, entranced by a power that had shown her what could be.

A taste—if she were to possess it.

There was a man—not quite a man anymore—with a rather large knife standing over the body of the fallen woman he'd just stabbed. He looked ashamed at what he had done.

The little girl had gone to her mother, pulling her dying form up onto her lap, rocking from side to side and repeating over and over, *"You're okay, Mommy. Please get up. You're okay, Mommy. Please get up. You're okay, Mommy. Please . . ."*

Delilah had no idea if the woman would be all right; nor did she care. All she was concerned with at the moment was what was inside that little girl, and how she needed it to give her back a world denied to her.

She sensed a moment at hand; a moment that she must seize with both hands, and throttle the life from, if anything beneficial was going to come from it.

"You," she said, looking toward the still-crying Mathias.

He responded with red, watery eyes, barely able to contain his emotions.

"You want your fantasy back?" she asked him. "Bring me the girl and we'll see what can be done about making your dreams come true."

The expression on his face became rapturous, as if he could never hope to bring what he had experienced back, but she had shown him otherwise.

She had shown him the truth. It could be so.

Mathias went to work, making his move toward the little girl.

"You're okay, Mommy. Please get up. You're okay, Mommy. Please get up. You're okay, Mommy. Please get up. You're okay, Mommy. . . ."

The child's father seemed to be in a sort of trance, gazing down at his former wife bleeding in the arms of his daughter. It was as if he were trying to make some sort of sense of what had happened.

Of what he had done.

It was obvious the poor soul had yet to understand that he was not in control of himself any longer, that a darker, more malevolent force now controlled his puppet strings.

Mathias saw his objective and went for it, reaching for the child to claim her.

The man became like a thing possessed, lashing out with his knife, slashing across Mathias' arm.

"You will not touch the child," the man said with a slow shake of his head, his eyes so dark they looked like dollops of tar hardening in his deep sockets. "She belongs to Dagon."

Mathias jumped back, the sleeve of his sweat-dampened shirt cut, blood dribbling freely from the gash in his arm. He reached into his back pocket and removed the Swiss Army knife he'd used earlier to pick the lock to the building. He briefly gazed at the tool, selecting what was needed for this particular job and unfolding the five-inch blade.

"It's not the size of the blade that matters, but how it's used." Delilah remembered these words of the many men who had often fought for her over the ages.

"Remember what you saw," Delilah said aloud to inspire her champion. "It can only be that way if the child is mine."

The words were just the catalyst required. Mathias sprang like a predatory beast, the small blade darting through the air, finding its prey multiple times, before falling back.

Carl was bleeding from many places as he maneuvered himself between his attacker and the child, who was cradling his dying wife.

Delilah was growing impatient, wishing the two would just kill each other and be done with it as she glared at her prize. She began to move around the men, as they continued their dance of death, moving closer to her objective.

If you want something done right . . .

She was close enough to speak to the child.

"Zoe," Delilah whispered, flexing the power of her voice. "Zoe, I was a friend of your mother's."

The child didn't seem to hear, hugging her mother and kissing her face and the top of her head, telling her over and over she was not dead.

"Zoe," Delilah said, trying again, flexing her vocal muscle.

This time it worked, and she caught the child's attention. Zoe looked up, her face flushed scarlet, her eyes swollen with tears.

"Come with me, child," Delilah said, holding out a hand. "I'll take you somewhere you'll be safe."

And as the words left her, Mathias screamed, lunging at Zoe's father. The two stumbled backward, crashing into the classroom desks that had been pushed to the side of the room.

The screams were wild, inhuman, like two savage beasts.

Zoe became distracted, staring in terror at the battle being waged across the room from her.

"Zoe," Delilah demanded, cautiously moving closer.

The child's attention snapped back to her.

"Take my hand, and everything will be all right," Delilah said as she willed the child to her.

Zoe looked about to do as Delilah wanted, when the damnable Deryn York fitfully twitched and let out a guttural moan.

Delilah rolled her eyes, furious that the bitch hadn't yet died.

Zoe's attention was back upon her mother.

"The specialness says I can fix her," Zoe said, patting her mother's hair.

"Perhaps we can," Delilah said, "but you're going to need to come with me before . . ."

The men thrashed upon the ground in an expanding puddle of gore. Whose blood it was exactly was not known, but Delilah guessed it was likely from them both.

"It says I have to take it back . . . take it back from the monster," the little girl squeaked, obviously afraid.

"Then let me help you," Delilah said. She'd dropped to her knees, sliding closer to the girl.

Close enough to grab her.

Delilah reached out, taking hold of Zoe's wrist and attempting to draw her near. She couldn't help herself, being this close to the force that would free her from her punishment and allow her to shape the world as she saw fit.

"You're mine now," the woman said.

Zoe's eyes grew wide, and a light began to fill them, growing so intense that it illuminated the child's entire head, making it appear on fire from the inside.

"I've got to take it back," she said in a voice no longer her own. "It must be whole again."

And there came a deafening silence, followed by a roar so loud that it could have been heard the day the universe was created.

CHAPTER SEVENTEEN

Even at the height of his power, Dagon had never felt like this.

The power of creation flowed through his veins, charging each and every muscle in his body with the power to transform the world.

It was what he'd always wanted; to take the world and bend it to its knees and make it learn who was its true master.

The old god had returned, filled with vim and vigor, and ready to challenge any and all for the domination of all things.

This was what he had been created to do, and soon the people of the world would awaken from their sleep, his name upon their lips.

Dagon.

But first he would have a snack, feasting upon the flesh and blood of one of Heaven's born.

Dagon found this one squirming in his grasp to escape, curious.

He wore the form of a mortal, but deep inside, locked and hidden away, was the power of Heaven.

Curious, yes, but not curious enough to stop him from dining upon the holy flesh of one of the Christian God's soldiers.

He brought the squirming angel closer, imagining what the

taste of his flesh would be like. Sweet, he guessed, opening his mouth wide so he could bite. Dagon could smell the blood; he could feel the life and the power pulsing through the man's body.

This will be a meal to remember, he thought as his jagged teeth sank into the man's throat.

And his mouth was filled with the blood of angels.

As much as he struggled, Remy could not free himself from the ancient god's clutches, but it did not stop him from trying.

It was all that he had now, the struggle . . . the fight.

All that he'd had for most of his existence.

He was created as a soldier to the Lord God, serving the Almighty in every manner, but it had become too much, and he had walked away. From one battle to the next; abandoning his true self, to wear the guise of humanity.

Every day was a battle, but every day, as he moved closer and closer to gaining that spark of humanity, he realized it was a battle worth fighting.

The memory of Madeline flashed before his eyes; the true prize to it all. Without her in his life, he would have attained nothing.

She showed him what it was all about; to embrace his newfound humanity, while helping him to accept what he truly was.

"You can't stop being what you are," she used to tell him. *"It'll eventually kill you to deny it."*

He knew she was right. . . . She was almost always right, and he begrudgingly accepted his nature. But it was his humanity, no matter how artificial, that he clung to the most.

Remy loved to be human, there was no doubt about it, but there were times—*times like this*—when being cruel, and a powerfully inhuman bastard, was just what the doctor ordered.

But there were no doctors handy; only the hot, rotting breath of a revitalized deity as his teeth drew closer.

Remy was thinking of Zoe and how he was going to be breaking his promise to her mother that he would find her.

He was thinking how sorry he was, when the teeth of Dagon bit down upon his neck.

A scream—and blood—bubbled up in his throat.

The blood rushed into Dagon's mouth, forcing its way down his eager throat.

And it began to burn.

At first he had no idea what was happening, the pain unlike anything he had experienced before.

Dagon tossed his prey aside, as he came to the fearful realization that he'd been abandoned; that the power of God had left him.

No, it had been stolen.

The Seraphim was free.

Remy had no idea what had happened, knowing only that the power of Heaven that he hid from the world was free, and there was no holding it back.

The Seraphim burned in its rage, shucking off Remy's disguise of humanity to clothe itself in the armor of fire and fury.

For the moment, Remy was gone, replaced by the angel Remiel. Placing a hand that burned like the sun against his throat, he closed the oozing bite with a hiss and turned his attention to the being that roused his anger.

"Dagon!" the Seraphim bellowed, as his wings of gold unfurled and he took to the air in pursuit of his foe.

*   *   *

The deity stumbled across the church grounds, the blood of the angel still eating away at his flesh—*his glorious new flesh*—like the most corrosive of acids.

The dead he had raised still walked, running by his side like a pack of obedient dogs, eager to please.

Dagon heard the sound of pounding wings behind him, and knew he was being stalked from the air. He stopped, turning to see the fiery form as it dropped from the early-morning sky. The angel landed in a crouch, his wings slowly fanning the air as he approached his prey.

Something had happened to the child, and the power that resided within her. Dagon needed to know the cause of his depletion, and whether or not he would be able get it back.

"Destroy him," Dagon commanded his reanimated troops, while running toward the classroom building.

Hopefully the dead would buy him the time needed to search out the problem and reacquire his godly manifestations.

The dead came at him in a wave, eager to do their master's bidding to the end.

Remiel smiled, an unfamiliar expression of feelings that normally he would not show. The Seraphim gathered that not all of his human traits had been cast aside.

But the angel was happy; happy to be free.

And doing what he knew how to do best.

The dead came at the Seraphim in an attempt to destroy him, and he met their attack in kind.

He would end their lives again, only this time permanently, leaving not even the smallest piece of flesh or bit of bone to be resurrected.

*   *   *

The dreams of a perfect world threatened to seduce her again, but Delilah did not want dreams; she wanted reality.

And in order for that perfect world to be hers, she knew what had to be done.

The child was using the power. . . . To the best of her limited ability, she was using the power.

Creation pulsed from her tiny body in waves, affecting their surroundings in the most bizarre of ways. The building in which they'd fought was coming apart, as if the glue that held the very structure together had come unstuck and all the pieces were drifting apart.

The room moaned like a beast in pain as it was slowly disassembled.

Delilah could see that the child was trying to focus, attempting to rein in the tremendous power at her disposal, and to use it to bring her mother back to health.

Such a small, insignificant feat it was for a power so great.

"Zoe," Delilah called again, climbing back onto her feet. She caught a glimpse of her hand, which had been holding Zoe's arm when the power had come alive. It was a shriveled black thing, barely functional, but this was just more incentive for her to obtain the prize.

She bravely approached the child again, dodging pieces of concrete and cinder block that floated in the air, their gravity inexplicably canceled.

The child had placed a glowing hand upon her mother's stomach, her eyes closed in deep concentration.

Delilah was afraid that the power would be wasted, that this foolish child would use up the greatness that had been hiding inside her on the single act of restoring her mother to life, when there were so many other, and far more important, miracles to perform.

"Zoe, please . . . ," Delilah began. "Let me help you."

The child stirred, her eyes languidly opening as if waking up from a dream.

"Mommy's hurt bad," she said. Her voice still sounded different, as if there were something else present. This seemed to be no longer Zoe alone, but Zoe joined with another. "I have to try and fix her."

Zoe's eyes closed again as she went back to concentrating on mending her injured parent's mortal wound.

It was more than Delilah could stand. To be this close and not have it be hers . . . To be perfectly honest, it drove her a little mad.

"Give it to me!" Delilah screamed, grabbing hold of the child; pulling Zoe away from the act she struggled desperately to perform.

The child was stunned, the amount of concentration she needed to maintain the power, or as she called it, the specialness inside her, temporarily interrupted. The power began to radiate from her tiny body again, the pieces of timber, glass, and stone floating in the air beginning to move faster, drawn toward some invisible current forming somewhere in the air around them.

The ceiling came apart with a scream, exposing them all to the dawn sky.

Delilah sensed it was only a matter of time before the power was fully unleashed, and she would be unable to control it. Through contact with the child she could feel it emerging, growing stronger and more confident, eager to do that for which it was intended.

It was the power of God . . . the Maker . . . a piece of the notion that had shaped the universe.

And for what she had endured, she deserved to have it.

Instinctively, Delilah resorted to her nature, the rumbling hunger that suddenly formed in her belly driving her to act.

She would take this power, as she had taken countless souls for sustenance throughout the ages.

Delilah leaned toward the still-startled Zoe, her full lips eager to touch the child's, firmly latching on and drawing out the immense power, like poison being sucked from a wound.

But this poison would not kill. *Oh no*, she thought, feeling the crackle of unearthly energy upon her lips just as they were about to touch.

This poison would bring her life.

She'd almost convinced herself that she had attained her goal, that finally, after so very long, she would at last have peace. But it was not meant to be, and she was sure the Lord God Almighty must have had something to do with it.

The horned god, Dagon, was suddenly amongst them, tearing the child from her grasp.

Delilah was hurled backward, a floating piece of brick wall violently halting her progress before she dropped to the ground.

"This power is not meant for the likes of you," he snarled with a shake of his great, horned head.

She was startled by the ancient deity's appearance, noticing the horrific burns around his mouth, neck, and chest, in direct contrast to the perfection of the rest of his body.

The look in the ancient god's eyes was fierce. She had seen that look many a time before, her own hungry reflection staring back at her.

He wanted the power as well and would move Heaven and Earth to have it.

Zoe, who had been tossed aside when Dagon made his appearance, let out a soft cry as she rose to all fours, scrabbling across the now-dirt floor—strips of linoleum soared in the air above them like awkward kites—to again be with her mother. The little girl's movement was enough of a distraction for Delilah to make her move.

"Now, Mathias," she demanded.

Her loving servant had been waiting, crouched in the darkness of a corner awaiting his mistress' ascension. He would do anything for her; she owned him body and soul, and now it was time for him to perform the ultimate sacrifice.

The former mercenary, his body beaten and bloody from his earlier conflict with Zoe's father, sprang from his waiting place. From the air he selected a jagged spear of something that had been broken into pieces when the power of creation had begun to dismantle the structure they were in.

Mathias had no concern for his own safety as he came up behind the horned god, thrusting the makeshift spear at Dagon's back, just as Delilah's rival for the blessed power started to turn.

The deity lashed out as the spear pierced his side, striking Mathias with such savagery that it snapped the man's neck, spinning his head entirely around and sending his body flying, dead before he even touched the floor.

Maybe in death he would find something close to what the power had enticed him with earlier, Delilah briefly considered, already forgetting the man who had given his life for her.

There were far more important matters to concern herself with.

She dodged the flailing arms of the horned god. The metal spear had come through at an angle, up through the rib cage and out the chest. If the ancient god still had a heart, and it was located in the typical spot as in most living things, it had either been narrowly missed or at least damaged by the jagged foreign object.

This gave her the advantage; this gave her those extra moments to achieve what she had to do.

Delilah moved through the field of floating rubble, feeling the bits of weightless debris grazing her face and body as she drew closer to her destiny.

Zoe was still beside her mother, though now the two of them floated above the dirt floor, encircled by a ghostly light. Deryn's blood floated as well, a crimson cord that extended from her mortal wound, to slither in the air around them. The power, as manipulated by the child, was healing the woman. She thrashed in the gravityless air, her breathing coming in short, pained gasps as the magick moved through her, doing as the child desired.

And Delilah prayed—to whom or what she really wasn't sure—that once she reached the child, and placed her hungry lips upon hers, there would be enough creation left to bring about her personal paradise.

She entered the corona of light around the pair, taking hold of Deryn York's floating form and pushing it aside in order to get to Zoe. With trembling hands, she reached out, taking the child's cherubic face and drawing it to her.

And in a moment of absolute bliss, their lips touched, and Delilah drank deep from the well.

The last of the walking dead were about to be vanquished, when Remiel felt the beginning of change in the world.

The angel felt it in his wings, the tips of his golden feathers feeling the ether torn apart like gossamer to reveal the beginnings of something new and fragile beneath.

A dead man, too stubborn to lie down, made one final attempt at attack, hauling his moldering carcass across the burning bodies of his brethren, attempting to sink his teeth into the angel's flesh.

He joined his brothers and sisters in final death just as his broken teeth touched Seraphim skin; a rush of heat and holy light incinerated the misbegotten thing before it could do any harm.

"Kinda like a bug light," a gravelly voice spoke.

Remiel whirled, always ready to continue the battle; he saw the large man and immediately recognized a kindred spirit.

"Samson," the Seraphim said, impressed that the warrior had survived the skirmish.

"Yeah, that's me," he answered. The big man looked around, tilting his blind head back slightly to smell the air. "Do you smell that?" he asked.

"Smell it. Feel it. Dread it," Remiel answered. "Forces are being played with here that should remain untouched."

The Seraphim reacted, spreading his wings and becoming one with the air. The very fabric of reality was being trifled with—the weave of God itself—and he would do everything in his power to see it protected.

Samson heard the angel go, and hoped he wouldn't be too late.

The warrior could feel that the change had started, but the existing reality wasn't giving up without a fight.

It was a difficult and dangerous thing, changing what was and attempting to replace it with something else. It was a matter best left to the gods.

The blind warrior stood for a little while, appreciating the deathly silence, but also cursing it. He listened for a sign of life, something that showed him that at least some of his children had survived.

Samson listened hard, straining his enhanced hearing for a moan, or a sigh, or a troubled breath.

But there was none of that to be heard.

And with a heavy sigh of his own, he knew he must follow the angel, for he still had a job to finish.

He had the Lord's work to do.

Delilah felt the world begin to change, just as it was torn away from her.

She was hurled violently back, landing upon the ground, just as she heard the lovely sounds of her children awakening from their beds after a long night's sleep; just as she heard the sounds of their eager feet upon the floors above her head as they were coming down to her.

But it was all gone in an instant, when Dagon reasserted himself.

The deity was in a bad way, the burns that had eaten away the flesh around his mouth and chest having spread across most of his once-impressive physique.

He looked as though he'd bathed in acid.

From where she lay, Delilah saw that Dagon had taken the child, pulling her from the air and dragging her down to the ground.

In one of his misshapen hands he held what appeared to be a piece of broken glass, and he was poised to bring it down upon the struggling child; to cut her open to remove the prize they both wished to possess.

The child squirmed beneath the horned god's attempts, but he held her pressed to the ground long enough to commit his act.

The glass blade descended. Dagon had aimed for the heart, but the child's squirming distracted his aim, and the tip of the impromptu knife went into her stomach instead.

It was as if all sound were suddenly stolen away, and time slowed to a crawl.

The child's mouth was open wide in a silent scream, and her eyes bulged with the horror of what had just been done to her.

And then her eyes closed, and she went very still.

Dagon perched over the child's body, waiting for a sign.

He did not have long to wait.

The energy erupted from the child in a burst of invisible force, picking up the ancient god and tossing him aside like a rag doll.

Zoe floated up from the ground, her bloodied stomach mended in a flash of white and the smell of burning ozone; even the scarlet stains upon her clothes were soon but a memory.

Gone was the frightened little girl, unsure of the power—the specialness—that lived inside her. Here was a being who had embraced this might and who was about to show those that hurt her what true power was all about.

Dagon seemed to know this as he hauled his broken body up from the ground where he'd been discarded. It wasn't the first time the deity had been cast aside for something stronger.

"Please," he begged upon his knees before the floating child, "just a taste . . . I don't want it all. . . . Just a taste again . . . not to be forgotten . . ."

Zoe looked down upon the lowly god and snarled.

"I used to think you were scary," she said, her child's voice oddly alien, "but you're no scarier than a bug."

A terrible smile appeared upon the little girl's face, the pulsing circle of energy that surrounded her momentarily expanding outward to touch Dagon with its might.

It happened so quickly that the old god wasn't even given a chance to scream. In a flash, his entire mass had been turned to bugs, golden cockroaches that for a moment held the form of Dagon, before they dropped to the ground in a squirming heap.

And Zoe eagerly returned to Earth to enthusiastically stomp upon their skittering forms, happily crushing their shelled bodies beneath her sneakered feet.

Making certain not to miss a one of them.

The Seraphim Remiel plummeted from the morning sky, drawn to the enormous power radiating from the body of one human child.

The child had become a receptacle for a tiny fraction of the Lord

God's power, but even a fraction of the Maker had more power than the puny human brain could ever hope to comprehend.

Here in the body of a little girl was the ability to create worlds, and from what the angel could see, it was driving her mad.

Remiel touched down upon the earth, avoiding pieces of the building that had somehow come apart and were now floating weightlessly in the air like an asteroid field.

The might of God was radiating from her in waves, growing steadily stronger as the child stood.

His human aspect felt sadness for the young one, eager to help in any way he could, but the Seraphim fought this emotion, seeing only the potential for extreme danger; danger to itself, as well as a threat to the world that God seemingly loved above all else.

It was the child who posed the threat with her inability to control the level of divine power that now coursed through her.

Remiel slowly approached, feeling waves of God's raw awesomeness radiating from the little girl; the potential to create . . . or to destroy.

"Child," Remiel called, his voice like the most beautiful of voices raised in song, "calm yourself."

Zoe looked at him in all his angelic glory and was terrified.

"Get away!" she screamed, and the ground spasmed violently, shaking him from his feet, the undulating earth carrying him away.

The angel spread his wings and took to the air, flying above the writhing earth.

"I mean you no harm," Remiel called down to her, but her fear was too great, and a terrific wind was summoned that was like the hand of a giant—*or God*—swatting him back to Earth like a bothersome insect.

The weather had started to react to the child's release; voluminous gray storm clouds, throbbing with electrical fury, were building over their heads.

"Mommy!" Zoe cried out as the thunder rumbled. "Where are you? I want my mommy."

Jagged bolts of lightning javelined down from the sky, attempting to skewer him with their electrical touch. Remiel scrambled across the ground, narrowly avoiding the deadly bolts raining from the Heavens.

The child was frightened, overwhelmed by what was happening to her; in a state of mind that could very well destroy them all.

The Seraphim was in a quandary. All that it knew was the option of battle, to wrestle something to the ground and end its threat by sword and burning all traces away with Heaven's fire.

But there was another way; a way the angel of Heaven did not care to recognize.

A human way.

The morning had become like night, the tumultuous air swirling the floating debris at greater and greater speeds, the other structures around the former building beginning to come undone.

The Seraphim momentarily struggled with its other side, the fragile human nature that it despised, this time proving itself to be the stronger. With a growl it allowed itself to be forced down, fully aware that if its weaker nature was not successful, it would be the Seraphim that reasserted itself, and the threat of the child would be put succinctly to an end.

Remy knelt upon the ground, feeling the physical characteristics of his warrior half recede. He was breathing heavily, his heart beating rapid fire in his chest as he glimpsed the nightmare he had been left to face.

The child had lost control, her fear causing the power to lash out uncontrollably and strike at the world that scared her.

She needed to see a friendly face; she needed to see someone who would tell her it was going to be all right. Not having any idea of what had happened to Deryn York, Remy took it upon himself to be that person. He hoped the little girl, filled with the power of creation, would recognize him, and not extinguish his life with a bolt of lightning.

The dirt and rock swirled faster in the air, stinging his exposed flesh. His clothes were in tatters, just one of the many pitfalls of assuming an angelic form, but he struggled on, shielding his eyes from the scouring grit, as he made his way toward the little girl at the center of the storm.

Through the maelstrom he saw her, a tiny, shivering figure lying upon the ground.

"Zoe," he called out over the howling wind.

Her eyes were closed, and she hugged herself into a tight little ball.

"Zoe, I'm here," he called again as he got closer.

Spears of lightning rained down in front of him, turning the areas struck to glass, but after a momentary pause, Remy continued on.

"Open your eyes, Zoe," Remy called out. "It's me . . . the one you drew . . . the one you said would protect you."

The wind picked up, roaring like a hungry monster, and Remy felt himself begin to be lifted by the intensifying conditions.

"Zoe, it's me. . . . Please . . . It's Remy."

Through the churn of dirt, he saw that she had opened her eyes.

The storm winds grew more powerful, and he desperately tried to hold on, sinking his fingers deep into the broken ground to anchor himself.

He knew he didn't have long. If the storm became any fiercer, he would be tossed away like the flotsam and jetsam that already clogged the air. This would be his chance . . . the human chance . . . and if he failed, there would be only one other way to put an end to the potential cataclysm.

The angelic way.

The Seraphim was there, waiting as always, waiting to prove that it was the superior nature, and as much as it pained him to admit, its solution was the likely answer.

The world was coming apart around him, and it was only a matter of time before he was torn apart by the storm. Remy was allowing the angel to flow through him again, to reassert mastery over their form, when the scouring winds almost instantly died down.

Remy dropped to the ground, covering his head as all the floating debris and rubble picked up by the power of the Almighty was released, and gravity reasserted its sway, raining it down upon the land.

Wiping grit and grime from his eyes, he raised his head to see what had happened and looked into the tear-filled eyes of a frightened little girl.

"Where's your dog?" she asked in a tiny squeak of a voice.

"He's home," Remy said, getting to his feet and brushing dirt from what remained of his clothes. "And he thought the pictures of him were really beautiful."

That almost got a smile, and as he drew closer, Zoe came to him. Remy knelt down, taking her into his arms. Squeezing his neck, almost to the point of choking him, she began to cry.

"Shhhhh," Remy said, patting her back. "It's all right. Everything is all right now," he said, comforting her.

He could still sense that she was in possession of the power, but somehow she had found the strength to keep it down and to gain control of her fear.

The Seraphim grumbled and roiled within him, unconvinced that the threat had been averted, but Remy believed it had.

"Would you like to go home?" he asked her. "How would that be?"

"Yes," she squeaked, still holding on to him for dear life. "Me and Mommy want to go home to Florida and swim in the ocean with dolphins," she said, hiccupping back more tears.

Gazing about the wreckage of the event that had transpired, Remy had no idea whether Deryn York had survived. His eyes immediately fell upon a form, carefully climbing over the rubble-strewn ground, and he was excited to see that it was Zoe's mother.

But she wasn't alone.

Delilah stood behind the woman, and the closer she got, Remy saw that the temptress had the tip of a large knife pressed to the woman's throat as they walked awkwardly side by side.

"Bravo, Mr. Chandler," Delilah said. "The power to calm a storm. I'm very impressed."

"Let her go, Delilah," Remy said, exasperated by the whole thing. "Don't you think we've all gone through enough?"

"No truer words were ever spoken," Delilah said. "Do you seriously think I'd walk away after this without my prize?" she asked.

He was still holding Zoe in his arms, and she lifted her face to see what was happening. Remy would have rather she didn't, but there was no stopping her.

"Mommy!" she screeched, seeing her mother .

"Hey, baby," Deryn said, trying to sound calm, but the blade's tip being pushed against the soft part of her dirty throat didn't make for the most calming situation.

"Put Zoe down, Remy," Delilah instructed. "And let the child come to her mother."

Zoe squirmed to be free, but Remy did not want to release her.

"Put her down now," Delilah raged, putting more pressure on the bayonet and causing Deryn to cry out.

The child was fighting him now, so he obliged.

"What are you going to do?" he asked, watching as the child ran to them.

"I'm going to make it all better," Delilah said, watching the child with hungry eyes.

Delilah released Deryn, just as Zoe reached her, allowing the two to embrace.

"Don't," Remy cried out, hoping there was a chance that . . .

"I promise you it'll be a wonderful world," Delilah said, snatching the child away from her mother, and preparing to kiss her—preparing to consume the power of God inside her.

The Seraphim emerged again, although Remy still managed to maintain most of his control, as he spread his wings and flew to the child's aid.

There was a flash of light so bright that it blinded him. Remy dropped from the air, rolling across the dirt. Blinding explosions of color erupted in front of his eyes as he struggled to regain his sight.

He could hear Zoe crying and Deryn's calming words of comfort, but he still had no idea what had occurred.

His vision finally clearing, Remy looked around. He saw a blackened and smoldering body upon the ground that must have been Delilah, and beside it, Deryn York clutching her child protectively as she gazed ahead, eyes wide in surprise.

"What now," Remy muttered as he slowly turned to see the cause of the woman's reaction.

The Retrievers stood like statues, staring intently at the mother and child. And suddenly everything made horrible sense. Remy knew why the angels had been in Methuselah's—and why they were here now.

He and the Retrievers had actually been searching for the same thing, the only difference being that he had been looking for the child, whereas they had been looking for what had been hiding inside her.

Still manifesting aspects of the Seraphim, Remy ruffled his wings threateningly as he moved to position himself closer to the mother and child.

One of the Retriever hosts raised his armored arm and pointed a sword that resembled a large splinter of ice at Deryn and Zoe.

"We want what is inside the child," the angel said in an emotionless monotone. "Allow us to relieve her of it, and we will be on our way."

Remy found it interesting that the Lord God had sent His bloodhounds to retrieve something that had been here since the beginning of the world.

Why now? he wondered. *What's so crucial that He would take back this power now?*

Deryn held her child all the tighter, looking at Remy and back to the fearsome pair.

"You can have it," Remy said, "but you must guarantee me the child's well-being."

He waited to see how the pair reacted.

They continued to stare, their shiny black armor glinting in the early sunshine.

"We want what is inside the child," the other Retriever said.

"I understand that," Remy said, "but you have to promise me the child will not be hurt."

The pair glanced at each other, a silent message passing between them.

"We cannot guarantee this," they said in unison.

"Then I'm sorry," Remy said.

"Sorry?" the Retriever questioned with an odd tilt of his head.

"You cannot have what the child possesses," Remy told him.

They again looked at each other.

"We could very easily destroy you, Seraphim," he said with

still no sign of emotion. "We could destroy you and take what we desire."

Remy saw the knife that Delilah had used to threaten Deryn upon the ground, and he reached for it. Holding the blade, he willed the power of Heaven into the metal, causing it to crackle with a powerful, holy fire.

"You're welcome to try," Remy told them, and he felt a rush of power flood through him as his warrior nature flexed its muscles in preparation for a battle to come.

He'd always wondered if he could take a Retriever, and now he was going to find out.

The bloodhounds from Heaven responded to the challenge, emitting a birdlike screech as their armor reconfigured into a more combat-ready mode, filled with spikes and many sharp angles. They raised their blades of ice and had started to advance, when they both halted.

At the ready, Remy watched with a curious eye.

The Retrievers appeared to be listening, listening to something that only they could hear.

And as quickly as they had prepared for battle, they stepped down, sheathing their swords, allowing their armor to morph back to its more streamlined design.

"What's happening?" Deryn asked, holding protectively on to her little girl.

"I don't know," Remy said, still watching the Heavenly pair.

The Retrievers stood there a moment longer, their ice-cold eyes darting from the mother and child, to Remy, and then back again.

Finally they spread their razor-sharp wings in unison, and with a final, hawklike screech, they leapt up into the air, and were gone as quickly as they had appeared.

Remy continued to hold on to the knife, waiting for something to happen. He was convinced that the Retrievers were going to drop from the sky in an attack, or that at least something would suddenly appear to challenge him.

But nothing appeared, nothing attacked from the sky, and he actually began to suspect it was all over.

He waited a bit longer, scrutinizing the area for any signs of potential danger and, finding none, allowed himself to relax. The Seraphim, temporarily satisfied, went down quietly, and Remy returned to his more human guise.

Turning, he found the mother and child both staring.

He looked down at himself, at his torn and bloodstained clothes, and self-consciously smiled.

"I knew there was something different about you," Deryn York said.

"You did," Zoe agreed with her mother. "I showed you in the picture I drew."

Her mother turned her face to the little girl. "You did, didn't you," she said, and kissed the child's cheek over and over again.

Zoe laughed sweetly, throwing her arms about her mother's neck and hugging her for dear life.

"I'd like to take my daughter home now, Mr. Chandler," Deryn said.

"Not yet," the little girl chirped, squirming in her mother's arms to be let go.

The child touched ground in a run, stopping a bit away from where they stood. She was staring sadly down at something.

Remy and Deryn followed the little girl, both stopping as they realized the child was looking at the broken and bloody body of Carl Saylor.

The child squatted next to him.

"Zoe," the mother cried out, "come away from there."

"He was a good daddy most of time," she said sadly, and Remy saw her hand reach out to place something that seemed to appear out of thin air upon her father's chest.

It was a purple flower that emitted the most wonderful aroma.

They stood there awhile longer, gazing down at Carl's body, before Zoe broke the silence.

"Can we leave now?" Zoe asked.

And the three walked from the compound into the surrounding woods, finding the path that would eventually lead them home.

Samson emerged from hiding after he was certain they were gone.

He had hated to hide like some loathsome coward, but he knew a blind man would have been useless against the things Remy had faced.

And besides, he had a special purpose to fulfill.

He moved out from behind the section of brick wall that had tumbled, following his nose toward the acrid stink of burned flesh and the supernatural.

Samson knew it was she; even though her flesh had been burned black, practically to ash, it still held the taint of what she was.

Of who she was.

The stink of cooked flesh grew incredibly strong, and he knew he was standing over her.

"Look at you now," he said, feeling a sudden surge of emotion threaten to overtake him.

He remembered how beautiful she had been and tried to keep that thought, even though by the smell, he knew that beauty had been taken away.

Delilah inhaled a rattling breath at the sound of his voice.

"Still alive," he said, and shook his head sadly.

Samson dropped to the ground, rock and bits of glass biting

into his ancient knees, and felt with his hands until he found her blackened remains. Gently he gathered her up, taking her frail body into his arms.

She could not speak, but he could feel her starting to quiver. He wondered how long it would take her to heal . . . how many souls she would need to consume before returning to her old tricks.

But that question wasn't relevant anymore because he knew this was the end. For millennia he had tracked her, and now he had her exactly where he wanted her.

Delilah was helpless in his grasp.

This is what I've been waiting for, he thought. Samson tried to find the anger . . . tried to find the fiery rage, but instead found only sadness—sadness over how far they both had fallen.

He brought her head up and laid it upon his shoulder, holding her tenderly.

"I've never loved anyone more," he told her, his emotion causing his words to break.

Delilah tried to speak, but it came out as only a scratchy croak, and he was certain she was telling him she loved him too.

And Samson took her life, as it was his job to do, the strongest man in the world broken by the memory of a love so powerful that it put his legendary might to shame.

A love that he would carry like the deepest of scars to the end of days.

The strange man was waiting for them as they came out of the woods.

He was standing on the opposite side of the desolate road, across from where the multiple SUVs had been parked, squatting on his hindquarters, and wearing far too much clothing for the warm and humid West Virginia weather.

At a glance, Remy suspected he was Vietnamese, and wondered why he was there.

The dark-skinned man stood to his full gangly height as they emerged, staring at them with dark, curious eyes. There were satchels at his feet, traveling gear, as if he were on a long journey.

Remy tensed, moving to stand in front of Deryn and Zoe; after the kind of night they'd had, he wasn't about to take any chances.

"What is it?" Deryn asked, not yet noticing the stranger.

"Could be nothing," Remy said, allowing his preternatural senses to test the air for potential danger, but getting nothing.

"Who is that?" Deryn asked, finally noticing the man.

"I haven't a clue, but he seems to know us."

There was the sound of movement, and Remy turned to see Zoe pull free from her mother's hand, then run past them into the road toward the stranger.

"Zoe!" Deryn screamed, making a move to grab the child, but for some reason—something in the man's stare—told Remy to let her go to him.

Remy held on to Deryn's arm.

"What are you doing?" she screamed, fighting him.

"Wait," Remy said, watching with a curious eye.

Zoe turned just as she was about to reach the man.

"I have something that I need to give to him," she said, before turning away from them again and joining the stranger on the other side of the road.

Deryn still fought to be released, but her struggles grew less pronounced as she watched the little girl and the man communicate. They stared at each other, a silent message passing between them.

Zoe finally nodded, squatting down to watch as the stranger dropped to his haunches as well, and proceeded to go through one of his satchels in search of something.

The last time Remy had seen the metal statue of the infant, its chubby legs crossed in front of it and arms spread open in acceptance, it had been on Delilah's plane in the possession of Clifton Poole.

"That's Poole's," Deryn said, curiosity in her tone.

The man placed the vessel down in front of the child, and she laughed happily, reaching out to hold one of the object's metal hands.

The stranger and the little girl smiled at each other then, and each nodded. The man reached out a long-fingered hand, and gently tapped the head of the infant's visage; the vessel snapped open of its own accord.

Deryn gasped at the sudden movement.

Zoe appeared to be in a kind of trance, as the stranger began to hum a simple yet beautiful song. There were no words, but Remy's mind was suddenly filled with images of a people who had sworn to safeguard a special gift that had fallen from the sky when the world was young, and who today were still performing their duty, as their ancestors had done.

The wordless song also told of a dark time, when their purpose had been lost to them, and how they had sent brave souls out into the world to find their purpose again.

Remy understood now, and by the expression on Deryn's face, so did she.

Zoe's body began to glow; a faint aura of yellow at first, gradually building to a nearly blinding white corona, before dissipating in a flash that left both Remy and the child's mother blinking away blindness that had temporarily stolen their eyes.

When their vision cleared, they saw that whatever had begun was completed.

They watched as the stranger reached for the child-shaped vessel, no longer open, and carefully—*lovingly*—tucked it back inside his satchel.

Zoe was standing now, watching as the man with whom she had just mysteriously communed gathered up his belongings in preparation to be on his way.

The child finally glanced over at Remy and Deryn, as if suddenly remembering they were there, and gave them a wave, before turning her attention back to her new friend.

The stranger bent down to the little girl with his palm extended, allowing her to give him a high five, before doing the same in return. And all this time not a word was spoken between them, because it wasn't needed.

They knew what had to be done.

The man watched as Zoe crossed the road. He turned away and started on his journey only when he saw that she had reached Remy and Deryn.

"We can go home now," she said, standing before them.

Remy looked away from the little girl to watch the man's progress down the road.

And not surprisingly, he saw that the stranger was gone, as if he'd never been there at all.

EPILOGUE

A month later

"What are you drawing?" Remy asked the little girl sitting across from him, hunkered over her sketch pad.

Zoe remained silent, busily working on her art.

"*Drawing*," Marlowe said with a tail thump as he lay at her feet.

"I know she's drawing," Remy said to the animal. "I was just curious as to what."

The little girl laughed. It sounded like tiny, delicate bells happily jingling.

"That's funny when you talk to the dog," she said, dropping one of her crayons on the desktop and choosing another from the box open in front of her. "My mommy says he can't understand you, you know."

"Your mommy said that?" Remy asked, leaning back in his office chair, enjoying the recently fixed air-conditioning. The chair squeaked loudly, making the child look up from her drawing to stare at him.

Zoe and Deryn had been staying with him and Marlowe since the business in West Virginia; just long enough to get their bearings so they could return to Florida. Finding out that their house had burned down hadn't helped matters, but Deryn was planning on staying with a cousin for a little while, until she got stuff straightened out with the insurance company, and then hopefully, she and Zoe would have a home again.

"Why'd you do that?" she asked him with a scowl.

"Do what?" he asked her, making the chair squeak again.

"That," she said. "Don't do that."

"Do what?" he asked again, playing dumb. "That?" He made the chair squeak again.

She had started to laugh, even though she didn't want him to see, pretending to be mad. "That noise, stop it now."

"What noise?" He bounced in the chair so it squeaked repeatedly. "This noise? You want me to stop this noise?"

She put her head back down, returning to her artwork.

"You're very silly," she said, grabbing the blue crayon and scribbling like crazy.

Deryn had gone out to run a few final errands before their flight back to Florida that night, leaving Zoe with him at the office. He didn't mind; he found the little girl fascinating and had no doubt he was going to miss her.

Remy watched her feverishly working on her project, relieved that everything seemed to have turned out for the best. With the power of creation removed from her, the little girl appeared to have been cured of her autism, receiving a clean bill of health from Franciscan Children's. It was almost as if Deryn and the little girl had been given a gift from a higher power for their troubles.

"Are you ever going to show me what you're working on?" Remy asked her as he came forward in his chair.

"Wait a minute," she said, frustrated by his impatience. "I'm almost done."

She dropped the crayon she was using and picked up the drawing to study it.

"I'm done," she said.

"Can I see?" Remy asked.

"You can have it," she said, casually tossing it on top of his desk. She was already pulling another piece of construction paper from the pad, getting ready to create another masterpiece, he guessed.

Remy picked the drawing up from atop the desk and held it out before him.

He was surprised at what he saw.

"So, what's this supposed to be?" he asked Zoe.

"It's you and Linda," she said matter-of-factly.

"Linda?" Remy began, for the moment not knowing whom she was talking about, but suddenly remembering.

Linda Somerset.

"How would you know about Linda?" he asked, looking up from the drawing to see that she had stopped scribbling with her crayon and was staring across the desk at him.

"I know," she said, annoyed that he had to ask, and shook her head as she returned to coloring.

Remy studied the drawing again of a man and woman holding hands in front of what looked to be a building. Through the windows in the building he could see other people, sitting at tables, who appeared to be eating.

"This is a restaurant?" Remy asked. "Linda and I are at a restaurant?"

"Yes, you're going to take her," Zoe answered, not looking up.

Remy felt immediately uncomfortable. He hadn't thought of the woman in a while, the last time being when he drove by Piazza, hoping to catch a glimpse of her working.

He decided to focus on some other aspects of the drawing, questioning her about the circular object that she'd drawn in the sky above them.

"That's pretty cool that you drew the sun with a face," he said, smiling. "I like that."

Zoe looked up. "That's not the sun," she said, shaking her head. "That's the lady in the sky watching you."

"Lady in the sky?" Remy asked, letting the drawing fall to the desk.

"She wants you to be happy," Zoe said. The little girl leaned on the desk and used the tip of a red crayon to point. "See, she's smiling. She's glad you're with Linda."

"But I'm not . . . ," he started to say.

"Not yet," Zoe interrupted.

Deryn opened the door into the office, plastic bags in each hand.

"Mommy!" the child cheered happily, as Marlowe barked. He had been asleep, and the sudden noise had startled him.

At the moment, Remy knew exactly how he felt, still staring stunned at the images drawn upon the construction paper.

"How's my big girl?" Deryn asked, coming over to kiss her on the top of the head.

"She hasn't been bothering you, has she?" Deryn asked.

Remy looked up with a smile. "Not at all. She's been perfectly fine," he said.

Marlowe had started to go through the bags she'd left on the floor, and she turned to shoo him away. "Hey, get outta there," she said to the Labrador, which got the dog's tail wagging. She bent down to pick up the bags and was rewarded with some awfully moist Lab kisses, which made her laugh.

Remy and Zoe stared at each other across the surface of the desk, the special drawing she had done between them.

"Not yet?" Remy asked.

"Not yet," Zoe said, finally climbing down from her chair to see what her mother had bought.

"But soon."